PENGUIN BOOKS

STUPID CUPID

Arabella Weir is a comic writer and performer, best known as part of the *Fast Show* team and as author of the bestselling *Does My Bum Look Big in This?* and *Onwards and Upwards*, which is published by Penguin.

STUPID CUPID

ARABELLA WEIR

PENGUIN BOOKS

PENGUIN BOOKS

Published by the Penguin Group
Penguin Books Ltd, 80 Strand, London WC2R ORL, England
Penguin Putnam Inc., 375 Hudson Street, New York, New York 10014, USA
Penguin Books Australia Ltd, 250 Camberwell Road, Camberwell, Victoria 3124, Australia
Penguin Books Canada Ltd, 10 Alcorn Avenue, Toronto, Ontario, Canada M4V 3B2
Penguin Books India (P) Ltd, 11 Community Centre, Panchsheel Park,
New Delhi – 110 017, India
Penguin Books (NZ) Ltd, Cnr Rosedale and Airborne Roads,
Albany, Auckland, New Zealand
Penguin Books (South Africa) (Pty) Ltd, 24 Sturdee Avenue,
Rosebank 2196, South Africa

Penguin Books Ltd, Registered Offices: 80 Strand, London WC2R ORL, England

www.penguin.com

First published 2001
This special sales edition first published 2002
1

Set in 11.75/13.75 pt Monotype Garamond
Typeset by Rowland Phototypesetting Ltd,
Bury St Edmunds, Suffolk
Printed and bound in Great Britain by
Bookmarque Ltd, Croydon, Surrey

For David Tennant, for his help, his knowledge
of farce and for being a very good pal.

Acknowledgements

Very great and eternal thanks in equal measure go to two ceaselessly supportive and long-suffering people – my editor, Simon Prosser, and my agent, Sarah Lutyens. They have both championed my writing efforts from the start – for that and much, much more I will always be extremely grateful.

Great thanks go also to: my mum, Alison Weir, for knowing words that no one else knows and how to spell them; Clare Ledingham, for her invaluable contribution, suggestions and unobtrusive amendments; Jon Canter, for being a pedant and good at commas; Juliette Mitchell, for her patience; and Rachel Norton, for being my reading 'guinea pig'.

And lastly to Jeremy, Isabella and Archie, without whom there would be no point in doing anything anyway.

1. The Elbow

Hat was reeling, literally reeling. She was so stunned that she was sure she was going to fall over – even though she was sitting down. She was absolutely convinced that her entire body was about to fold in half and crumple into a crinkled heap underneath the table. Hat didn't know what had hit her. Catastrophic, cataclysmic destruction had struck and she hadn't seen it coming. To make matters worse, it wasn't as if she hadn't spent her whole life waiting for disasters – she had. She had spent it on the look-out for calamity. She'd always kept an ear open for tragedy's timely rat-tat-tat on the door. When anything pleasant happened to her, Hat would be happy in that moment and perhaps for a while after. But way off, in the back of her head, she'd always be thinking secretly, Bet I'll have to pay for this later.

So, generally speaking, Hat mistrusted agreeable events; she viewed them with suspicion, as if they were tricks. To her, a nice thing was all well and good but it inevitably came with a hefty price tag. Not that she was a miserable person – she wasn't: she was kind, lively and solid. It was just that she didn't assume good things would happen to her; to other people, to her friends, yes, but not to her. Of course, good and bad things occurred all the time but Hat always felt more comfortable when the bad things came along, as if they were an old friend she'd waited ages to see. Hat nurtured this characteristic because, above all, it made her feel safe. It was one of Hat's things.

But not even her own personal lifetime of low expectations had geared her up for this. Yet here she was, Harriet Grant, known to all (excluding her parents and sometimes her sister) since she couldn't remember when as Hat, a thirty-three-year-old gardener and office-plant maintenance officer (why 'officer' she'd never worked out) left high and dry six weeks before her wedding. Her fiance James Mackenzie, known to all since he couldn't remember when as Jimmy Mack, had called the whole thing off. Forty-bloody-two miserable, sodding days before her big day Jimmy Mack had taken it upon himself to give her the big heave-ho, the elbow, the brush-off, the right-royal chuck, the pathetically insufficient, laughably (if she'd been in the mood for laughing) cliched it's-not-you-it's-me speech.

Hat's mind was spinning and it wouldn't stop. It was twirling around on its own thoughts so fast that if it had been wearing a kilt it would have been Scottish dancing. She was rooted to the spot. She wasn't going to crumple on to the floor any more: crumpling was off the menu, because now she felt like she'd lost the use of her legs. Now, she realized with horror, she was paralysed from the waist down. For a split second the idea flashed across her mind that Jimmy Mack might come back out of pity once he discovered she'd been in a wheelchair since the day he'd left. She dropped that notion as soon as it dawned on her that paralysis would mean she wouldn't be able to ride pillion on his motorbike and Jimmy Mack loved that bike.

Hat was like that: she was one of those people who are always sensible even in a crisis. At least, she saw herself as sensible, her friends saw her as a tad neurotic. She was the sort of person whose house might be consumed by fifty-foot-high flames and who wouldn't leave until she'd made sure she'd locked the back door. So, not so much a sensible swot as a double-checker – well, a triple-, no, quadruple-checker. This practical-at-all-times trait complemented always-keeping-an-eye-open-for-a-debacle perfectly and, in Hat's view, meant that she was always prepared for the worst. Until today.

Once again Hat went over the dreadful, terrible, end-of-her-world-as-she-knew-it moment.

'You what?' Hat spluttered, spraying coffee over the faded red Formica table at which she and Jimmy Mack were sitting. She was instantly and painfully aware that this wasn't the *most* attractive thing she'd ever done.

'Oh, God, Hat, don't make this any harder than it is. Ah just . . . erm . . . cannae.' Jimmy looked down into his untouched coffee and shrugged his shoulders in that hey-I'm-just-a-helpless-guy way that Hat ordinarily thought adorable.

'C-c-can't what?' Hat urged, knowing full well what he couldn't now do.

'Hat, please, look, it's no *that* big a deal. Well, sorry, no, it probably is quite a big deal but, you know, Ah mean it might not be. If we knock it on the head now, you know, it won't . . . it shouldnae . . . erm . . . be completely disastrous, eh?'

'But we've already sent out the bloody invitations, and people have started replying! My dress is nearly ready! My mother's going to burst a blood vessel! And what about the flowers, the food, the booze, everything, shit, the hall, it's all been paid for. Oh, God, and our honeymoon,' Hat whined, knowing that not only was it untrue that *all* of these things had been paid for but that they weren't really the point anyway.

'Yeah, but only the deposits on most things, eh? Not the whole amount, that's right, in't it? We . . . erm . . . you weren't goin' tae havtae pay the balance until much nearer the time,' Jimmy Mack replied lamely.

'How much nearer the time do you want to get? It's in six weeks! Anyway, I don't think we get any of the deposits back if we cancel so soon before . . . before . . . the . . . our . . .' Hat couldn't bring herself to say the word 'wedding'. She couldn't believe he'd just sprung this on her out of the blue and they were arguing the toss about deposit losses versus full refunds. Talk about rearranging deckchairs on the *Titanic*.

'Still, that's better than losing *all* the money, d'you no reckon?' Jimmy Mack said cheerily, with a crooked come-on-it-can't-be-that-bad smile that made Hat feel like gouging his eyes out with the stained teaspoon that lay buried in the sugar bowl.

'Never mind about the bloody deposits. Why? Why aren't you going to . . .' The word stuck in her craw. She had to force it out. '. . . marry me? Why now? What, I mean, what?' Hat knew she wasn't making sense but, then, the whole thing didn't make sense.

Jimmy Mack and Hat were in a coffee bar round the corner from the church where their wedding was supposed to take place. It wasn't one of those ubiquitous, trendy coffee-drowned-in-milk-and-old-buns-made-of-grated-carrots-pretending-to-be-more-tasty-because-they're-called-muffins type of imported-from-America-and-therefore-better-in-every-way bars. It was one of those dreary old cafes decorated with dusty plastic fruit and faded murals of Naples Bay run by depressed old Italian couples who hate the British for not knowing the difference between linguine and spaghetti. They'd arrived way too early for their first meeting with the new vicar. That was Hat's doing: being cautious, she'd insisted they set off in ludicrously good time so that they'd make a favourable first impression by not being late. It was a lady vicar. 'How lovely, how modern,' Hat's mum had said unconvincingly, on the phone from Canada where she and Hat's dad had lived for the last ten years. They'd been torn between there and Jersey as the ideal destination for their retirement. They'd chosen Canada because, in Hat's view, a greater number of boring old people lived in North America even than in Jersey.

The church had been booked as soon as they'd decided to marry but the vicar they'd met originally had since moved on to another parish. The new one had understandably requested a meeting to familiarize herself with the couple before she married them. Neither Jimmy Mack nor Hat had ever been church-goers, nor had they been brought up as believers, but Hat had wanted a proper, brass-knobs-on, all-the-trimmings wedding. Jimmy Mack hadn't seemed to mind either way – until today he had never expressed strong feelings about anything. Even so, Hat wasn't to be blamed for choosing a grand ceremony. She'd never expected to find anyone who would be happy to go through a palaver like that, and when Jimmy Mack had proposed, she'd felt she'd better seize her chance and do it properly for fear of appearing to look a gift-horse in the mouth. She'd been swept away by it all, especially since she'd never expected to get married. She'd never thought she was the type of girl men would *want* to marry – the type of girl they went out with, had a laugh with, had good chats with, yeah, but marry? Never. Hat had always imagined that marriage was the preserve of girls who were petite, delicate, fluffy and feminine, like her sister Penny.

Hat wasn't overweight but neither was she slender and petite. Her work had led to the development of some strong muscles, and although she didn't look like a shot-putter, she wouldn't have been mistaken for a ballet dancer either. She was statuesque with long sandy-coloured hair that went streaky blonde in summer. She was attractive without being beautiful, and strong without being masculine. All the same, she had never felt entirely at ease with her body. Her older sister's fragile little frame had always been the mirror in which she had been reflected and she felt that, by comparison, she fared poorly.

'The thing is, Ah don't really have a clear idea why. Ah just know that Ah don't want tae go through with it right now. Maybe Ah just need some time on ma own, some space tae try and work things oot.'

Great, because time and space are the last fucking things you've got right now, Hat thought angrily.

'You know, this is not you it's me . . .' Jimmy continued, as if he were offering a rare and inspired insight into what might be wrong with their relationship.

'Bollocks!' Hat barked. 'It's me that's bloody well not going to be walking up the bloody sodding aisle, so you can stuff the it's-not-you-it's-me speech.'

'Erm, well, yeah, Ah get whit you're sayin' . . .' Jimmy Mack replied hesitantly. Unhappy as she was Hat could tell that he wasn't enjoying this either.

'But fur now, you know, Ah think it's for the best if we forget aboot it . . . just for now, yeah? Maybe if Ah spend a wee bit of time on ma own it'll change things, you know?'

Hat couldn't believe he kept referring to their wedding plans as if they could be put on hold, like a video or something. And even though he'd trailed off, it was clear to her that he had something more to say, something that would make her feel as if she had been slapped round the face with a large wet fish. She wanted desperately to clamp her hands over her ears and start singing loudly, but she didn't have a great voice and decided against it, reasoning that she might look a bit childish – not to say mad.

'The thing is, this is best for me, I think, you know?' he mumbled, concluding his uncomfortable speech.

'Best for you? When have you ever known what's *best for you*? Why do you have to realize what's *best for you* six weeks before our bloody wedding? Couldn't you have decided what's *best for you* after the wedding? Couldn't you have thought about what was *best for you* before we decided to get bloody well married? Oh, Christ . . . my mum, oh, help, help, shit, fuck, what's my mum going to say? I thought we loved each other,' Hat wailed, in an agonized, strangulated voice.

The glorious event she had organized single-handedly would have been the first time in Hat's life that she'd made her mother see her for all that she was and wanted to be. So much more than just the tomboy to her sister Penny's princess.

A heavy silence hung between them until eventually Jimmy spoke again. 'Look, Ah really *am* sorry, you know.'

'Yeah,' Hat replied feebly. She knew she was being pathetic, but how else was she supposed to react? It all seemed so final and what was worse, so . . . so valid. How does one argue with another's claim that they are doing what's best for them?

Hat tried frantically to come up with a reason for why he could not, must not, *would* not leave her in the lurch six weeks before their wedding. Before she was able to come up with anything more appealing than leaping across, clutching him by the collar of his jacket and yelling, like a banshee, 'I want to get married! I want my bloody wedding day!' Jimmy eased himself across the bench seat, got up and shuffled out, giving Hat a sad little wave. As she watched him go her heart wrenched. It felt like a sopping wet towel being wrung out by a Sumo wrestler.

As the door swung closed Hat saw her future happiness evaporate. She couldn't see how she was ever going to get over this. She had loved and trusted him and now he'd gone. They had had a strong, mutual love and understanding, or so Hat had thought until now. It might never have been a bubbling cauldron of rampant passion, but it had been all that Hat was looking for. She had agreed to marry Jimmy Mack because she'd thought she'd met the love of her life, and had been content with the style of their partnership from the beginning – cosy and safe.

And now what? Where had cosy and safe got her? Dumped and heading fast towards a wedding day with no groom. About as pleasurable, Hat thought, as being trapped on a runaway train with no driver. She ordered another coffee: she needed time to gather her thoughts and she didn't think the grumpy old waitress would take kindly to her sitting there, trying to sort out her life without paying for the privilege. Once the woman had plonked the cup in front of her, Hat decided to start thinking about what the steaming, bleeding, arsing hell she was going to do next.

2. Thirteen Months Earlier, When Hat Met an Alien

'Ah gotta persil heer that needs synin fur,' a voice mumbled from across the other side of the room. Hat's back was to the door: she was working at the trough of Japanese orchids that ran the entire length of a huge waist-to-ceiling plate-glass window. It formed the exterior wall of the reception area of a small but successful textile design company, Styles and Stripes. Hat had a contract with them to tend their collection of beautiful and, fortunately for her, high-maintenance plants. She turned round, hands covered in soil, to find a motorbike messenger holding a package. He was still wearing his helmet.

'A persil. Can you syne furit?'

'Sorry, I can't understand what you're saying. Would you mind taking your helmet off?'

'It's no the helmet, it's ma accent you cannae understand,' the messenger said, but pulled off his helmet.

Hat smiled. 'I've got no problems with a Glasgow accent. That thing muffled your voice and made you sound like an alien.'

The guy laughed. 'How'd ya ken it's a Glasgow accent?'

'Cos I was at the horticulture college near the botanic gardens.'

'What? So you huvtae go tae college now just tae learn how tae do a wee bit of weedin'?' he said, putting the parcel and his helmet on the reception counter.

Hat realized he was flirting with her and her stomach did a flip. She was fazed. She couldn't remember the last time someone had flirted with her – well, not someone she liked. And Hat liked the look of this man. He was tall and wiry with sunken cheeks and a pale complexion. He had dirty-blond hair – a muddier version of her own colour – and piercing blue eyes. There was a worn, lived-in air about him that just stopped him being classically handsome. Hat guessed that he was probably around her age. She had a hunch that his weatherbeaten look was the result of having been completely out of it more than a couple of times in his life. Not so much drop-dead-gorgeous as drop-dead-drunk – not now, but frequently and in recent history.

'So, can you syne furit? Otherwise Ah'll huvtae cum back.'

'No, it's all right, I'll take it.'

As Hat handed back the receipt she wished she'd pretended she couldn't sign for it so that he'd be forced to return later and she could see him again. The courier picked up his helmet and walked towards the door. It dawned on Hat that she might have misread him: maybe he hadn't been flirting. She found she was disappointed.

Then he turned round. 'Anyway, you were wrong. It's no a Glasgow accent, Ah'm from Paisley.'

'Oh,' Hat said lamely.

'And, another thing, Ah'm an alien, as it goes,' he said, threw her a crooked smile and left.

Hat was so thrilled that she blushed and her stomach turned another somersault. She knew exactly where Paisley was – it was just outside Glasgow – and, even better, she knew that that had been definitely, *definitely* a flirty thing to say.

'A motorbike messenger?' Mish howled.

'Yes, a courier. So what?' Hat asked defensively, sensing that her flatmate and best friend wasn't going to approve of the Scottish boy she had set her sights on.

'Calling him a "courier" doesn't make his job any posher or more permanent.'

'I know. But maybe he's really a writer, or an actor, or a chef or something. Maybe the couriering is only to tide him over until he starts doing well in his proper job.'

'Hat, don't start this all over again. Maybe he's *just* a messenger and that's it. But he probably isn't. It's always a filling-in thing, like being a waiter or something. He probably hasn't found his feet, doesn't know what he wants to do in life. That's much more likely than that he's doing motorbike messengering because he can't get anyone to notice he's discovered a cure for the common cold or that he's got some revolutionary way to cook prunes. Don't start building up yet another man you fancy into something he's not. If he delivers letters and stuff for a living, and that's OK with you, fine, but don't try to pretend he's really a tortured novelist, or an Oscar-winning actor-in-waiting, or an unrecognized scientific genius, and that only your love will help him find the key to his hidden talents. For Christ's sake, don't open up your hospital for wounded puppies again, Hat, promise me. I thought we'd finished with Pet Rescue.'

Although she was absolutely sure that the alien wasn't from the adorable-hurt-puppies stable of men, Hat knew exactly what Mish was referring to. She was confident that she'd got out of her Pet Rescue phase. Not that she'd ever been totally convinced that that was what she did when she was picking a partner.

In her friend's opinion, the three major relationships in Hat's life so far had been with men straight out of the Damaged Goods Department. And, if truth be told, none of them had been much cop. They hadn't shaped up on any level but – vitally, from Hat's point of view – had shown massive potential for improvement. With her support and devotion they would turn into something special. Her taste for this kind of man wasn't based on an egomaniacal, power-crazy, I'm-so-wonderful-I-can-change-them self-belief. In fact, it was quite the reverse. Hat always felt slightly diminished in the presence of confident, happy, sorted-out men. It was as if, being already content, there was nothing she could offer them. With their full lives what would they want with her? But when she found a man with nothing going for him, then, hey, what's not to love? She wasn't looking for gratitude or servility: she wanted copper-bottomed, Grade-A security. She reckoned that a loser wasn't likely to dump you anything like as quickly as a winner

13

might. Not that Hat ever saw any of the men to whom she was attracted as losers: she saw them as people who simply hadn't yet found their way in life, who needed redirection and someone to love them before they blossomed.

As far as Mish was concerned they were men who could never give back to Hat what she gave them. Just like a pet, according to Mish, you gave them love, support and friendship only to find that they still shat all over the place.

A week later, as Hat drove her beaten-up two-seater half-car half-van towards the office of Styles and Stripes, she could hardly contain the feelings of wild anticipation whizzing around inside her. The alien had occupied her every waking thought since she'd last seen him. She'd been invaded by an alien.

'Do you know how many bike messengers come in here every day, Hat?' Gerry yelled at her, over the hissing and groaning of the espresso machine that lived in a little cubby-hole off the main reception area. He was Hat's other best friend and the receptionist at Styles and Stripes.

'You *must* know him. I'm sure he'd been here before, he looked like he knew his way around.'

'Hat, see that?' Gerry said, leaning out of the coffee nook and pointing at the only door leading to the reception area. 'We call that a door. It opens, inwards usually, and you enter. Most people are familiar with the procedure. It's not very difficult to look like you know your way around.'

Hat ignored Gerry's camp sarcasm. 'Scottish, tall, lanky, sort of good-looking in a kind of lived-in way?'

'Mmm, he sounds delicious, I must look out for him. I'll toss you for him, ha, ha. Anyway, no, he hasn't been in, as far as I know. But if he turns up I'll be sure to tell him you were asking for him.'

'Don't do that, Gerry, please. I just thought he was nice.'

'He's tickled your fancy, yeah?'

Hat looked at him and pulled a reluctant face, conceding that he was right, as usual. 'Yeah, but I'll never see him again now and he was probably The One.' She grinned – it was supposed to be a joke but as she made it she'd felt a bit funny.

'Oh I see, he's "The One", is he? My goodness and after only a glimpse. What is this? *Brief Encounter?*' Gerry handed Hat an unperky-looking cappuccino. 'I have something in my eye. Do you think you could help me?' he continued, pouting and fluttering his eyelashes theatrically. It was a fair imitation of Celia Johnson's upper-class uptight housewife from the famous film.

Hat looked down at her mug and raised her eyebrows.

Gerry was quick to pre-empt any negative remark. 'Don't start. I'm having trouble getting my froth up.'

She giggled, and went back to pruning the splendid lemon tree that stood in a large terracotta pot beside the desk. 'I'm not saying he's my Rhett Butler, I'm just saying that something clicked between us, OK?'

'Well, whatever, as long as he's not another from

Pet Rescue,' Gerry said, and added a puppyish whimper as he settled himself at his station.

All Hat's friends had adopted Mish's turn of phrase, unanimously agreeing that it described her choice of men to a T.

Gerry was an old and loyal friend to Hat – they'd known each other since their schooldays. Gerry had been a quirky child with a precociously camp manner, and few kids had been prepared to risk being seen anywhere near him. Although he'd had no idea at the time what made him stand out he'd always known he was different. And Hat had been the only one who'd happily befriended him. She'd never mentioned his oddity, never asked why he was so unlike the other boys. She'd simply accepted him as he was and they'd become lifelong pals. Gerry was sure that, despite the vicious jibes of others, she'd never noticed anything unusual about him. After school and during their college years they'd lost touch. Gerry had eventually recognized his sexuality and had thrown himself headlong into gay life, preferring gay friends and gay venues. Then, Hat had been away at college, which made their friendship even harder to maintain, but since she'd moved back to London and got him the room at Priscilla's they had begun to see more of each other and re-established their old rapport.

Later, as Hat made her way out of Styles and Stripes she felt crushed. She knew it was mad, that it was nuts to talk to someone for a few minutes then obsess about them for a week but she hadn't been able to help herself. She'd been sure that she'd see the alien again, that, somehow, he'd turn up. Like an alien would. Something about him had struck a chord in her – and if only she'd known what it was she might have had the good sense to run a mile.

'Hullo,' the alien said, stepping out of the doorway of the next building as Hat arrived on the pavement. 'Ah thought you could use these,' he continued, handing her a pair of gardening gloves, 'you know, fur your weedin' an' that.'

'Thank you.' Hat looked down at them and broke into a broad smile. The alien had been waiting for her and he'd brought her a present. She didn't know what else to say. After a few awkward moments it was clear that the alien didn't either: he'd got himself there, he'd waited for her, he'd even got it together to bring an ice-breaker but, evidently, not an ice-pick as well. Hat wasn't sure what to do. She couldn't believe he'd waited for her just to give her some gardening gloves then go on his merry way. But he wasn't volunteering any more information.

She steeled herself to take the plunge. 'Thank you, these are great. Erm, have you finished work? Do you want to go for a drink?'

'No, Ah cannae. Well, see, Ah don't drink . . . well, not any mair,' the alien replied, looking down at the pavement. Instantly Hat knew she'd been right about where his worn-out look had come from. This time, she didn't hear Pet Rescue warning bells ring out loud and clear.

'But we could go and get a tea or somethin', if you like,' Jimmy Mack continued, gesticulating towards a cafe on the other side of the road with the hand that held his helmet.

And that was how it had begun: not so much with a bang as with a whimper.

3. What Hat Did Next

The truculent Italian trout displayed even more spectacular grumpiness during the few minutes it took Hat to pay for the coffee. She was feeling utterly wretched now that the reality of Jimmy's words had sunk in, and couldn't understand why the woman felt entitled to indulge in such gracelessness when her customers had to pay nearly a fiver for three mugs of dishwater masquerading as an authentic Italian beverage. She took revenge by sticking out her tongue at the sulky old bag – after she'd turned away, naturally. Hat wasn't the cheeky, rebellious kind. That was more Mish's area of expertise.

Hat left the cafe marginally cheered by having further irritated the woman: she had ostentatiously failed to drop an offering into the saucer that stood next to the till with a bold scrawled note demanding 'TEEPS' stuck to it. With no idea of where to go, she shuffled along in a daze. She felt as if all the direction and purpose in her life had been sucked out of her by a turbo-charged vacuum cleaner. She couldn't get things straight in her head. Twenty minutes ago everything had been going along just tickety-boo. Now the entire train had derailed and gone arse over tit.

A few minutes later, she found herself standing on the vicarage doorstep and ringing the bell. It was a balmy evening in late summer and, even in her current low state, Hat couldn't help drinking in the scent of the roses that grew in rampant abandon around the porch. Roses were Hat's favourite flower. She planted them wherever she could and often found herself persuading clients to give homes to the many different varieties she yearned to grow but couldn't accommodate in the pot-crammed tiny terrace of the flat she and Mish shared. Oh, God, I was going to have roses in my bouquet, she thought helplessly, as she waited for someone to open the door. Given that there was now no bridegroom, she hadn't a clue what she was hoping to achieve by coming here.

As she heard footsteps coming towards the door she decided that she had come to tell the vicar face to face that the wedding was off. It was the polite thing to do, but she felt strange as she wasn't given to spontaneity: she was the sort of person who liked to know exactly what she was doing well ahead of time. Mish called it her proper-advanced-planning thing. This was Hat's first unplanned move as a grown-up.

'So, that's all settled. I'll read the banns on the first three Sundays in September and very much look forward to seeing you *both* next week at the service. We'll have our chat after that,' the vicar was saying to Hat, in her sing-song nearer-my-God-to-thee voice.

She was a tall, bony woman with the drawn, emaciated look of a retired ballerina. Hat had found everything about her soothing – in fact, practically hypnotic – so much so that she hadn't wanted to disrupt the lovely floaty atmosphere with bald facts. But the way she had said 'both' snapped Hat back into the present. As they stood in the hallway shaking hands Hat realized that this was her last chance to set the record straight. She couldn't believe she had just spent twenty-five minutes in this woman's company, drinking tea so strong you could stand a spoon up in it, and not tell her that there wasn't going to be a wedding. That there wasn't, as it turned out, going to be any *both* coming to any Sunday service, and, by the looks of it, no bloody *both* going to be doing any-sodding-thing.

'What the hell do you mean you didn't want to disappoint the vicar? What's *her* disappointment got to do with it? What about *your* disappointment? Hat, for once in your life, think about yourself. You're the one who's been let down. Now's not the time to worry about other people. It's not like the vicar's some ancient old granny of yours who's going to drop dead when she hears you're not getting married after all. It must happen to her all the time – people are probably always calling off weddings. Hat, are you out of your bloody mind? What on earth are you going to do?'

Hat wasn't sure how to answer Mish's obvious and, indeed, rather pertinent barrage of questions. All she knew was that somehow she had succeeded in leaving the vicarage without cancelling her wedding. She felt as if she'd been having an out-of-body experience ever since she'd watched Jimmy walk out through the café door. Somehow she'd made her way home, and was now sitting in the living room having brought her pal up to date on the bizarre catalogue of events that had befallen her since they'd last seen each other just a couple of hours before.

After a few moments when Hat hadn't offered any clues as to how she was going to handle her new dumpedness, Mish calmed down and plonked herself next to her friend, who was sitting on the huge beaten-up old sofa that dominated their living room. Evidently hoping that straight talking might get her pal to snap to, Mish began again, but in a softer tone. 'Listen, Hat, I know you must feel absolutely terrible, really awful, but maybe it's for the best. Jimmy wasn't good enough for you – to be honest, he was another puppy from Pet Rescue. Maybe he's seen that. Maybe he thinks you deserve a better lifelong partner.'

Hat was only half listening. She knew her friend had never believed Jimmy was The One – none of her friends had approved of him. But although he might never set the world on fire, Hat knew that he wasn't a Pet Rescue type. He hadn't expected her to sort out his life: he didn't want it sorted out, he liked it as it was. He hadn't leant on her, then collapsed when she'd leant on him. He'd been her friend. She'd been able to talk to him about things. He didn't say much in return, but he wasn't hopeless, just unambitious. She wondered now if the whole thing had been too much for him. She just wished he had said something she could get her teeth into – like there was another woman, for instance. Well, obviously she didn't want *that* to be the case, but she wanted there to be something solid that would help her understand. Then perhaps it wouldn't hurt so much.

Hat had been surprised by how enthusiastically she'd taken to the idea of getting married after the notion had raised its unlikely head. Once they'd decided to go for it, the whole thing had taken on a momentum of its own. It had become like a train with more and more carriages being added on as it chugged along the track. And with each carriage it had picked up speed. The things required for the type of wedding they had chosen appealed to Hat's hidden sense of femininity. She had felt liberated to dive into the whole gamut of girly frippery that she had previously found somewhat embarrassing and which had felt like prohibited territory for which she didn't have the right pass. She had opted for the kind of wedding that meant she was duty-bound to have a big dress, masses of flowers, caterers, a reception, the works. The kind of day that would mean *she*, for once, would be the centre of attention.

When Hat was a child, her mother had always referred to her as her little tomboy. Hat had long suspected that she really meant 'truck-driver'. Hat hadn't been chunky or boyish, she simply hadn't been a little blonde angel like her sister Penny. Penny was three years older than Hat and liked playing with dollies and tea-sets, and loved wearing dresses with sticky-out skirts, which Hat hated because the nasty material scratched her thighs. Penny squealed when she saw a worm while Hat picked them up with her bare hands and fed them alive to her goldfish. Hat liked climbing trees, didn't like having her hair brushed and refused point blank to wear shiny party shoes. All the same, as they grew up there had been times when Hat thought she might like to wear a pretty dress or try on some of her sister's makeup or buy something different from Dr Marten's but the die had been cast. She couldn't shake off the image – at any rate, not within her family. To make matters worse, it had always been clear to her which kind of daughter their mother preferred.

As they grew older, nothing had changed. Predictably, Penny had married young, straight out of university, and 'very well', according to their parents. In fact, so well that their mother had nearly passed out with joy. Penny's husband's father was a knight and their mother never forgot it. Guy worked for his dad's firm in the City. Hat didn't know exactly what his job was but she knew he earned loads of money. She wasn't that keen on him as he tended to think he had the answer to everything. Penny and Guy had had a lavish wedding, which Hat had decreed to her friends was her idea of a living nightmare. Not for her all that getting trussed up like a toilet-roll cover, wearing a chunk of contorted metal on your head and listening to people you didn't like making speeches that weren't funny.

Hat never consciously envied Penny and her fairy-tale wedding, or her perfect match. However, as she'd got older she had found that she wouldn't mind sharing her life on a more permanent basis than the endless 'going-out' state she'd become used to. And then she'd arrived in her early thirties and met Jimmy Mack. Sparks might not have flown but there was real love between them and they got on well. One day, out of the blue, after they'd been going out for five months Jimmy had asked her to marry him. His proposal had turned him magically from her reliable, gentle boyfriend into the most fantastic guy in the world.

4. The Iceberg

The next morning, after a night devoid of repose, Hat got up at a quarter to eight. She had accepted at last that there was no point in trying to sleep and heaved herself up with the greatest of effort. Her mind was willing but her flesh was weak. She felt like a pile of hot, sweaty crap. She had spent four and a quarter hours thrashing about in a series of different positions: she'd twisted, turned, sat up, lain on her front, her back, with her head dangling over the edge of the bed (having heard somewhere that a rush of blood to the brain makes you sleepy), all without achieving even nineteen winks, never mind forty. She was exhausted but her mind just wouldn't rest. It was consumed by misery, confusion and bewilderment.

At three thirty in the morning Mish had begged to be allowed to get some rest. After hours of speculation on what Jimmy's motives might have been, she'd tried to persuade Hat that they'd drawn a blank. Left to her own devices Hat had spent the rest of the night listing every little thing she suspected she could have done differently to have averted the disaster. She had gone over and over everything she had not done right, refused to do, pushed Jimmy into. She'd even got down to things she'd worn that he might not have liked. Hat knew vaguely that she was clutching at straws and pretty short ones at that. Jimmy never expressed his feelings about anything much and when he did he meant it.

Having dragged herself into a sitting position, Hat sat on the edge of her bed. She began a half-hearted search for her moth-eaten but much-loved sheepskin slippers. As she glanced around her ramshackle room, she thought suddenly of the last time Jimmy had slept there, two nights previously. We didn't make love, she remembered sadly. In fact, what with all the wedding shenanigans, sex had taken a bit of a back seat recently. She wondered pathetically if Jimmy had minded. It wasn't as if he'd constantly tried it on and she'd rejected him. Most of the time he had seemed just as happy to cuddle and kiss in bed . . .

Hat and Jimmy Mack had started seeing each other fairly regularly after that first date, if it qualified as such. Initially Jimmy had begun to appear, as he had the first time, once a week outside Styles and Stripes just as Hat was leaving. After that they fell into a pattern of meeting up two, three, sometimes four times a week. They had first slept together eleven days into their relationship. It was different from anything Hat had experienced before. Although Jimmy knew what he was doing in the bed department he didn't have the same urgent hunger that most men exhibit, which had made her like him even more. He was considerate and gentle, and although the earth didn't move she had felt instantly comfortable with him. He was a great cuddler, which was rare in a man, she'd thought, and he seemed to love stroking her hair for hours on end. So, in her view, they had gelled sexually. Right from the beginning Hat had felt she could trust him. On the rare occasions when she had questioned the lack of roller-coaster element in their life, she'd always come to the satisfying and comforting conclusion that it was as good as it got.

Particularly since Paul, whom she'd met during her last year at college and stayed with for two and a half years. Neither Mish nor Gerry could fathom what Hat had seen in him. He'd said he was a painter but never seemed to paint anything – nothing that anyone ever saw. He didn't want to live with Hat because he claimed to need independence but ended up with his mum when he couldn't find a flat. He said that Hat and he couldn't see too much of each other because it would sap his 'creative drive' but spent most of his spare time – which was all day every day – in the pub.

None of these things had mattered to Hat, because she was convinced that through their love his talent would blossom. At moments when hard-hitting clarity threatened to open Hat's eyes, Paul had a knack of using his one tangible talent: he was a top-of-the-range shag. When it came to bedtime his inventive energy knew no bounds. He was a shagger *par excellence*. Hat would never have allowed herself to believe that this was his *only* redeeming feature, or that without it she probably wouldn't have given him the time of day. Her belief in the other merits of the relationship was only put to the test when he announced that he intended to abstain from physical relations: the energy he was 'wasting' on sex would be better redirected into his art. Mish had nearly died laughing when Hat had told her this, particularly since she'd long suspected that it had been his chief attraction for her friend, much as Hat protested otherwise. The relationship had ended shortly after Paul implemented his work-to-rule. Hat had come away from that relationship mistrusting great sex. She had resolved to search for deeper qualities in a man, even if top-quality bonking blocked out all else. This decision complemented a vague notion that infrequent shagging equalled a high-quality relationship.

Now that she was forced to reflect on every detail of her recent past, she wondered where on earth that idea had come from. Eventually she dimly recalled her mother once announcing that 'If a lifetime commitment is based on sex, it has no chance of survival.' As Hat couldn't imagine her parents ever having done it, let alone enjoying it, she could see where her mother had got *that* theory from. If, according to her mother, passion needn't be a motive for getting married then a couple was likely to stay together, just as long as neither party ever caught a glimpse of somebody they really did fancy.

The ghastly spectre Hat had conjured up of her parents on the job snapped her out of her reverie and she spotted her slippers peeping out from under a pile of clothes – a lifeline back to normality.

She shuffled into the kitchen and was glad to find Mish making tea and toast. She settled down at the table and, without planning to, found herself launching straight into the of-all-the-things-I-might-have-done-wrong-which-do-you-think-made-Jimmy-leave catalogue she had constructed overnight.

Mish listened patiently for a few minutes then cut her off mid-flow. 'Look, I'm not being cruel but you've got to stop this, Hat. You're doing what the captain of the *Titanic* must have been doing while the ship was going down.'

'Eh?' Hat was bewildered.

'It wasn't that that particular iceberg had the *Titanic*'s name on it, and if only he'd steered the ship a tiny little bit to the left everything would have been OK. It's that the ship shouldn't have been in the bloody iceberg-infested waters in the first place. Don't you see?'

'No,' Hat replied grumpily. She was too tired to try to work out the seafaring analogy.

'Hat, I'm going to be absolutely straight here. You knew I thought you shouldn't be with Jimmy Mack at all, let alone be marrying him, so now that the ship has sunk, let it go. Let this be the final resting place for your Pet Rescue. Don't try to mount a salvage operation.'

'Will you give it up with the Pet Rescue thing? Jimmy Mack was never like the others.'

'Yeah, it really looks like it from where I'm standing.'

'He just doesn't realize what he's done is all. And you don't understand either!' Hat yelled at her friend. It was as if every single one of the glaring realities and all their ramifications had crashed simultaneously into her consciousness. 'The wedding is up and running! It's like a runaway train. It's got a life of its own. I can't write it off, chalk it up to experience. We're already on board. You can't turn your back on a wedding like this six weeks before it's due to happen and just hope it goes away! Jimmy Mack *asked* me to marry him, I said yes, and that was supposed to be that! He can't just wobble out and leave me in the lurch. We've spent the last three months talking about nothing else. We've spent hours and hours discussing stargazer lilies and roses nestling with forget-me-nots surrounded by appropriate foliage and more hours choosing fillings for vol-au-vents, and knife and fork sets and soup tureens, and arguing about naff crystal bowls that blokes think you need for making foul concoctions that nobody ever drinks at the kind of party we wouldn't ever give – I've never made a bloody punch in my fucking life!' With that, Hat reached across the kitchen table, grabbed a piece of toast and took a huge bite. For a few moments the pair sat in stunned silence. Mish was the first to speak.

'All right, OK. Leaving vol-au-vents and punch-bowls aside, do you want to spend the rest of your life with him?'

'Of course I do. I love him,' Hat wailed. 'I know you probably think I said yes just so that I could get married and have a big day but it's not true. I'm not like that. You know I'm not. I want to be married to him. I felt safe with him. I trusted him. But I want my wonderful dress, too, and my lovely bouquet and the big reception and all-night dancing. Why shouldn't I? I want the fantastic day that was going to be all about me. Oh, why did Jimmy do it? Why did he leave me so soon before our wedding?'

'Would you have preferred it if he'd left you *after* the wedding?' Mish asked.

'Maybe.' As soon as she'd spoken Hat looked up at Mish and, realizing what she'd just said, began to laugh. Then she said, 'I do want to be with him, Mish. But in all honesty, once all this other stuff gets involved, it turns into a nightmare. Suddenly it's not about you two any more. It's about how many tiers to have on the cake, and whether his one-legged uncle from Dunoon who's got a prison record should be invited, and worrying about whether my mother will be able to behave herself for one sodding day.'

'Maybe Jimmy just got overwhelmed by it all,' Mish suggested, although they both knew that he wouldn't have noticed much of anything that was going on.

'Maybe,' Hat agreed forlornly. Then, all of a sudden, she sat bolt upright, her face brightening as if she'd just had a brainwave. 'Yeah, maybe that *is* it. Maybe I should have protected him more from the organizational side of it. Blokes are famously bad at coping with that sort of thing, aren't they? That's it! I just need to find a way to make the whole thing seem more casual, more fun, more normal for him.'

Mish nodded, smiling nervously, then stood up. She had to get to work. As a makeup artist she was freelance and couldn't afford to be late, particularly as she was doing a magazine shoot that day with a photographer she'd never worked with before. 'Look, Hat, I'm glad you've perked up. I'm not too keen on the idea that Jimmy just needs a pair of blinkers and some earplugs to get you back to where you were.'

Hat didn't respond: her mind was elsewhere. 'Hat, I've got to get ready for work now, OK? Why don't we talk about this when we get in tonight? We'll get a take-away.' She headed down the hall towards her bedroom. 'We could make a dolly of Jimmy and stick pins in it,' she called back over her shoulder. While Hat was grateful to her pal for having stayed up nearly half the night helping to perform the autopsy of the freshly dead relationship, even so, she wasn't ready to accept that the corpse was completely stiff: she'd found the answer to why her fiance had left. Now she was focusing on one thing and one thing only: how to get Jimmy Mack back in time for their wedding.

5. Later that Same Iceberg Day
Hat Decides that Priscilla Has
the Answer

As soon as Mish was safely out of the door, Hat headed straight for the telephone, despite having made her friend a solemn promise not to. It was the first chance she'd had: aside from trips to the loo and the time they'd spent in their respective bedrooms, she and Mish hadn't been out of each other's sight since the debacle. Still in her slippers and pyjamas she stood over the phone, racked with nerves, rehearsing some possible opening lines for the forbidden call to her ex-fiance.

'Hi, it's me, how are you doing?' No, too silly and chirpy, we've just broken up. He knows I'm upset, he's going to think I've had a lobotomy if I start like that. I mustn't steam straight in with the protecting-him-from-everything routine, he'll smell a rat straight away. I'll do that gently once he's back.

What about a simple 'hello' followed by total silence, leaving the ball in his court? Yes, I quite like that, she thought, moody and powerful at the same time. Oh, God, that's no good – he won't say anything either and we'll both be hanging on the phone for hours on end not getting anywhere.

'Hello, it's me. Look, I think we need to talk.'

Nope, too direct, he'll run a mile. Hat knew from experience that Jimmy wasn't a great one for let's-sit-down-and-thrash-this-out heart-to-hearts. Actually, come to think of it, she remembered, he's not a great one for heart-to-hearts full stop.

She searched for another option. What about starting up as if I've forgotten the split happened? 'Hi, Jimmy, just a quick call to let you know your suit's ready to be picked up, that your uncle Hector from Dunoon has accepted – oh, yeah, and our rings are ready too.' Hat was cheered momentarily by this approach. Yeah, she told herself, that's what mums are like when you've had a fit – they ignore it, no matter what you say, and just carry on as normal, and when you finally realize it's like talking to a brick wall you give in! After a couple more seconds' thought, Hat threw it out. It was one thing ignoring a tantrum, but she could hardly *ignore* Jimmy into marrying her.

She was waging a messy and totally unfamiliar internal wrestling match between this new desperate, frantic, panic-stricken self and her old, familiar, capable self. It wasn't clear which was going to win until Hat took a hold of herself and blurted out her last pitch: 'Hi, it's Hat. Listen, I know you've just walked out on me six weeks before our wedding but I wondered if you'd like to meet for a coffee or something?'

Well, it can't be faulted for accuracy, Hat decided. Knowing she was making a huge mistake, but unable to stop herself, she took a deep breath and reached for the handset. Just as her fingers touched it, it rang and Hat nearly jumped out of her skin. It had never sounded so loud and shrill before. She was certain it must be Jimmy. As it continued to ring she stared at it. She didn't want to answer it too quickly, convinced that if she did he'd know she'd been standing there trying to pluck up courage to call him. Finally, after an agonizing wait, she picked it up.

'Good, I've caught you. Although why you haven't left yet is beyond me. You're supposed to start at nine thirty and you've certainly got your work cut out for you with that Godforsaken privet of mine. It's gone berserk, which it's got no business doing at this time of the year. However, as you haven't left could I prevail upon you to pick me up a pint of semi-skimmed on your way here?'

Hat didn't answer. She was still grappling with the realization that it wasn't Jimmy Mack who'd rung but an old friend of her mother's, and Hat's longest-standing client: Priscilla.

'Hello, Hat, are you there?'

'Yes, pint of milk, OK, see you soon, I'm on my way,' Hat replied automatically.

'I know I could shuffle round to the corner shop myself – God knows, I need the exercise – but I can't face another mind-numbingly tedious conversation with that wretched little man. He's kind enough but he really is a crashing bore! I'd rather have molten lava poured into my ears than listen to him whinge on about whose responsibility the pavement outside his shop is. It's not that I don't like him. Ye gods, I certainly appreciate having a shop so close by that's open all hours and, in his own way, he's sweet enough.

But, my word, two yards of pavement and their attend-ant problems are not my idea of a fascinating way to pass a morning.'

Ordinarily Hat would have cut off Priscilla mid-rant, way before she'd got this far, but she hadn't been listening to her. She was still reeling from the conviction that it should have been Jimmy at the other end of the line.

'No, it's fine, Priscilla, I'll get the milk.'

'Semi-skimmed, mind you. None of that skimmed filth you young people drink. Revolting stuff, might as well put Tippex in your tea.' And Priscilla rang off, confident, as ever, that her orders would be fulfilled.

The call had thrown Hat completely off course. She'd been so fixated on finding the right thing to say to Jimmy Mack that she had forgotten what she was supposed to be doing that morning. Now, reminded that she was expected at Priscilla's, she was intensely relieved. She felt as if she'd been pulled in the nick of time from the jaws of a man-eating lion. The sensible side of her had known all along that ringing him would be a mistake, but until now the mad side had been winning the argument. She felt like falling on her knees and offering thanks to God for making Priscilla the laziest, bossiest woman on earth.

'Pre-wedding nerves, that's all it is. Typical man, yes, pre-wedding nerves, nothing more, nothing less. I only wanted a pint, I won't be able to use all of this before it goes off,' Priscilla barked, waving the litre carton Hat had brought her. They were sitting in

Priscilla's shambolic kitchen having a cup of coffee before Hat began her weekly attempt at maintaining the vast arrangement of lawn, shrubs, trees and plants that surrounded the once grand, now dilapidated house Priscilla had inherited from her parents.

Priscilla Montagu and Hat's mother, Margaret, had been at school together. They were unlikely friends, particularly in adulthood. Hat had always thanked her lucky stars that her rather ordinary, small-minded mother had managed to hang on to the friendship of someone as unusual as Priscilla, who had led a flamboyant and action-packed life since her days as a debutante model in the late 1950s. Now in her early sixties she'd slowed down a bit. She had never married, or had children, and had been like a wonderful aunt to Hat and, latterly, to Gerry to whom she rented a room. Although somewhat eccentric, she was a vital, independent woman with no regrets to haunt her. It was she who had encouraged Hat to take up gardening professionally, having nurtured her childhood interest in all things green. To Hat she was, in every way, a more appealing person than her mother. She could, and did, tell her anything.

'Cats won't touch it. It has to be full cream for those girls or they just turn up their noses at it. You can't fool them. Yes, I once knew a chap did exactly the same thing.'

'Turned his nose up at semi-skimmed milk?' Hat asked, bemused. Although she'd known Priscilla for years and was familiar with her machine-gun fire, rat-tat-tat-tat style of speech, always jumping from one topic to another, she was having difficulty keeping up. Maybe it's lack of sleep, she reasoned.

'What? No, you fool, balked just before his wedding. The girl's father found him, took him by the scruff of the neck, gave him a good talking-to and the wedding went ahead as planned.'

Hat was immeasurably glad to hear this. 'And did they live happily ever after?' she asked, a little nervous of the answer.

'No, or that is to say they might have done but we'll never know now. A couple of months later the poor chap shot himself, so there's no telling how it would have turned out. Still old Grizzle had her wedding day and the family could hold up their heads in the village high street so all's well that ends well.'

Priscilla missed Hat's horrified grimace. No matter how much she wanted her wedding day she didn't want Jimmy to commit suicide as a result of it.

'Oh, right. Well, I don't think I'd want my dad to give Jimmy Mack a good talking-to, he hasn't even met him yet. It's a year since they've been over. "Hi, Dad, this is Jimmy Mack, er, Mackenzie, my fiance. Well, I say fiance but technically he isn't any more. I just thought it'd be nice for you two to meet anyway. I'll get the drinks in while you have a chat, get to know each other, not that there's going to be much point, seeing as Jimmy's –"'

Priscilla cut her off. 'Of course not, my dear! One can't do that sort of thing nowadays, totally ridiculous. No, *you* have to find a way to make Jimmy see sense. You'll have to cook up something that knocks him back into play. That's all it needs.' Priscilla dropped some withered-looking smoked salmon she'd found at the back of the fridge on to the floor. Her three beloved cats appeared from nowhere and pounced on it. Although they were often fed the finest foods, Hat suspected that, given the choice, they'd choose regular meals of any old cat food over haphazardly supplied caviar.

She was thinking hard now, her mind had gone back into maximum whir mode. *Priscilla is brilliant! It's perfect, that's exactly it! I just need to think up something that'll make Jimmy laugh. Something that'll make him remember all the good times and why he wanted to be with me in the first place . . . something to make him think about what it was like before we got caught up in all the wedding preparations.*

Hat spent the rest of the day in the garden, hacking away at the notorious privet hedge with a religious mania. She could feel an optimistic excitement rushing through her, filling her with energy and joy. She was absolutely sure that, thanks to Priscilla, she'd found the solution to getting Jimmy Mack back.

Hat Discovers that Jimmy Mack Has a Roomy Hall Cupboard

Hat spent that evening at home, mulling over a variety of gimmicks, ideas, surprises, ploys and strategies that she might spring on Jimmy to bring about the desired effect. She was convinced that the perfect one would hurl him back instantaneously to his pre-chucking self. She had wisely elected not to share her recovery package with Mish: her friend would think she'd lost her mind.

In a way, on a small scale, Hat *had* lost her mind. She was in the grip of a manic obsession, which was – at least temporarily – keeping her out of a slough of forlorn despondency. Priscilla's approach appealed to Hat's sense of order and control, none of which she ever displayed domestically but which was always evident in her work and the way she led her life. Naturally, it had extended itself into her wedding preparations. The gardens Hat created were wild, exotic, labyrinthine, twisty and tangly. During winter, as she'd intended, each was enjoyable to its owners in a quiet, subdued way. Come spring and summer, they erupted into glorious technicolour, giving the same impression as an explosion in a paint shop – exactly as Hat had planned. She always positioned plants with military precision, knowing exactly how they would perform when they bloomed. As a gardener, the patience and forethought she displayed were exemplary but these virtues had disappeared as she contemplated her options as a jilted woman.

Hat had stopped being able to see the bigger picture, if there was a bigger picture to be seen. All said and done, she'd probably stopped seeing the bigger picture on the day she'd agreed to marry Jimmy Mack. She was oblivious to the fact that his proposal had opened up her own particular can of worms. The zeal with which she had accepted him then dived into planning the big day made it clear that not only had that can been festering away for years but that the worms were bursting to get out.

And what was she supposed to do with all that energy and enthusiasm just because Jimmy Mack had gone and changed his mind? Plans don't evaporate overnight because one of the participants has withdrawn his involvement, however much the quitter might like that to be the case. And you don't stop wanting someone the very second they announce they don't want you. You don't stop thinking about someone because they die. It would be great if life were like that, and a lot less painful, but it isn't. The prospective groom had made a decision for himself that, unfortunately for Hat, reverberated resoundingly upon her own plans. But for now, at least, she simply wasn't having any of it.

In the middle of yet another sleepless night the longed-for inspiration came to Hat and the next day she set off for work bursting with excitement. *En route* she made a short detour to buy the items she required to pull off her plan. With a great deal of huffing and puffing, she managed to stuff her booty under the bench seat of her little car/van – she needed to hide it until she could put the whole operation into action.

It was getting dark by the time she reached Jimmy Mack's flat and she was relieved to see that his motorbike wasn't outside. She had banked on him still being at work. Thanking God that he hadn't asked for the keys to his flat back, Hat let herself in. As she rooted about his kitchen for the piece of equipment she needed she felt a mixture of nerves, terror and elation. Mainly, she was convinced that when he saw what she'd done, he'd laugh like a drain, realize what an idiot he'd been and beg her forgiveness. It can't go wrong, she thought, after she'd completed everything and hidden to wait for Jimmy. It just can't.

6. Hat Relives the Awful Event

'Oh, God, oh, God, oh, God! I thought I was going to pass out! I'm so embarrassed, I want to curl up and die. I'm never going out again. I can't look at either of you. I'm such a twat!' Hat wailed, as she rocked back and forth on one of the wobbly kitchen chairs she and Mish had rescued from a skip and painted in a variety of Caribbean colours.

Fresh from her excruciating failure at recapturing Jimmy's heart, Hat had hotfooted it home prickling with shame. On arrival she was surprised, and eternally grateful, to find Gerry sitting in her kitchen chatting to Mish, a newly opened bottle of wine standing on the table.

'Calm down, have a drink, and tell us what happened,' Mish commanded, handing Hat a glass of wine.

'I don't think I can. I'm too humiliated. Oh, God, what was I thinking? He'll never come back after this.'

Gerry and Mish exchanged bewildered glances. They'd both hoped, a little prematurely, that Jimmy's coming back wasn't an option. They'd fondly imagined that that dish was permanently off the menu.

'Take your time. There's another bottle of wine in the fridge,' Gerry said encouragingly. 'Looks like we might need it,' he added.

Hat gave him a half-hearted smile by way of thanks, then burst into another drawn-out moan. 'Oh, Jesus Christ, I do not believe I did what I did! Mish, why didn't you stop me? I've completely buggered everything up now!'

'I didn't know you were going to do anything,' her friend replied hotly. 'How *could* I have stopped you? Anyway, I bet it wasn't that bad. Just tell us what happened, yeah?' she said, gingerly settling herself on another of the jauntily coloured but precarious chairs.

'Oh, I might as well get it out,' Hat said, with a resigned air. 'Yeah, maybe if I talk about it, I'll realize it isn't terminal after all. You know, a problem shared and all that . . .'

'So?' Gerry pressed.

'All right, but when I tell you, please remember that it was supposed to be a joke. Don't go thinking I've gone bonkers, OK?'

'No need to worry about that – I'll knock you senseless with this bottle if you don't get the story out right now!' Gerry barked. Patience was not one of *his* virtues.

'Right, OK, here goes. When I talked to Priscilla about it she was convinced that it was all nerves and stuff, so I got it into my head that Jimmy just needed to be reminded of the fun times, the laughs, you know? Take his mind off the nightmarish aspect of it all.'

'Please don't tell me you went round there and tried to get off with him?' Mish interrupted.

'Oh, God, no. It's much worse than that.'

'It can't be,' Gerry said. 'Go on.'

'Right, so I went round to his flat and . . . and . . . well, I got a pan, filled it with water, put it on to boil and . . . and boiled a load of bunnies in it,' she explained, in as throw-away a style as she could manufacture.

'*What?*' Gerry cried. He was a big animal-lover.

'Not real bunnies, you dork,' Mish butted in. Even in her present demented state Hat was unlikely to torture rabbits in pursuit of her ex.

'You see, when Jimmy and I saw *Fatal Attraction* we absolutely pissed ourselves and every time we saw another film after that with any woman who was a bit keen we'd shout out, "Oi, watch out, she might be a bunny-boiler!" I thought he'd think, Oh, she's pretending to go a bit mental like Glenn Close, and laugh cos he'd know I hadn't gone really mental.'

'Oh, yeah, he'd obviously realize you hadn't gone *really* mental,' Gerry drawled. He couldn't believe the story he was hearing.

'And what *did* he do?' Mish asked, throwing Gerry a mean look.

'Well, for a start, he was late coming in so the whole thing backfired. Normally he goes straight home after work so I thought I'd be fine putting the bunnies on to boil when I did. I wanted to get the timing right, have them bubbling away for exactly when he walked in. But he didn't get back for ages and the pan was spitting and crackling. As it got later and later I began to worry, but I'd put loads of water in, so I thought it'd be all right. I was hiding in the cupboard opposite his hall, with the door a tiny bit open – you can see

46

the front door and the kitchen from in there. Actually, that was a stroke of luck because I hadn't thought about where I'd hide before I got there. Anyway, there I was waiting for him to come in, see the pan, take off the lid, clock what was inside and start laughing, you know, and then I'd come out, ta-dah! But when he *did* come in, he started looking around with a weird, suspicious look on his face. The pan was giving off a terrible smell. When he saw it, he went over to it, got a fork and fished out something that didn't look anything like the toys I'd put in there at all. The fucking bunnies had been on the boil for so long they'd gone all manky! They didn't look like rabbits any more, looked more like diseased albino aubergines! One looked like a bleached ox tongue or something. All sort of grey and floppy. Or like tripe, pale and sickly and all runkled up like a prune. It looked like a very old man's cock that hadn't seen the light of day for fifty years.'

Gerry and Mish burst into wild guffaws.

'Don't,' Hat pleaded, 'it isn't funny. I could kick myself for not thinking about the plastic in those bloody things. I checked the safety label on them and it said, "Keep away from naked flame," but I thought they'd be OK in hot water. Shit! Bollocks! It might have gone all right if the bunnies hadn't mutated.'

'Do you really think so?' Mish said gently, once she'd stopped laughing.

'Oh, yes, if you'd gone for a higher quality toy rabbit the whole thing would have been a tremendous success,' Gerry added, still snickering.

Hat ignored him and replied to Mish: 'I don't know but it couldn't have been worse than it was.'

'What did Jimmy say when you emerged from your hidey-hole?' Gerry asked, perhaps trying to be a bit more helpful than he'd been so far.

'Nothing – well, nothing to me. I was so paralysed with embarrassment that I stayed in the cupboard. I mean, I could hardly have come out and asked if there was any chance of him reconsidering now that I'd ruined his pan and stunk his flat out, could I? When he left the kitchen and disappeared from view I sneaked out of the flat. So that's something – at least he doesn't know it was definitely me.'

Mish and Gerry erupted into hysterical laughter again.

'Are you mad, Hat?' Mish burst out. 'Of course he knows it's you! Who else would do something like that?'

'I don't know – a burglar maybe?' Hat suggested weakly.

'Yes, and why not?' Gerry jumped in. 'I can just picture the scene. A burglar who happens to have a detailed knowledge of film breaks into Jimmy's flat without any sign of entry. He is so annoyed to discover that there's nothing of any worth that he takes time out of his busy burgling schedule to boil the toy bunnies he has handily brought with him in case just such an opportunity should arise – the opportunity to express his extreme displeasure at the absence of valuables via movie trivia. He finds a pan and pops the bunnies on to a low simmer, making his getaway filled with the happy knowledge that his victim, upon seeing his dastardly act, will forever rue the day he didn't buy the full range of tip-top electrical equipment available from Bang and Olufsen.'

'Yes, OK, so Jimmy probably knows it was me but he didn't actually *see* me. He hasn't rung, has he, Mish?'

Mish shook her head.

'See? He hasn't rung, so he's probably not going to. Maybe he did think it was funny after all. Maybe I haven't completely blown it. Maybe he's laughing to himself about it right now,' Hat said cheerily, and leant forward to pour herself some more wine.

A quick exchange of looks between Gerry and Mish was all they needed to acknowledge that they were in silent agreement. Hat had had a hard enough day as it was. They had planned to give her a supportive, but serious, talk about how she needed to face facts, but they had understood that, right now, she didn't need to hear the home truths. Without words, they agreed that that sobering moment could wait.

Hat Fails to Get a Grip

The next day was Saturday, which was just as well because after the effort and trauma of the last forty-eight hours Hat was finally sleeping – and, even better, like the dead. Mish was pottering about their flat, trying to keep quiet so as not to wake her, when the door bell rang. She rushed to answer it and was dismayed to see who was standing outside.

*

'What's all this?' Hat asked sleepily as she shuffled into the living room sometime after noon. Every inch of floor-space – and it was not a spacious room at the best of times – was piled high with cardboard boxes of various sizes sealed with broad white and green tape. The smallest could have housed a domestic cat and the largest a Dobermann dog – probably with its owner.

'This lot,' Mish said, throwing out her arm and making a flamboyant sweeping gesture that took in most of the boxes, 'is some of your wedding presents, according to the men from John Lewis who delivered them a couple of hours ago.'

'Oh, fuck,' Hat said, and slumped into the armchair nearest the door.

Mish waited in vain for Hat to say more. Eventually she decided to press her friend into making a more illuminating comment. 'I take it you were so busy catching and cooking bunny rabbits yesterday that you didn't inform the John Lewis Partnership that your wedding was off.'

Hat took a moment to reply. 'No . . . I mean yes, no, whatever. I didn't ring them.'

Now was the ideal moment for home truths, Mish thought, even if Gerry wasn't there to help her lay them out.

'Hat,' she began, 'you must start facing facts. This wedding is not happening, you have got to accept that.' She paused to see if the message was getting through. From Hat's blank expression, she couldn't tell. 'You know, if you start dealing with all the admin bollocks, like cancelling the caterers and telling John Lewis and all the other people, I'm sure it'll make you feel better. Sort of taking control.' Mish was a great believer in getting on with things. She wasn't the sort to stand about weeping and wailing over spilt milk, although this laudable characteristic didn't make her any more gung-ho and courageous than Hat. Because neither was she the sort to get a mop and clean it up. She was more the walk-away-and-get-a-fresh-pint type.

Ordinarily a girl in Hat's predicament would have been able to rely on her mother's help to pick up the pieces: traditionally she would have been involved with the wedding plans. However, Hat's mother wasn't. Hat had wanted to do everything herself. Her parents knew that she was getting married, of course, but she had wanted to surprise them with the grandeur of it all. Margaret had been under the impression that the wedding was to be a low-key affair, and hadn't been too forthcoming with offers of help, while Philip, Hat's father, conventional to the last, had offered financial help in the form of eight thousand pounds. 'Exactly the same, taking into account inflation and interest, that your sister had for her wedding,' he'd informed Hat, in the prosaic, no-need-to-beat-about-the-bush letter that had accompanied his cheque. So far, she'd enjoyed her autonomy, and had budgeted the money carefully, but she wasn't so sure about having to do the cancelling on her own.

'I tell you what,' Mish said suddenly. They had

been quiet for a few minutes. 'Give me the list with everyone's numbers and I'll start ringing round if you think it's going to be too hard. Might as well put your redundant bridesmaid to good use, eh? I'll phone John Lewis first – the guys said they might be able to come back later on today if we, er, you, needed them to. Who else? Where's your list of who's accepted so far? I don't mind ringing Jimmy's lot and telling them it's been called off,' she said helpfully. 'And there's the caterers, the florist, the vicar, the photographer, the video bloke, the jeweller's, the hall, the butcher, the baker, the candlestick maker, ha, ha.'

Hat took a hold of herself and made a firm, positive decision. 'No, you don't need to ring them,' she announced.

'OK, great, so you'll ring them. Do you want me to do anything else?'

'Yeah, you can help me pile up these boxes where they won't be in the way.' Hat pointed at the longest bit of empty wall.

'*What?*'

Hat looked her in the eyes. 'I know you're going to think I'm mad, Mish, but I'm not. I've made up my mind. This wedding is going to happen if it kills me. I am going ahead with everything. I am not cancelling anybody. I'm not going to tell anyone. Only you, Gerry and Priscilla need know. For everyone else it's business as usual. If I believe with all my heart that it's going to happen then it will. Jimmy Mack is going to come back. I know he will and I need to make sure that everything hasn't fallen apart by the time he does.

I am getting married at two o'clock on Saturday the seventh of October at St Cuthbert's if it's the very last thing I do.'

7. Hat Realizes She'd Better Get Her Thinking Cap On

Later that day Hat had an appointment for her third fitting with the woman who was making her dress. Given her new it's-all-going-to-work-out-fine attitude she was keeping the appointment. Mish had attended the last two with her but this time Hat went on her own. Things had turned decidedly frosty between the pair in the hours that had elapsed since Hat's conversion. Mish had done everything possible to persuade her to abandon her determined journey towards, as she saw it, self-destruction. She'd gone from reasoning to yelling to cajoling via blackmail and threatening, even making a brief pit-stop at begging. Having failed at every stage she had sent her to Coventry. Unfortunately for Mish, Hat had taken on a kind of Joan of Arc conviction, a sort of everyone's-against-me-but-I-know-I'm-right stance, and her resolve was thriving on Mish's fierce opposition. The more Mish went on and on about what a mistake she was making, the more Hat believed she was doing the right thing. Having always seen more potential in Jimmy Mack than everyone else, she was even more determined to maintain her faith in him and his goodness. She was not going to allow any new evidence to the contrary to sway her from her chosen path of righteousness. And, for now, that was that.

Hat had found Mrs Kostas, the dressmaker, through a contact of Mish's. As a makeup artist Mish often worked with costume designers and fashion people, and when she had mentioned that her flatmate was looking for someone to make her wedding dress, a colleague had given her Mrs Kostas' name. She'd turned out to be perfect for Hat. Mrs Kostas was a small, dark woman of Greek-Cypriot origin. She had an unfussy manner that had set Hat at her ease right from the off. Despite having opted for a big wedding, Hat was not the sort of person who would ever be comfortable in flounces and she had chosen a simple Empire line dress with three-quarter-length sleeves. Although Mrs Kostas' workshop walls were lined with photographs of customers wearing, in Hat's view, preposterously swishy dresses, the dressmaker had not murmured a hint of disapproval and had set about creating exactly what Hat had envisaged. The body of the dress was more or less ready and today, according to Mrs Kostas, who spoke with a heavy Cockney-Greek accent, was 'slivs' day.

The bride-to-be, as it were, stood and looked at herself in the long mirror as Mrs Kostas pinned one sleeve into an armhole. She was quietly delighted with the way she looked. She'd never been given to dressing up and only owned one dress – which she'd worn to Penny's wedding twelve years earlier. Her job demanded practical, hard-wearing clothes, and when she was not gardening Hat wore less battered versions of her workwear – trousers, T-shirts and vests. To be happy and, what was more, comfortable in a full-length, slub-silk dress was quite an achievement for her, but its clean lines and high waist complemented her tall physique and its understated style suited her personality perfectly.

'So, nothing too frilly, I hope, Hattie. With your figure you need plain simple lines. That's what you'll look best in,' Penny pronounced authoritatively, as she finished her second cup of tea.

'You sound like Mum. I think I'm capable of choosing my own wedding dress, thank you. And please don't call me Hattie – it makes me feel like some fat old comedienne. Everyone's called me Hat for years,' Hat snapped. She felt just the same as she had when, as children, they'd argued over the frou-frou party frocks into which their mother was always trying to force Hat.

'OK, keep your hair on. So, what's it like, then?'

Hat resisted the temptation to launch into a description of an absurd crinoline, knitted-loo-roll-cover type of Princess Di's wedding dress: she knew her sister would think she was serious. 'It's an Empire line dress in a very pale green.'

'Green!' Penny exclaimed, in a tone that made it clear to Hat that she might as well have said shit-brown.

'*Yes.* Very pale, though, almost minty.'

'Do you think that's a good idea?'

'Well, I wouldn't have chosen it if I hadn't thought so, would I, Plopie?' Hat replied calmly. It was a cheap thrill to use the baby name she'd bestowed on her sister. It had stuck for years with Hat and their father. Penny and their mother, for obvious reasons, had hated it.

'Don't call me Plopie.'

'Sorry.'

The sisters were sitting in Tea-Time, a chintzy tea-shop close to Hat's dressmaker. Penny had suggested it. Hat hadn't noticed it until today, but it was her big sister all over, she'd thought as she walked in. The walls were covered in a boisterously patterned wallpaper depicting garden trellis entwined with unfeasibly pink Bourbon roses. The large, self-consciously homely room was dotted with small tables, each of which boasted a stiffly ironed white lace tablecloth. Instead of ordinary seats there were pastel-coloured Lloyd Loom chairs with padded seats. Hat felt as if she was having tea in their granny's bathroom.

'Should be called Twee-Time, not Tea-Time,' she'd mumbled to herself, as she'd sat waiting for her con-sistently late sister – Hat guessed Penny only did this to make her life seem more glamorous and action-packed. After all, it wasn't as if she had any real work to do.

Although Hat had made the plan to meet Penny before her world had gone belly-up she hadn't thought of cancelling. On the contrary, she had relished the prospect of the meeting: she had decided to regard it as the first hurdle. If sheer doggedness was going to be the determining factor in bringing off her wedding successfully then there were going to be many such moments over the next few weeks when her personally manufactured rock-solid faith was going to be put to the test. And Hat couldn't crumble under a little interrogation. She couldn't collapse in a heap of tears admitting that it had all gone skew-whiff because Jimmy had walked out. Just as the Christians had when they were thrown to the lions, she would hang on to her beliefs, no matter what wild beasts presented themselves in the shape of probing questions from people who hadn't yet met Jimmy, and badgering from the few who knew what had happened. He was coming back – she was sure of it. In the meantime she had to remain strong. It would all be all right in the end.

'You know, Hattie – sorry, Hat – a wedding has nothing to do with being married,' Penny announced suddenly, breaking the uncomfortable silence that had fallen between them.

'What? Sorry, I don't understand.' Hat was unaccustomed to her sister making deep and possibly personally revealing comments.

'A wedding isn't about married life. I just wanted to warn . . . oh, perhaps that's not quite right, let me think . . .' Penny jiggled her cup around in its saucer while she struggled to find the right word. Hat was transfixed: she couldn't imagine what her sister was trying to say. They rarely shared secrets and even more rarely discussed their private lives – they'd never been that chummy. The marked difference between them as children, added to how close Penny had always been to their mother, had ensured that a sisterly bond had never really taken hold. However, a natural fondness existed between them, albeit distant.

'Advise, yes, that's better. I wanted to advise you that a big wedding is great but it bears no relation whatsoever to the ordinary, mundane business of living with someone.' With a throaty chortle that Hat didn't find convincing Penny continued, 'You could almost marry one man on your wedding day and live with another for the rest of your life, there's so little connection between the two.'

Hat was astonished. If she hadn't known better she'd have thought Penny was trying to tell her that there was trouble in paradise. 'Is everything OK with you and Guy . . . erm, at home, Penny?' she asked.

'Yes, absolutely fine,' Penny said quickly. 'Everything's great. I just wanted to give you some big-sister, old-married-woman words of wisdom so that you didn't have any romantic illusions.'

Hat thought that that was a pretty stupid thing to say. There wouldn't be much point in getting married at all if you didn't have *any* romantic illusions. You might as well say cooking's got nothing to do with eating, or ballet's got nothing to do with dancing or shagging's got nothing to do with sex. At that point Hat stopped making comparisons. She'd suddenly recalled some grim times when for her shagging hadn't had much to do with sex.

'So, is Jimmy looking forward to meeting us all?' Penny asked, as she and Hat prepared to leave the tea-shop.

'Oh, yes, he can't wait,' Hat barked cheerily. Christ,

she thought, wincing at her strangled, high-pitched tone, I'd better work on my acting skills or I'm never going to get away with this.

'Good, because I can't wait to meet *him*. He must be absolutely great if you want to marry him,' Penny said, with genuine affection. Then she gave her sister a quick kiss on the cheek and climbed into her shiny car, leaving Hat with a gnawing pain in the pit of her stomach.

As Hat's family hadn't yet met Jimmy Mack, Penny had organized an informal (ha, ha, Hat had thought) pre-wedding dinner. It was scheduled to coincide with their parents' arrival two weeks before the great day. Hat had been dreading it from the moment her sister had made the offer. However, she hadn't seen how she could reasonably decline. The family had to meet him at some point and in a toss-up between a restaurant and Penny's house the latter just about had the edge. To the untrained eye it had been a kind gesture on her sister's part, but Hat suspected her secret motive was more sinister. She feared that Penny wanted to indulge in a fest of hey-everyone-look-how-fabulous-my-husband-is-in-comparison-with-this-impoverished-motorbike-messenger-my-sister-is-saddling-herself-with-for-life. Hat knew that to their parents (and possibly a few other people) Jimmy would compare unfavourably with the fabulous Guy with a knighted father. And while Penny wasn't always overtly competitive with her, Hat often wondered why, if her life was so perfect, she seemed driven to draw constant attention to it.

But that was beside the point. Until now she hadn't even begun to contemplate what she was going to do if Jimmy hadn't come back by the day of the dinner. She'd only thought about getting through the next hour and the one after that. She hadn't got round to thinking about how she was going to pull off the impending occasions when Jimmy's presence, as her fiance, would be, to put it mildly, vital. Finally it dawned on her that it was all very well having made her mammoth screw-my-courage-to-the-sticking-place-and-I'll-not-fail decision, but getting the fucking machine to work without having all its parts to hand was an entirely different matter.

8. Hat Tries in Vain to Enlist Mish's Help

'Mish, Mish – Michelle!' Hat called frantically, as she opened the front door to their flat.

Mish, who was still freezing her out, eventually deigned to pop her head out of the kitchen. 'What?' she said, frostily.

'You've got to help me think of something. It is absolutely vital that I get Jimmy Mack back.'

'We've been over this, Hat. You know I don't agree with what you're doing and I don't think that –'

'Never mind that now! Christ, the wedding's the least of my problems. I've got to get him back *before* the bloody wedding! Forget about the sodding wedding,' Hat said, pulling off her coat. 'Well, no, don't forget about it, but I'll worry about that later. I've got to get him back in time for the arsing dinner at my sister's! You know the meet-the-family-and-probably-go-right-off-me-straight-afterwards? I'd completely forgotten about it!'

'Oh, yes, that,' Mish drawled. 'And let's not forget the rehearsal.'

'What rehearsal?' Hat cried impatiently. She didn't want to be distracted from the hideous dinner issue.

'Your pal the vicar just rang. She wanted to know if three weeks on Saturday, the thirtieth of September, would be convenient for the wedding rehearsal. I said you'd get back to her. Oh, yeah, nearly forgot, she also said she was looking forward to seeing you *both* at church tomorrow.'

'Church?' Hat howled. 'Oh, fuck, I forgot I'm – we're supposed to go to the service. Shit. *And* I'd forgotten about the rehearsal.' She plonked herself on a chair in the kitchen and tried to take it all in, fiddling with her hands. She felt like all this information was packing itself into her head, jostling for first position with all the other stuff she had to consider. She couldn't stop fidgeting – she looked like someone awaiting urgent medication.

'You'll be glad to hear I didn't tell her that at this particular moment in time you were trying to locate your fiancé and that therefore *actually* booking a day for the rehearsal right now might be just a tad hasty,' Mish went on.

'Yes, good idea, thanks for that.' Hat had missed the irony in her friend's voice. 'OK, right, got it. I'll go alone to the service tomorrow and say Jimmy's not well. I'll worry about the rehearsal later. Now, about the dinner, how am I going to get round that?'

'The dinner?' Mish cried, her tone loaded with incredulity now. 'Hat, I don't really think you're focusing on the main issue here. The dinner is the *least* of your worries. You haven't got a boyfriend any more. Jimmy has left! You can't get married without a groom. And, in case it's slipped your mind, there's a living room filled with presents you can't keep. *And* you've done nothing about anything else. You're still committed to spending thousands of pounds on food, booze, a venue, flowers, and the rest for an event that is not going to take place! Will you wake up and smell the coffee, please?'

Hat gave her a blank stare, evidence that Mish's words had bypassed her. 'It is. It has to. I am having my wedding. You've got to remember how unsure of himself Jimmy Mack sounded. He's panicking, that's all. He just needs breathing space. But for now, *I* have to think of a way to get round this whole dinner problem.' She got up, went into the hall, where she flung her coat on to one of the pegs, then marched into the living room. Every coat she and Mish had ever owned hung from those few pegs and they were straining under the weight. One day they would crash down in a huge pile on top of someone unlucky enough to be passing at that moment and cause them to suffocate in an avalanche of fake fur, Gore-Tex and boiled wool. Until such a disaster happened neither girl was likely to do anything about it. In fact, if that unhappy accident did take place, so haphazardly did the two run their domestic affairs that the body would probably go undiscovered for weeks.

Mish turned on her heel and returned to the kitchen where she had been in the middle of making supper. She was stumped. Under normal circumstances her friend's determination stood her in good stead – when she had to work outside in cold, hard conditions, for example – but now, Mish realized, it was being woefully misapplied. She wondered if she should get out the *Yellow Pages* and look under L for Lunatic

Asylum, but decided against that course of action. She wasn't confident that you could have someone sectioned for wanting to go through with a groomless wedding. All the same, just to be on the safe side, she rang Gerry to request an emergency summit meeting. This was getting too big for her to handle on her own.

'Gerry, it's me.'

'Why are you whispering?'

'Cos Hat's in the other room and I don't want her to hear. Look, she's gone sort of mental – she's carrying on as if nothing's happened. As if Jimmy will be back. She went for another dress fitting today. The fucking thing's nearly ready!'

'Oh, God. Have you tried talking to her?'

'Er, doh, no, Gerry,' Mish hissed. 'Of course I didn't think of that! Yes, I've tried talking to her but there *is* no talking to her. She's decided that if she just has faith it'll all work out.'

Gerry broke into a robust but poor rendition of George Michael's 'Faith'. The ubiquitous pop star was one of his many icons.

'Gerry, for Christ's sake, this is serious! We've got to do something.'

There was a pause. Then Gerry said, 'Listen, bring her round for dinner tomorrow night. I'll make sure Priscilla's here too. We'll all talk some sense into her, she'll be fine.'

Mish was relieved that Hat's other two closest friends were now going to get involved. She knew that neither of them could be described as practical and straight talking, but surely they'd back her up.

Then she remembered that Priscilla's initial reaction had been responsible for encouraging Hat to keep going with everything. But something had to be done before Hat went completely round the bend. For now, Mish resolved, she would tread carefully with Hat: she didn't want to fall out with her again. She felt it imperative that the lines of communication were kept open: that way she could, ever so subtly, keep plugging away at her.

'That was Gerry,' Mish announced casually, as she strolled into the living room with a tray of food.

'What was Gerry?'

'On the phone.' She handed Hat a plate and settled into their solitary armchair. Unusually for them, it hadn't come out of a skip, but had been a rare joint purchase. Neither girl was disposed to spend money on furniture or things for the house.

'I didn't hear the phone,' Hat said, without looking up.

Mish panicked. 'I picked it up very quickly. It only had time to go bri–' she tried unsuccessfully to imitate the half-ring of a telephone. 'Anyway, he wanted to know if you, we, fancy dinner there tomorrow night. Priscilla's going to be there too, I think.' Mish crossed her fingers while she waited for a reply. She was waiting for Hat to decline on the grounds that she'd be too busy chaining herself to the railings outside Jimmy's flat or setting fire to herself in front of his work.

'Yeah, whatever, fine,' Hat replied absently. She was deep in thought.

Mish sighed with relief and turned on the TV. Maybe after all things could get back to normal soon.

About ten minutes later, Hat piped up brightly, 'Now, what do you think? Terminal illness or a dozen red roses?'

'What?'

'Which do you think would be more effective, a terminal illness or some flowers?'

Mish had a strong suspicion that she knew what her friend was talking about but she didn't want to encourage her. 'More effective at what?' she asked innocently: if she pretended not to know what Hat was talking about, her friend might be too embarrassed to persevere. She was on the wrong track by a million miles.

'More effective at getting Jimmy back. You see, if he thinks I've got a terminal illness then he'll feel really guilty and definitely come back, I reckon. And then later I can miraculously not have it after all, or I can say they've found a cure for it or something. On the other hand, that's quite a biggie, it might be worth keeping it up my sleeve until the last moment, you know, if all else fails. Whereas flowers show that you care. And they are my thing, after all, and he might like that. Boys don't often get flowers, do they?'

'I don't know, they probably get a bunch or two at their funerals,' Mish muttered. She'd better arm herself with the number for the loony-bin after all, she thought.

'Yeah, flowers, much better. I don't want to go

right over the top and make him think I've gone mad or anything.'

'Oh, no, you wouldn't want to do that.' Mish rolled her eyes to the heavens. She couldn't wait for tomorrow night when the cavalry arrived.

9. The Tangled Web We Weave

As the vicar came towards her, Hat's stomach slithered down and hid in her bowels. She had the same awful feeling she'd had at school when her name was called out during assembly to go and see the head teacher. The vicar was still wearing her cassock and, as she approached, Hat noticed that she looked more like she was gliding than walking. The idea that, for speed's sake, she might be wearing roller skates underneath her robes flitted across Hat's mind.

'Hello, Harriet. It's nice to see you. I hope you enjoyed the service.'

'Oh, yes,' Hat replied earnestly. In truth, she'd spent its entire duration so firmly in the grip of terror that she'd barely noticed what was going on. For all the attention she'd paid, they might have been sacrificing live goats and young virgins. From the moment she'd entered the church and settled down on a pew among the sparse congregation, she'd been convinced that every single person was going to turn, point at her, and exclaim loudly, 'What are you doing here? You've been dumped. You're not getting married any more!'

'Yes, it was lovely. I – I – always love a good hymn,' Hat continued. Oh, Christ, she thought, could I sound more guilty?

'And is your fiancé not with you?' the vicar inquired gently, looking behind Hat as if he might be hiding somewhere.

'No, no, sorry, he's – he's – indisposed … not well.'

'Nothing serious, I hope?'

Hat decided she'd better come up with something mighty quick. She was being offered a golden opportunity to give Jimmy an illness serious enough to explain his absence for the entire time up to the wedding in five-weeks-minus-a-day's time. She racked her brains trying to conjure up an affliction that wouldn't necessarily affect the way a person looked (just in case Jimmy *did* reappear) but would mean that they couldn't go out much. 'Cancer,' she said.

'Cancer,' the vicar echoed. She was clearly deeply shocked.

Hat realized that this had been a very bad choice. 'No, ha, ha, no, sorry, I meant he's a Cancer, which means he's very prone to – to –' Hat was frantic '– to – to foot conditions.' Not only was Jimmy Mack not a Cancer but Hat had no idea what she was talking about.

'Foot conditions?'

'Yes, like boils and bunions and verrucas and – and –' she was struggling to find a slightly more serious foot condition – verrucas don't keep people at home '– gout.'

'I see, poor chap. And that's because he's a Cancer.'

'Not just because he's a Cancer but that does make it worse. You see, Jimmy and I practise astrological health care and your zodiac sign can tell you a lot about your particular area of weakness and for Cancers it's teeth – I mean feet.'

Hat hadn't a clue where she was getting the stuff she was spewing forth but, as it seemed to be working, she didn't dare stop.

'I see, how interesting. Well, I'm a Gemini. What are my weak spots?'

Oh, fuck, Hat thought, desperately wishing she'd stuck to something of which she had, at least, a vague grasp. 'Gemini, er, let me see if I can remember. Gemini, oh, yes, Geminis that'd be – ah – your internal organs.' She made a circular movement above the general area between her breasts and her groin. She reckoned that that covered a good catch-all, non-specific region, her total ignorance of which would probably remain undiscovered.

'That's funny because I do have problems off and on with my bowels, as it happens.'

I don't want to know what happens to you when you go to the loo, Hat screamed inside her head. While she was relieved that the vicar appeared to be buying this nonsense she certainly didn't want to hear any of the woman's hard-stools-that-I-have-passed stories. She decided it was time to get out while the going was good. 'Well, I'd better get back, Jimmy's laid up and probably needs something.'

'Right-oh. Please wish your fiance better from me. I do hope he's well enough to come next week. After all, I can hardly meet him for the first time on the day I join you in holy wedlock, can I?' she said laughing, clearly under the impression that this was a hilariously unlikely eventuality.

'I wouldn't bank on it,' Hat muttered, as she walked out of the church.

Although evening was falling, it was mild for September and Hat decided to walk home. It wasn't far and she needed time to think. Her resolve wasn't shaken yet but it was certainly getting a good beating. The heat was on. She started going over the increasing number of obstacles that kept popping up to thwart her. She didn't blame herself: she put it down to all the outside forces conspiring to bring about her downfall – the bunny plan backfiring, the dinner, the vicar's irritating request to meet Jimmy, her mum's imminent arrival. Hat suspected that, if she didn't watch herself, the latter might prove her undoing. She knew that if she didn't come up with some bloody good reason as to why Jimmy wasn't glued to her side, her mother would smell a rat quicker than you could say 'jilted'. And Margaret was expected from Canada in just over three weeks' time. She'd made a great song and dance on the phone about how she was flying over early to help Hat – making it clear that she regarded this as an act of great sacrifice. Hat, though, was sure that her mother just wanted to get her oar in – and visit a poncy milliner to buy herself some truly appalling headgear, whose only real purpose would be to embarrass her younger daughter.

'For my money I think Hat *has* decided on exactly the right course of action,' Priscilla announced, to Mish's dismay, as she ladled out the stew she'd prepared into four chipped bowls, each from a different dinner service. As with everything in Priscilla's home, the china had once been very grand. It was exquisitely delicate hand-painted porcelain, now reduced to various states of disrepair. Some of it would have been too cracked and chipped to pass muster in a soup kitchen, but that didn't deter Priscilla. She'd never kept anything for 'best' and stacked it all together in her cupboards willy-nilly. Consequently a visitor was as likely to be given tea in an old tooth mug as a Limoges cup and saucer from a set made expressly for a Russian empress. It was the same with all the stuff in Priscilla's house – furniture, carpets, lamps. Along with the house, she'd inherited its contents and had never replaced or renewed anything. Some of it was in a respectable, usable state and some looked as if she'd nicked it out of a squat. 'Shabby chic', Gerry called it lovingly.

'She can't be paying any attention to his namby-pamby, shall-I-shan't-I meanderings so close to the big event. No, she simply has to knuckle down, keep her eye on the ball and go full steam ahead. At the end of the day men appreciate a woman who refuses to be budged – it means they know where they stand. All men are babies. Ultimately, they are all as weak as each other. Whether or not they are aware of it, they invariably take their lead from women. Think of the great words of Nancy Astor, I think it was her, that all women marry beneath them.'

Mish shot Gerry a despairing glance, hoping to elicit his support if no one else's. His reply was to raise his eyes to heaven then tuck into the food that had just landed in front of him.

Until this moment, Mish had fondly imagined that she'd come to the right place for some solid back-up. So far, it was looking increasingly unlikely that she was going to get any at all. She decided it was time for the truth. 'Priscilla, Jimmy Mack wasn't being indecisive. Well, OK, he probably was by most people's standards but for him to say something like that was quite a big deal, considering he's dumb most of the time.'

Hat looked at her indignantly, but Mish ignored her.

'For him, he was quite forthright, don't you think, Hat?' Mish said.

'Not *really*, no,' Hat began. 'He said he didn't know why he was doing it, just that it was probably for the best. And, more importantly, that he just needed some time on his own. I agree that, for Jimmy, you could see what he'd said, for him, as quite decisive, but you've got to remember he's given no concrete reason for backing out and that is definitely proof that he isn't sure.'

'Of course he's got no reason! As I said before, it's just pre-wedding nerves. All men need to be told what to do,' Priscilla pronounced confidently. She was keen on sweeping statements that neatly endowed entire gender groups, usually men, collections of people or even whole nations with one single characteristic.

'Would that be why you've never been married?'

'Among many other reasons, yes,' Priscilla replied, oblivious to the affectionate sarcasm in Gerry's question. 'None of the men I would have married were free to do so at the time,' she continued, 'and the ones who were I didn't fancy hitching myself to for life. So what with one thing and another I ended up a spinster and jolly glad about it.' The only spinster-like thing about Priscilla was her unmarried state.

'The thing is, pressure's mounting. Mum's coming over soon and you know how nosy she can be,' Hat said, looking at Priscilla for support.

'What? You mean a little thing like wanting to meet your intended? Yeah, I agree that is *really* nosy,' Mish said.

'Oh, he'll be back long before Maggie gets here, mark my words,' Priscilla announced, and knocked back the rest of her wine. 'You just have to think of something irresistibly seductive. Wonderful saucy lingerie, for example, no man can resist that.'

Hat winced.

Mish couldn't picture her friend in a Jackie Collins-type scenario, turning up at Jimmy's flat wearing nothing but a peep-hole bra and matching thong – apart from anything else, she'd said only the other day that those knickers made her feel like she had dental floss wedged in her crack.

'And what if he hasn't come back by then?' Mish

snapped. She was determined to inject a note of reality and get everyone to face the music.

'You get a beard!' Gerry cried.

'A what?' the women asked in unison.

'A beard. If Jimmy's not back by then, Hat'll have to get a beard.'

'You think if she grows a beard that'll change Jimmy's mind?' Priscilla inquired.

'No, a beard is what you call the girl a gay guy uses as a decoy, when they don't want people to know that they're gay. The list is endless – Rock Hudson, Michael Barrymore, Elton John, every one of them was married at some point in their lives. For crying out loud, just take George Michael – he used to have girlfriends all the time.'

'Couldn't George Michael just have been bisexual before?' Mish suggested hopefully. She was a big fan.

'What – and then went off it when he found the right boy?'

'Greedy poofs, that's what we call bisexual boys, isn't it, Gerry, my darling?' Priscilla called out from the kitchen's walk-in larder. She was rummaging around trying to find something that would do as a pudding.

'Yup,' Gerry said, arching his eyebrows. 'You're one thing or the other and if you can't decide which team to play for it's because you're a greedy poof.'

'Not an indecisive straight?' Mish teased.

'No, they are always definitely, indisputably gay.'

'So you're saying I should pretend to be gay and get a girlfriend?' Hat asked. She wasn't keeping up.

'Don't be daft. Although they do say all boys fantasize about having sex with two girls . . .'

'Yeah, and that's what we girls call a greedy straight,' Mish chipped in.

'Anyway, no, I'm not suggesting you do that although it might be a good fail-safe idea to keep in mind. I'm saying you find a man who'll pretend to be Jimmy while you're working on getting the real Jimmy back – so that your mother doesn't cotton on.'

'That's a brilliant idea, Gerry.' Hat looked delighted: she'd been thrown another lifeline.

'Yes, it *is* quite a clever idea,' Priscilla agreed, returning to the table with some moth-eaten fruit, half an ancient fruit cake and a packet of biscuits. Mish was thunderstruck. 'Hello? Sorry to rain on your parade, everybody, but just a small point. What's going to happen on the actual day if Jimmy does come back? You think Hat's mum, never mind anyone else, won't notice that it's not the same bloke she was introduced to before?'

The table fell silent as everyone pondered Mish's valid remark. For a moment or two it looked as if her pragmatism had won the day. Until Priscilla had a brainwave. 'No, he'll just have to wear a thick scarf and hat when he meets Maggie, pretend he has a bad cold or something.'

'Yeah, that wouldn't be too hard to carry off,' Gerry enthused.

'What? Are you both mad?' Briefly Hat came to her senses. 'I can't take someone round for dinner at my sister's house, which by the way has all mod cons *including* central heating, and expect no one to notice that my fiance won't take off his hat and scarf. They'll think he's Secret Squirrel or something!'

'Nonsense. He could say he had any number of throat or mouth ailments,' Priscilla retorted. She was probably the only person in the world who'd accept at face value a person who came into her home dressed like that and making such an extraordinary claim.

'Well, yeah, maybe,' Hat said, not sounding entirely convinced but evidently keen to give the idea some serious thought and unwilling to give up *any* options yet, no matter how far-fetched.

'All the same,' Priscilla added, 'I'd persevere with the first course of action – entice him back with a few womanly wiles. That's what's called for here. The last thing you need right now is to have to go rooting about for a moustache.'

'A beard, Priscilla,' Gerry reminded her affectionately.

'I know, I understood perfectly,' Priscilla retorted, 'facial hair serving as a metaphor for a disguise, beard, moustache, whatever, it hardly matters.'

'Anyway, the saucy gear is bound to work, isn't it?' Gerry said, putting his arm round Hat's shoulder.

Mish threw him a murderous look but to no avail: when it came to heterosexual to-ings and fro-ings Gerry always deferred to Priscilla's vast and lengthy experience.

10. When Push Comes to Shove

The next morning Hat woke up with a start. Adrenaline was coursing through every vein in her body. And, what's more, it was turbo-charged. She reckoned this must be how a soldier felt on the verge of going into battle. She had to steel herself for the week ahead, knowing that its developments were crucial. The impending arrival of her usually less-than-supportive mother in exactly thirteen days' time made her feel as though an ignited professional-display-sized firework was stuck up her bum and about to be lit.

Hurriedly Hat pulled on a random selection of clothes – the end result was Worzel Gummidge goes combat training. Never a dedicated follower of fashion, Hat wasn't focusing on teaming her fatigues with her fleece. Instead, she was cursing the fact that she couldn't put work on hold. She wanted, more than anything, to be able to concentrate full-time on the pressing matter of retrieving the life she had enjoyed up until nine days ago. Not that she didn't enjoy her job, she loved every aspect of it. She tended each garden and office array, no matter how functional or commonplace, with maternal devotion. She fretted over any plant that showed signs of fading. She nurtured back to erect, proud life any that drooped with the care most people reserve for dying relatives. Not that Hat was one of those types who believed in talking to her flora: she didn't hold with any of that hippie claptrap, dismissing anyone who did with the observation that 'You might as well talk to the trowel for all the good it's going to do.' Hat was anything but a romantic but she felt a passionate loyalty and deep sense of duty towards the living things under her protection. She was intensely proud of all her charges, and often wondered if she went for high-maintenance men because she had to expend the same amount of energy in keeping their balls in the air as she did on keeping alive capricious orchids.

For Hat the next two days of work were singularly unexciting and, consequently, offered no distraction from her obsession. She had three gardens to see to, all of which needed nothing more mentally taxing than routine pruning, weeding and mulching. However, Hat was glad of the opportunity this provided to come up with a fab new scheme that would change Jimmy's mind. It came to her via a gardening fork.

After an uneventful first day, Hat began the second allowing reluctantly that reality might beat her after all. Then, as if by magic, her faith was rescued by an inadvertently self-inflicted injury. When it happened she was alone at a client's. He was a concert pianist named Hermann Muller, and was away on tour. He was often out of town and Hat was accustomed to letting herself in via his back gate and getting on with things. That day, she was kneeling on the grass mulching a delicate plant and accidentally drove her fork into the ground with such force that the handle broke. As it snapped she lost her grip and fell twisting her wrist and a couple of fingers. The pain was excruciating. She shook her hand violently then held it under her armpit, squeezing it tight. She waited for the pain to pass, but the fingers swelled and were hard to move. Eventually she decided that she'd better get them checked out in case she'd broken something. Using her one good hand, she gathered up her stuff and climbed into her little car/van.

She drove herself to the hospital with one hand and the elbow of her other arm. She was aware that, as she hunched forward, attempting to negotiate the traffic, she was eliciting some peculiar looks from fellow drivers. Also the car/van handled about as well as a dodgem car: the steering-wheel had a will of its own, often taking her in directions she had no intention of going. As she grappled with her new driving style, she vowed to get something done about the wilful wheel.

Hat threw down the six-year-old, dog-eared magazine she'd been leafing through and cast a guilty look around the waiting room in case someone had caught her reading *Woman's Realm*. It was forty minutes since she'd seen the doctor and she was getting bored. As her gaze wandered around the room, she noticed a couple sitting across from her. The man had his arm around the shoulder of the girl, who was doubled over and seemed to be experiencing stomach pain. As Hat watched them, she envied the girl the tenderness her boyfriend was showing her. And then it came to her. Of course! That's it! This was just the chance she'd been waiting for – a no-fault-of-her-own-copper-bottomed-excuse to ring Jimmy. No need to fake a terminal disease, this is much better, she thought excitedly. I've genuinely hurt myself. Nobody turns down an injured ex. Hat skipped over to the public phone attached to the waiting-room wall.

'Hello, Jimmy, it's me, ah – ah – Hat.' She was suddenly painfully aware that that special it's-me greeting is reserved for the confidently-mutually-in-love crew and is unbearably embarrassing when used by the just-chucked brigade.

'Hullo,' Jimmy replied.

Hat tried to work out whether this was an oh-fuck-she's-rung-what-am-I-going-to-say-wish-I-hadn't-answered-the-phone hello or more of an oh-hi-thank-God-you've-rung-because-I-haven't-had-the-nerve-to-ring-you-but-I've-wanted-to-so-much-can-we-make-up hello. She decided that one word wasn't enough material to subject to a full analysis, and persevered.

'I'm in hospital.'

'God, whit's the matter? Whit's happened?'

Great, Hat thought, he still cares, he must do, otherwise he'd have just said, 'Oh, really,' or 'Why?' but he wants to know what's happened, that's a good sign.

'I've hurt my hand.'

'Oh, right. Whit – gardenin' or somethin'?' Jimmy asked, clearly having concluded that it was nothing serious.

Fuck, no, this is no good, Hat panicked, he thinks this is just an ordinary job-related run-of-the-mill accident, which it is, strictly speaking, but he's got to think it's worse than that for it to have the desired effect. She decided to up the ante. 'Yes, erm, but my hand's quite badly damaged,' Hat lied.

'Can you still use it?'

'No.'

A silence fell as Hat waited for Jimmy's question and he waited for her to elaborate.

'So is it broken?' Jimmy asked eventually.

'Er . . . no.'

A longer, heavier silence passed. Again, Jimmy was the first to speak: 'Well, is it in plaster, then?'

'Not exactly.'

Hat saw she was pushing her luck, and knew she had to be a bit more forthcoming but she couldn't think straight. She was making it all up as she went along. She realized now that she'd been wildly foolish not to have established with herself the severity of the injury prior to picking up the phone, and cursed herself.

'Is it sprained?' Jimmy continued.

'Ah – ah, no.'

'Hat, look, Ah'm sorry you've hurt yoursel' an' everythin' but Ah dinnae really known why you're ringin' me,' Jimmy mumbled.

Hat knew she'd better jump in quick. 'My hand's been amputated.' Oh, my God, she howled inside her head, what have I done now?

'Jesus Christ, Hat! Are you serious?'

'Erm, well, no, not yet, as such. But it might have to be.' Hat was thinking as fast as she could. She meant to raise the threat of a stump but wanted to hold back on a total amputation at this stage.

'Hat, has your hand been amputated, yes or no?' Jimmy said, evidently shaken.

'No, but they are saying it might have to be if it doesn't improve overnight.' Bollocks! Hat screamed, to herself, I should have said over the next three weeks and then I could have held it over his head until after we were married. I mean, no one would dump someone who might be facing amputation, would they?

'And whit do you want me tae do?' Jimmy asked – not unsympathetically, Hat noted.

What do you think? Go through with our fucking wedding, you plonker, she shouted inwardly.

'Erm, I wondered if you'd come down to the hospital and hold my hand – so to speak.' Hat wanted to kick herself – I'd hardly be likely to make jokes if my hand was really going to be cut off, would I? Act more devastated, she urged herself.

'Hat, Ah dinnae want to be mean but d'you no think it'd be better if Mish came doon?'

'No! She can't, she's away at the moment. I wouldn't have bothered you if she'd been around . . .' Hat cried forlornly.

It worked. Jimmy agreed to come.

'Miss Grant? Hello, we've been looking for you,' a nurse said, tapping Hat's shoulder as she put down the phone.

Hat wasn't confident she'd made the best move of her life but, what the hell? she had achieved the desired result. She was finally going to see Jimmy and she was ecstatic.

'Good news, the doctor's had a look at the X-rays and there's nothing broken, just some bad swelling, but that should come down over the next day or so. Your hand will feel a bit tender but that'll go as the swelling reduces. If you'd give the receptionist your GP's details, we'll send him or her the X-rays and you can see them for any follow-up.'

'No, no, I've got to stay here,' Hat practically yelled at her.

'I'm sorry?'

'I've got to stay here! I'm not feeling very well. I've lost all sensation in my hand – I think it's got worse. You can't discharge me, please, please,' Hat begged.

'Now, calm down. There's really nothing wrong with you. Your hand is bound to feel a bit funny but it's going to be fine in a couple of days. It shouldn't even affect your ability to work.'

'No, no, you've got to at least bandage it up. It's got to look awful. It's got to look terminal.'

'Terminal?' the nurse repeated. 'I've been a nurse for twelve years, Miss Grant, and in my experience a bruise doesn't usually lead to loss of life, not even a bad one,' she continued, smiling at her little joke.

'I don't mean terminal like that. I mean my hand's got to look like it's very, very seriously damaged and possibly even gangrenous.'

'Gangrenous?'

'Yes, you know, when a limb goes all funny-coloured and dead-looking.'

'I'm familiar with the condition of gangrene but –'

'Look, I can't explain why, it's too complicated, but can we get the doctor to pretend that he might have to amputate? It's really important,' Hat interrupted. She felt that no matter what it took she just couldn't let her opportunity slip away.

'You want me to find a doctor who will *pretend* that your hand may require amputation?' the nurse asked slowly.

'The thing is, I'm supposed to be getting married but my boyfriend has sort of gone off the idea. And it's occurred to me that I might be able to get him to change his mind if he thinks I'm going to have a stump,' Hat explained.

'I see.' The nurse had adopted a decidedly nursy, more gentle manner than she'd employed so far.

'You see, I know it sounds a bit silly but I've told him I might have to have my hand cut off. And because of that he's coming down to the hospital now, which is fantastic and I'm hoping that he'll come back to me, you know, *because* of that,' Hat rambled on.

'Well, I think you should come with me. You can have a nice lie-down and we'll find a doctor you can have a little chat with, OK?'

'Great, fantastic. Obviously I don't really want my hand cut off. I'm a gardener and I couldn't do without both of them. I just want him to think that there's a real danger of me losing it, do you see?'

'Oh, yes, perfectly,' the nurse replied, leading Hat smoothly back along the corridor.

'You see, when I boiled the bunnies round at his house that didn't work at all. I *had* thought he'd think that was hilarious but instead of floating in the pan like the one in the film did mine all melted into weird shapes. Oh, yeah, and they stank to high heaven but I didn't know because at the time I was hiding in the cupboard. You've seen that film, yeah?'

The nurse indicated that Hat should lie down in the bed she had revealed behind a curtained area removed from the main body of A and E. 'Oh, yes, of course, I know the one. Now, if you'd like to take these and have a little rest while I find the doctor and explain the situation to him . . .' the nurse said, handing Hat a couple of pale pink pills.

She swallowed them. 'So, what I'd really like is for you to wrap my hand up with masses of bandages, like I've done something awful. What were those pills, by the way? My hand's only aching a bit – it's just that I need . . .'

11. The Calm Before the Storm

Hat was waking up from a deep sleep she hadn't even been aware she'd fallen into. She tried to open her eyes and couldn't. She tried again but to no avail. The normally simple procedure was turning out to be a lot harder than it was ordinarily. Her eyelids felt like they'd been tied shut with tent ropes. After really putting her back into it, she managed to prise them open only to find that the world had turned white as snow. The entire place seemed to be neon lit. Hat emitted a low groan. Her head felt like hefty farm workers had been baling hay inside it.

'Good, you're awake – at last,' Hat heard Mish say. From her tone, Hat could tell that she was in a less than sunny mood. 'How are you feeling? Are you all right to get up?' she continued crisply. Before Hat was able to form a reply her friend leant forward and whispered in her ear. 'I think we should try and leave as soon as poss. I need to get you out of here before they insist on getting "Psych" down, as they keep calling it. Bet they didn't use that expression before *ER*. Anyway, I've had a hell of a job convincing them that you're not round the twist, which, seeing as I think you actually are, wasn't that easy.'

'Have they amputated my hand?' Hat asked wearily.

She had a vague memory of asking to have it chopped off.

'No, they bleeding well haven't, although it would have served you right if they had. In fact, they should have lopped both off. That way you wouldn't have been able to use the phone again to call Jimmy. Honestly, I've never heard the like, asking a nurse to mock up a serious accident to get your boyfriend back!'

'Oh, my God, Jimmy Mack! Where's Jimmy Mack?' Hat asked, instantly coming back to life.

'He's gone.'

'Gone? Gone? You mean he's been here and left? He was actually here and I missed him? Oh, God, I can't believe it! How did I miss him? What happened?'

Mish gave her pal a long-suffering but sympathetic smile then embarked on an explanation of what had happened. 'Apparently the nurse decided that you were mad, can't think where she got that idea from, and, I quote, "presenting the classic symptoms of a person who might be a danger to themselves or others". She gave you some sedatives because she said you were raving on about self-mutilation and how that would get someone back and make them love you again. Then Jimmy turned up, he said you'd rung him and told him I was out of town . . .' she gave Hat a sideways glance, making it clear that she took a poor view of this lie '. . . but thanks to the pills you were already asleep when he arrived. When he realized you weren't in any danger he guessed you'd probably lied about me being away too and called me.

I came down, having stopped off on my way to buy you a one-way ticket to Loonyville, which if you don't give up this nonsense you will definitely be needing.'

'Oh, shit, Mish, it's gone all wrong again. I wasn't supposed to be asleep, Jimmy was supposed to find me with my arm all bandaged up looking all woebegone and helpless.'

'Oh, very you,' Mish drawled sarcastically.

'Exactly. Not very me at all, which is why I thought it would work. I thought if he found me like that it would make him feel all protective and sorry for me, what with my heavily bandaged, possibly-going-to-be-cut-off hand. You know, sort of attractively-injured-and-needy-but-not-in-a-hideously-deformed type of way.'

'Were you looking for a charity shag, then?'

'Not a shag, course not, well, not here, just for him to feel responsible towards me and –'

'Same diff. Charity shag or charity marriage, it's all about forcing him into pitying you so much he'll do what you want, isn't it?'

'Yes,' Hat replied, instinctively blurting out the truth. 'Well, no, actually, I don't see it as *forcing* him, more as *persuading* him to see the error of his ways.'

'However you dress it up, Hat, does it seem fair?'

'Maybe not – oh, I don't know, but is it fair that I have to cancel my wedding, all my plans, everything, just because the groom's changed his mind all of a sudden?'

Mish didn't reply because she knew that it wasn't

fair. But she also knew that Hat was going to have to wake up and smell the coffee before too long or she was going to be dealing with a lot more trouble than a groomless wedding.

After her brief and unsuccessful dalliance with amputation Hat kept a low profile over the next few days. In fact, so low did she keep it that she succeeded in appearing to have returned to her normal self. She even managed to con Mish into believing she'd seen the light. She didn't go so far as to tell any bare-faced lies, she simply elected not to share the new idea she'd had. This fresh brainwave had served to renew and invigorate her strength of conviction. She had got her groove back. Nothing in her manner betrayed that she had decided to hurl right out of the window the minuscule reserve of caution she'd kept in place for the if-all-else-fails emergency. She was going to pull the ripcord, dive in feet first and ram her head right between the lion's snarling jaws.

In the unlikely event of Hat having taken time out to draw up a chart headed Ten Top Ways To Get Your Boyfriend Back, then the bunny-boiling episode and the amputation scene would have appeared as numbers one and two when compared with the advisability of her next planned move. Indeed, they were stark stand-alone symptoms of a lost plot but by contrast to what was next on the agenda they were positively enlightened, win–win manoeuvres. Hat was about to do something from which, if it failed, there would be no way on earth of regaining ground.

Her plan was bold. It was daring. It was top-of-the-range cream-of-the-crop bonkers. But it might just work.

Hat, the jilted bride, was in the grip of an obsession. It had mutated and grown into something much bigger than she was. And, like most people held in the grasp of an entity like that, she couldn't see the wood for the trees. Anyone could have walked up to her with a pine plank, forced her to eat it and she still wouldn't have seen the proverbial lumber. And, to be fair to Hat, total responsibility for her actions didn't rest entirely with her: the obsession itself was partly to blame. No self-respecting obsession can claim membership to that exclusive club Obsessions Are Us without ensuring the sufferer gives themselves up body and soul to its mighty will. A real obsession wrestles its hostage into a powerful head-lock then niggles and gnaws until it possesses all of its victim's reason, to the extent that they lose sight of the true worth of their object. If the obsessee becomes aware that what they desire isn't the real thing, the spell is broken. But that rationale had not yet descended upon Hat. No, she was smack bang, neck deep in the middle of a full-blown fixation. She was going full steam ahead, ensuring that she kept her eyes tight shut against hurdles, road-blocks and brick walls.

Until the joyous moment when she'd lit upon her latest plan Hat had kept herself busy. In the middle of every night since Mish had escorted her home from hospital she had beavered away at her wedding plans. She dashed off thank-you notes for the gifts that had already arrived. She tried on her veil, about which she'd never been sure. (In it, she felt as if she was making a phoney attempt to emulate the virginal brides of yesteryear, who, one presumed, would never have seen a man's unclothed penis before the wedding night. She'd only agreed to it because Mrs Kostas had insisted that it was a vital component of the outfit. She was pretty sure she'd dump it before the day.) As per the instructions in the step-by-step wedding-day-countdown pamphlet *Your Very Special Day* that Hat had found invaluable (although, she'd noticed, irritably, that it didn't give you any pointers on what to do if the groom does a bunk), she'd been padding around her bedroom in her wedding shoes. She had also spent hours moving little pieces of paper back and forth on the old piano stool (specially cleared of its customary pile of discarded underwear) trying to work out the seating plan for the reception.

However, although the plans were bobbing along, the run-in at the hospital had knocked Hat back. Part of her motive in continuing with everything now was to block out that hideous experience. Since then she had spent most of the time trying *not* to think about Jimmy having been there, seen her and stood, she presumed, only a few, tantalizing inches away from her. Instead she focused on the future and on all of the things that had to be sorted out to ensure that everything didn't fall apart. All Hat's hopes and dreams were invested in this one day going without a hitch and she wasn't going down without a fight. And, boy, was she putting up a good one!

If a relationship was a car, Hat had always been the driver of the vehicle she and Jimmy had shared. In fact, it would be fair to say that Jimmy didn't have his own set of keys, or even a relationship licence. However, all of this had been taken on with Jimmy's tacit consent. He was one of life's dreamers and had drifted along with the flow without revealing any worries. Which was why, after his revelation that he had some real ones, Hat felt entitled to cling to the conviction that his change of mind had been an aberration. Even though there was now strong evidence to the contrary, which was flapping its arms and screaming for attention, Hat felt justified in believing that he couldn't really have meant to break her heart, that he could not have understood how big a cat he was setting among the pigeons. And, to some extent, she was right.

Jimmy *didn't* know just how massive a tarradiddle he'd walked away from. Inadvertently she had protected him from most of the balls-achingly tedious paraphernalia that comprises the lead-up to a wedding. Apart from the one entire day – and it wasn't as though it'd been a match day – they'd spent traipsing around John Lewis's, wedding list in hand, trying to decide if a fondue set really was too naff and how many matching plates were likely to be needed in a lifetime, the whole process hadn't been too heavy for Jimmy. He wasn't the sort of person who could be relied on to sort things out, and Hat had willingly let most things fall on her. Now she was convinced that when he grasped how immense was the production he had walked out of, as an honourable, decent person he'd come back. Her new plan, she was sure, would bring that about.

12. Warning – Saucy Lingerie
At Work

Hat made sure she'd picked a night when Arsenal, Jimmy's 'when in Rome' team, were playing at home. (His first love was Partick Thistle but, as they hardly ever played outside Scotland, he'd had to have something to keep him going when he'd moved to London.) She knew she would have ample time to execute her plan: Jimmy was a creature of habit and Hat knew that, without fail, when he was coming home from a game, he went via the chip shop. All the same, as she let herself into his flat for the second time since he'd left her, she did so with stealth worthy of a diamond thief. She was acutely aware that this was likely to be her last chance and she couldn't afford to blow it.

Once inside she fed the front door back into the frame as gently as if it were made of hand-blown Venetian glass and stood, for a moment, frozen to the spot listening for any giveaway sounds. Nothing. Just to be on the safe side she called, 'Hello? Anyone at home?' It didn't dawn on her until it was already too late that if Jimmy *had* been there she was going to look a bit of a prat standing in his hall calling to him as if nothing could have been more normal. Luckily, no one responded and, for now, she was in the clear.

Hat made her way down the hall, past the kitchen,

where she was surprised, and more than a bit embarrassed, to see that the scorched bunny was still sitting at the back of the stove. How unlike Jimmy to have done nothing about it, she thought, as she opened his bedroom door. Then again, maybe he left it there deliberately as a reminder of me and the laughs we used to have.

She was delighted that Jimmy's room looked exactly the same as it had the last time she'd seen it and from this she took comfort. She read it as a sign that his astoundingly unexpected withdrawal from their marriage couldn't have been as a result of any major internal change, as she'd feared. His bed, as ever, was neatly made. His meagre assortment of clothes hung from the dress-rail that stood in one corner. His princely array of shoes, all three pairs, bar the ones he was presumably wearing – unless he'd started going out barefoot – were lined up on the bottom rack of the rail. His vast collection of motorbike magazines stood in chronological stacks on the bookshelf that ran the length of one wall. He'd made it especially to house them. His beloved cracked leather armchair sat in the corner opposite the dress-rail. It was here that he always settled himself to read his new copy of *Bike-you-Like*, or whatever those boys'-toys magazines are called – Hat was ashamed to admit she could never remember.

Jimmy hadn't always been neat. In fact, once his life had been terrifyingly chaotic in every respect. He'd changed, he'd told Hat, when he'd moved away from Scotland where apparently he'd been unhappy. At home, bad schooling had led to terminal unemployment, which had led to terminal unemployability. After a few months in London, having secured his job and just before meeting Hat, he had wholeheartedly embraced order in every area of his life. He'd found that it had brought with it calm and a sense of control, neither of which he had previously experienced. It was one of the things that had drawn him to Hat.

With a valiant sigh in place of a battle cry, Hat threw off her coat and climbed on to Jimmy's bed. As she struggled into position it dawned on her that accomplishing her mammoth task was going to demand a great deal more ingenuity than she'd originally anticipated. But she wasn't going to give up now. Finally, after a considerable struggle, and with renewed admiration for Houdini's skill, she succeeded in preparing herself to lie in wait for Jimmy's return. She looked down, giving herself the quick once-over before adding the final touch and was quite pleased with the result. She was pretty sure that, when he saw her like this, Jimmy would be unable to refrain from tucking right in.

After what seemed like the longest wait she'd ever endured, Hat heard the front door open. She'd only been in the flat for just over an hour but the wait had seemed longer because of the sensory deprivation she'd inflicted upon herself, on top of the other considerable physical impediments she'd engineered. Her heart pounded in her chest and her whole body stiffened with tense anticipation. She prayed she wouldn't break out into an unattractive nervous sweat, which might take the edge off what would otherwise be, she hoped, the epitome of erotic male fantasy. Suddenly she was grasped by a fervent wish to bottle out but, given the position she had got herself into, she knew she was stuck and that was that. As she lay there listening to Jimmy moving around his flat she thought she was going to pass out with the strain. And then abruptly, out of nowhere, the notion of adding some sound effects popped into Hat's head: the perfect icing on the cake. Confident that no man could resist a woman panting while she was awaiting his attentions, Hat began to emit a series of low breathy moans. After what felt like ninety-seven years, she heard the door open. This was the moment of truth.

At first he said nothing. All Hat could hear was an interminable deafening quiet, which seemed louder and a million times more painful than if someone had been blowing performance-standard tubas into both of her ears at the same time. What with the blindfold and all, she couldn't decipher precisely what Jimmy's reaction was but she didn't need vision to deduce that it was bad. Very bad. It quickly became skin-crawlingly clear to Hat that he hadn't leapt on top of her, wild with passion. Evidently he was more than capable of resisting her. She wanted to die and ached for a big black hole to appear and swallow her up.

Unfortunately, trussed up like a Christmas turkey as she was, even if the hole did appear it wouldn't be taking her anywhere. And, to make matters worse, she had broken out into the mother of all sweats.

Hat had banked on several different reactions but none had included total silence. She had anticipated sex, of some description, anger, dismay, bemusement. Anything, she felt, would have been better than the numbing *nada* to which she was being subjected. She lay there, stock still, in the vain, pathetic hope that maybe he hadn't seen her – it was dark, after all – and maybe he'd leave the flat before he realized she was there.

'Er, erm, ah, hullo. Are you . . . erm . . . awright? D'you need a hand, at all?' said a soft Scottish male-barely-past-puberty voice, clearly racked with electrified embarrassment.

An awful, totally-unprepared-for catastrophic eventuality thundered into Hat's head. Something that had not occurred to her had happened. The voice didn't belong to Jimmy! She was consumed by a whirlwind of shame, humiliation and desperation.

'You were probably, erm, expecting Jimmy, weren't you? See, erm, he's no here. He's gone back tae Scotland for a wee while. Did he know that you were, er, comin'? Ah mean, you see he, er, gie'd us a loan of his flat, said it'd be OK to stay an' that . . .' the boy stuttered.

It was obvious that he had never seen anything like this before and that he had no idea what best to do. And he wasn't the only one: Hat had never done anything like this before and the display she'd prepared had been intended for Jimmy's eyes only. The look she'd been going for was saucy-yet-irresistibly-inviting, a picture so completely alluring that no man could resist, no matter what decisions he'd made. And tied up spreadeagled to her ex-fiancé's bed, wearing little more than a smile, some skimpy lingerie and a blindfold, had seemed just the ticket. It might – men being aroused, traditionally, by overt visual stimulation – have had a tremendous result if only *Jimmy* had happened upon it. As she lay there, Hat wished she'd checked Jimmy's whereabouts before embarking on the plan. But it was way too late for hindsight now. She was torn between wondering frantically what possible motive Jimmy could have had in going back to Scotland so close to their wedding (well, currently, *her* wedding but she wasn't in the mood for splitting hairs), and how on earth she was going to get out of the mess she'd got herself into.

'Will Ah get you a blanket?' the boy asked, displaying impeccable manners.

'Yes, please,' Hat squeaked.

While she waited for him to return, Hat consoled herself with the thought that at least she didn't have to worry about the boy getting any ideas of his own – evidently that was the last thing on his mind. Once she was sure he had left the room she began a frantic attempt to wrestle her wrists out of the homemade self-tying contraption she'd fashioned to ensure that she could get both arms tied up at the same time. She'd known that she'd be able to tie her legs easily enough but, after that, she'd needed help with her hands. Now it seemed her handiwork had been too good: she was getting nowhere, except on a fast track to really sore wrists. She groaned as she thought of the interrogation Mish would give her when she saw the marks. She was pretty sure her flatmate wouldn't believe that she'd gone to an S- and M-club for a laugh.

'Here you go,' the boy said, entering the room and laying some sort of cover over Hat. It was a damp sleeping-bag, Hat guessed from the feel of it, but she wouldn't have cared if it'd been infested with fleas so grateful was she to be covered up. She was sure now that, rather than an irresistible sex-crazed goddess, she looked like some old slapper from the Readers' Wives section found in the back pages of the more cheesy top-shelf magazines. She knew she couldn't get undone without the boy's help, and she guessed that this had probably occurred to him too, but as he was so young, she realized that she would have to ask for his assistance, rather than expecting him to offer it.

Half an hour later, the liberator and the failed sex-slave were having a cup of tea together in Jimmy's sparsely furnished living room. Hat, now fully clothed, was pleading with the boy not to tell Jimmy in as grown-up and non-hysterical a way as she could manage.

'Oh, please don't worry. Ah won't, Ah mean Ah wouldn't even know how to begin tae . . . er, Ah won't tell anyone, ever,' the boy said, looking down at the floor.

Hat believed him. In fact, she thought, shuddering with shame, he probably won't even want to think about it again as long as he lives. She smiled at him and for the first time took him in properly. He was a cousin of Jimmy's, it turned out, and was in London for a last interview at an art school he was hopeful would accept him. He was about nineteen, fresh-faced and adorable. Hat felt like squeezing him to death with gratitude for saving her, for promising to be discreet, but most of all for being a nicely brought-up boy. Luckily for her, Hat concluded, his mother had obviously done sterling Presbyterian work by ensuring that, when faced with a near naked female stranger, her son would instantly shoo away all carnal thoughts and replace them with practical ones. She prayed that the experience wouldn't put him off women for life.

Tears were practically spouting out of Mish's eyes. She was clutching her stomach and gasping for air between guffaws. Hat sat waiting patiently for her to get over the hysteria she'd provoked, having recounted her attempt at down and dirty irresistibility. She'd guessed that Mish would react in one of two ways: she would either throttle her or see the funny side, and Hat was forced to admit that there was more than ample of that on view. She watched her friend without resentment. She was accustomed to Mish dining out on her disasters, particularly lately when she had provided so many juicy ones.

Eventually Mish's merriment died down. 'Please, please, tell me this was the last try. I mean tying yourself to his bed! Had you lost your mind?' Mish burst out again into uncontrollable laughter. 'It's the sort of thing people who've been married for forty years do to spice up their tired old sex lives. Not attractive, brilliant women like you who should know better. That's the sort of advice they give to those saddos who ring up daytime TV shows with tales of woe about how their husbands aren't interested in them any more,' Mish continued.

'I know, I know. But Jimmy did once ask me if I'd ever been tied up and I just thought that given what Priscilla had said and everything . . .' Hat tailed off.

'Jimmy probably *would* have fancied you if he'd seen you like that – you know what blokes are like. But, let's face it, indulging in a bit of bondage isn't a very solid basis for a lifelong commitment, is it? I mean, setting out all your gift-wrapped essentials for him isn't the best foundation to get you through all the boring chores that married life's made up of. A wild night of rampant sex is all very well but it doesn't get you over the problems Jimmy has right now. It doesn't get either of you over the stuff like the weekly Sainsbury's shop, school runs and which end of the toothpaste tube he squeezes. Solutions to those kind of issues don't magically appear after an evening of sweaty S and M, do they?'

Hat shrugged.

'You've got to work out if you want him back for life or just so that you can have your wedding day. Because it is *for life* that you've got him – at least in theory – once he comes back. And you know what they say – never want anything too much because you just might get it.'

Hat had not heard these words of wisdom before, but the uncomfortable thought struck her that they might have been written specifically to describe her and her quest. She erased it from her mind: it was not a philosophy she was ready to delve into. All the same, warning bells had begun to ring, albeit in the background. The possibility that maybe she wanted to get married more than she wanted to marry Jimmy had presented itself to her.

13. Can Soup Kill?

The following day was Hat's day to do Priscilla's garden and it was with a heavy heart that she heaved herself round there. Against all the odds, she was beginning to lose faith. Having failed at last night's do-or-die deed of gladiatorial proportions she was feeling very bleak indeed. She felt as if she'd put every single one of her eggs into a basket only to find that the whole lot had been shattered. She couldn't see how she was going to get Jimmy Mack back in time for their wedding in twenty-eight days' time. No matter how much of an arse she made of herself, she couldn't get her ex to return. In fact, she couldn't even manage to clap eyes on him for two minutes, let alone long enough to coax him into marrying her. Fate was conspiring against them . . . well, against her, it having given Jimmy the thumbs-up to walk away without so much as a backward glance.

She arrived at Priscilla's and wrestled her car/van into what, for any ordinary vehicle, should have been a perfectly adequate parking space, but with her steering-wheel it proved harder than manoeuvring a wonky shopping trolley packed to the rafters with food into the five items or fewer queue. To make matters worse, and befitting her mood, it was raining heavily. Hat was not looking forward to tackling the ever-needy privet hedge. She decided to delay things until the rain eased off a bit, and headed straight for the house.

'Hello, anyone in?' she called from the back door, which, against all her friends' advice, Priscilla always left unlocked. So far, her philosophy was holding good: she hadn't been burgled. She believed that bad things only happened to those who expected them to happen. And, what with the tragedy that had befallen her recently, Hat was coming round to Priscilla's way of thinking.

'Hat? Is that you?'

'Yes.'

'I'll be down in a minute,' the lady of the house bellowed from the upstairs landing.

Hat made her way across the hall into the kitchen, wondering why Priscilla never worried about a madman creeping in with an axe and hacking her to death. With that morbid thought in mind she nearly jumped out of her skin when she saw a stranger sitting at the kitchen table. She calmed down when she realized they weren't frothing at the mouth or waving a machete. The stranger was female. She was smoking a cigarette and flicking through an ancient copy of *Vogue* – Priscilla had kept every one she'd ever bought. Some dated back to the late fifties and often contained photos of Priscilla in her debutante prime.

'Oh, hello,' Hat said.

'Gloria,' the girl replied, standing up and stretching out a slender, elegant hand. Hat shook it.

Gloria had a dark, Mediterranean complexion with big black eyes and a mane of glossy deep chestnut hair. She stood nearly six feet tall. Hat wondered where on earth she'd popped up from: unless she was a fantastically successful sex-change she wasn't one of Gerry's conquests. That was unlikely, anyway, as Gerry tended to go more for the builder-cum-boxer-cum-market-trader-with-a-soft-centre look.

'Do you want a cup of tea?' Hat asked, making for the kettle.

The girl smiled and shook her head slightly. 'Gloria.'

Hat had assumed that this was the girl's name not an answer to a question. She decided to try again. 'Or perhaps you'd prefer a coffee?'

The girl shrugged her shoulders. 'Gloria.'

Hat wondered if she was about to break into a mass. Puzzled, she decided to go for a more general theme of conversation while she put on the kettle. 'It's tearing down out there, I got soaked just walking from my van. I'll have to face that hedge soon enough, though, even if it doesn't stop.'

'Stop,' the girl repeated, as if she was trying the word for size in her mouth.

'Very good,' Priscilla said, walking into the room before Hat could take offence. 'You see? Won't take long.'

'Jess. Stop,' the girl said, as she sat down again to resume her perusal of *Vogue*.

Hat couldn't work out what was going on. Who was Jess and what was she supposed to stop?

'You're going to get drenched out there today, hope you brought your waterproofs,' Priscilla said.

'Yes, I was just saying so to . . . erm, your friend.'

'Gloria. Well, wasting your breath there. Can't speak a word of English, apart from "yes" and now, apparently, "stop". I think that's a new one. We mastered "yes" earlier this morning, although Ys are a bit of a struggle and tend to come out as Js.'

Hat winced: even if the girl couldn't speak English she could surely understand when somebody was talking about her. She looked at her, intending to make a silent show of support. She got no response. Gloria didn't seem to be aware of anything: she was more interested in the cocktail dresses of yesteryear than she was sensitive to Priscilla's huge capacity to embarrass.

'She's South American, I believe. Quite a beauty, don't you think?'

Hat grimaced. Although she would have liked to know more about Gloria and where she'd popped up from, she didn't want to encourage Priscilla to keep talking about her as if she were a deaf mute.

'Stop making faces, Hat. I assure you, she cannot understand a word. Sam's Spanish must be very good – unless they only communicate in the most obvious way, but in the long run that won't butter any parsnips.'

'Who's Sam?' Hat asked, clanking her teaspoon loudly in the cup in the hope that the noise would drown Priscilla's voice.

'Didn't I say? This is Sam's wife, and they're just back from wherever it is she's from – I forget. They're staying here till they get on their feet. I'm giving a temporary home to love's young dream. They're newlyweds, isn't it sweet?'

'Adorable. Who's Sam?'

'Haven't you met him? I was sure you had. He's the son of an old boyfriend of mine. Although I'm not absolutely sure he knows about his father and me, and as his mother is a dear old friend, probably best if you don't mention it.'

'Fine, fine, fine, Priscilla,' Hat hissed, desperate to change the subject.

'Hat, don't flap! For the last time, she cannot understand what I'm saying. However, what with you hissing like a snake and hopping about like a nervous major-domo she's bound to think something's awry.'

'Yes, all right. I'm going to make a start in the garden,' Hat replied sulkily. She decided that getting soaked to the skin would be miles better than hanging around to hear about happily married couples who had everything in the world going for them.

The rain had reduced Priscilla's garden to a series of mud trenches. Hat pulled on her wellingtons, and as she squelched her way round beheading plants and hacking at the hedge she found herself wondering what kind of bloke Sam was. He must be something to have bagged a girl like that, Hat thought enviously. He probably wouldn't mind if she never learnt English or anything else intelligible when she looked like that. It was uncharacteristic of her to be jealous of others' good fortune, but the burgeoning prospect of having to admit failure was making her feel so bleak. She was finding it difficult to believe that the entire world wasn't in the middle of enjoying the nicest, most perfect, most complete, most never-going-to-break-up relationship. Everyone out there, except for her, was on the brink of a romantic, never-a-cross-word, guaranteed-to-succeed marriage. And now, just when she needed it least, a prime example of that breed had landed bang in the middle of her world to rub large granules of salt into her freshly opened wound. Mrs Hair-like-a-prize-stallion-probably-had-seven-million-proposals-but-she-couldn't-care-less Gloria and Mr I'm-so-wonderful-I-don't-even-need-my-wife-to-be-able-to-speak-my-language-just-being-near-her-is-enough-for-me Sam had come to live at her friend's house and Hat felt dreadful about it.

'Hello! Priscilla says do you want to come in for some lunch?' a male voice called across the lawn through the driving rain. Hat looked round and could just make out a man with blondish hair waving to her from the back door. Sam, she thought.

'Thanks, I'll be in in a minute.'

So now I have to eat with Romeo and Juliet as well, Hat thought grumpily, as she pulled off her boots and shook out her soaking wet parka, leaving them to dry in the porch. She padded through to the kitchen in her socks and, as she went, quickly checked herself in the hall mirror. Her hair was drenched and had separated into long stringy rats' tails.

'Goodness, you look like a sodden crusty!' Priscilla exclaimed, as Hat entered the room.

'Thanks, Priscilla. That's just the look I was going

for,' Hat replied darkly. She wasn't in the mood for teasing and felt like strangling her friend. At that moment she caught the eye of the blond guy. He raised his eyes to the heavens and threw her a conspiratorial what-is-she-like? look. He obviously knows Priscilla well, Hat thought, and smiled at him.

'Hi, I'm Sam. This is my . . . ah . . . wife, Gloria,' he said, half rising from the table and indicating the exotic woman, whose head was still buried in the same copy of *Vogue*.

'Hi. Gloria and I met earlier,' Hat replied.

Sam sat down, turned to his wife and began to talk to her in what – judging by the amount of heth-heth-heths mixed with that noise a cat makes when it's clearing its throat – Hat guessed was Spanish. She was surprised by Sam's ordinariness in comparison to the flaming beauty beside him. He was tall with dirty-blond hair, and although he was tanned and fairly muscular, he was nothing special. Hat had been expecting nothing short of Brad Pitt with a dash of that bloke out of the Fun Lovin' Criminals to match up to the vision that was his wife. All the same, she was pleasantly surprised and less intimidated at the prospect of breaking bread with the pair.

'Hat's getting married too in a few weeks,' Priscilla announced, plonking a vat of soup in the middle of the table.

'Really? Congratulations,' Sam said, and turned to Gloria. Hat presumed that he was translating the happy news.

'Ah, *felicitaciones, muy bien*,' Gloria said – Hat guessed by way of approval.

She felt deeply uncomfortable. While she was fractionally cheered to learn that Priscilla hadn't given up the fight she didn't want to go public with it. And, given her current mood, she definitely didn't feel up to an in-depth breakdown of the story-so-far, least of all to a couple of newly married strangers.

'When is it?' Sam inquired, obviously attempting to make conversation.

'Um, well, in theory the seventh of October,' Hat mumbled.

'In theory?'

'Yes, there's a bit of a hiccup,' Priscilla butted in. 'Her fiance, Jimmy Mack, has done a bunk – or "wobbled out", as I believe the modern expression goes. Can't be found for love nor money. I am convinced that it's simply a bad case of pre-wedding nerves. Hat is working on it and I'm sure will win him round in time. However, so far, poor girl, she's not having much luck, are you, Hat?'

Hat wanted to die. She'd rather Priscilla had insisted she welcome her guests by performing a table-top naked belly-dance. Anything rather than throw open for general discussion her failed attempts to change the hideous course of events that had beset her so far.

'Shall I dish out the soup?' Sam said and seized the ladle. Hat could tell he wanted to have this conversation about as much as she did.

'You see, I still hold by my saucy underwear idea –

simply don't see how it can go wrong. All men love that sort of get-up, don't they, Sam?'

Hat was heartened to notice that he was nearly as embarrassed as she was. And there was no way on earth that she was about to tell their hostess that the underwear idea had been a disaster.

'But if that doesn't appeal I think you should give Gerry's idea a go. Get yourself a moustache.'

'*Mostaza?*' Gloria said, looking up from her magazine.

'Apparently that's what gay men do when they don't want people to know they're gay. They get a girlfriend. It's called a moustache.'

'Beard, Priscilla. Look, I really don't want to talk about this,' Hat hissed. She felt like sinking her head in the bowl of scalding soup Sam had just put in front of her. Right now, she'd have happily singed her entire face off – anything, as long as it would get Priscilla to shut up.

'Don't be silly. Sam's going to be around for a while so he might as well know about it. He might even have some bright ideas,' Priscilla replied crisply, settling down to her meal. 'My goodness, that's it! Sam, *you* could be Hat's beard!'

'*What?*' Sam and Hat burst out together, united in horror at Priscilla's suggestion.

'Well, you need someone for that dinner, assuming Jimmy's not back by then. Ye gods, it's soon enough, isn't it? And you're perfect, Sam! You see, Hat needs someone unknown to her family, and as you're happily married, you pose no threat of messy complications.

You bear more than a passing resemblance to Jimmy – you've got the same colouring and roughly the same physique, I'd say, don't you think, Hat? You can simply perform a service, as it were, for my friend in need, with no strings attached.' Priscilla was clearly delighted by her own genius.

Hat looked down and wondered if her soup bowl was deep enough to drown herself in.

'I – I – wouldn't . . . I'm not sure . . . It's not really my . . .' Sam spluttered.

Hat could see he was trying to demur without being rude to either his hostess or her and she felt for him. 'Don't worry, I wouldn't think of . . .' Hat couldn't think of the right word. 'Priscilla, in the unlikely event of my deciding to use a beard, I'll find my own, OK?'

'Well, I think you're mad. Sam is simply perfect and you'd be happy to do it, wouldn't you, Sam? Where else would you find someone as ideal as him? For the love of God, there's only one dinner involved here! After rebuilding flood-damaged villages in South America it'd hardly be the most difficult job you've ever undertaken, would it?'

Before Sam could reply, Hat cried, 'Look, Priscilla, as it happens I'm probably going to call the wedding off anyway! I'm giving up, I don't think he's coming back. I don't know why he left and I can't seem to find him anywhere. Mish is right. It's time I faced facts. He obviously doesn't want to marry me. I can't keep believing it's going to be all right when it's obviously not! I have to stop!'

Hat's outburst was met by an embarrassed silence around the table.

It was broken a few moments later by Gloria: 'Jess. Stop,' she said, evidently delighted with her powers of retention.

Not much later, a fuming Hat dragged her rake aggressively across the dead autumn leaves that lay scattered over the fading lawn. She was performing her task with such force that entire clods of turf were coming up. Having no desire to add reseeding the lawn to her list of tasks she threw down the rake: she needed to calm herself. She settled on the bench that stood under the magnificent magnolia tree planted sixty-three years earlier by Priscilla's father to celebrate the birth of his only child.

Hat had never before been on the sharp end of Priscilla's wilful lack of sensitivity and she was feeling the after-effects acutely. She knew that Priscilla was *trying* to be helpful, but she felt as if a pair of her least attractive old pants had been produced at the lunch table and everyone invited, non-English speakers included, to comment on their lack of appeal. She wished she'd never talked to Priscilla about the whole thing in the first place.

'Hello.'

Hat looked up to see Sam and Gloria standing a few feet in front of her.

'Oh, hi, I was just having a rest, quite sweaty work raking, ha, ha.' Hat wondered why she'd said something so stupid and, for that matter, inaccurate.

'Yes, I can imagine. We're just going for a walk but I wanted to tell you that I don't mind doing it, if you need me to. I'll pretend to be your fiance at that dinner, if you like.'

Hat's skin was still crawling from the humiliation she'd experienced at lunch. She didn't know what to say and wondered if he was taking the piss.

'I've talked about it with Gloria and she doesn't mind at all. She thinks it's rather funny, actually, and typically English,' Sam added, as if this would ease Hat's mind.

She wasn't sure whether his wife's approval made her feel better or worse. 'Thanks, that's very kind of you but I'm fine, really. Priscilla's gone a bit off the rails with all this. I mean, she's been great but I'll sort it out. Thank you anyway.'

'OK, but if you *do* decide you need a beard, I'm your man.'

Hat watched as they walked off down the path together. She was overwhelmed by envy of the closeness they must share if Gloria could sanction her brand new husband offering himself as another woman's decoy. All the same, she thought, as she resumed raking, I wouldn't choose *him* as my beard. I need someone much less geeky.

14. Mummy Dearest

Later that day Jimmy came back. Much to Hat's astonishment. In the middle of the night, when it was darkest, coldest and scariest, he returned. He chose that eerie time when, if you wake up with worries, they instantly take on mammoth proportions, seeming more desperate and life-ruining than they ever do in the cold light of day.

Hat woke up to find him creeping naked into her bed. She was instantly engulfed by the million things she wanted to ask him, but she found she couldn't say a thing. He didn't say a word either but began to kiss her as he'd never kissed her before. Hat wrapped her arms around him and kissed him back with a passion she'd never before felt for him. She was overcome with joy – not only had he come back but he felt like a different person. His absence had changed him. She hadn't remembered his body being so firm or his kisses so provocative, so exciting. As they made love Hat climaxed more powerfully than she'd ever done in her life. His touch, his embrace, his skin, his rock-hard penis – everything about him seemed new and wonderful.

Afterwards they lay entwined in each other's arms and Jimmy, who hardly ever uttered more than three words in a row, talked and talked and talked. He told her about the Vespa hire business he had started (it was something he'd waffled on about for as long as Hat had known him). He talked about them buying a house together when they were married. He talked about the children he wanted her to bear him. He talked about how much fun they'd have spending the rest of their lives together. He talked about all the things they'd never talked about.

Hat was astonished. She was delighted that he was declaring so much of himself, that he'd at last got himself together and, most of all, that he had come back of his own free will. If this was the payoff then everything she'd been through since he'd left had been worthwhile. All the same, she was thrown. It was as if Jimmy Mack had come back in some other, much more evolved, mature bloke's body (and, apparently, that of one who went to the gym a lot). She didn't dare burst the bubble by asking him what startling revelation he'd had while they'd been apart, what had led to this miraculous change of heart. It was enough that he was here. It was all going to be all right after all.

'Oi! For the last time, do you want a flaming cup of tea?' Hat heard Mish shout. She cursed her flatmate as she wrestled herself out of the deep, delicious slumber she'd fallen into once she and Jimmy had stopped talking when first light had broken. Then she sat up.

'Where's Jimmy?' she asked, looking round the room frantically.

'Hat, please, it's too early in the morning to start all that again.' Mish was already going back up the hall towards the kitchen. 'Anyway, I've made some tea. It's on the table if you want it,' she called.

Hat was confused and panic-stricken. She threw back her duvet wondering if Jimmy was hiding underneath it. He wasn't. For a daft second, Hat thought he might be cowering under the bed – he'd have good reason to fear seeing Mish, who was likely to give him an earful when she got hold of him. She swung her legs over the side of her mattress and felt around on the floor for her slippers, trying to work out where Jimmy had disappeared to. Then the truth crashed in on her. Jimmy Mack hadn't come back. She'd dreamt the whole wretched thing. So strong was her desire to get him back that she'd conjured him up in her sleep. And she hadn't simply conjured up any old him: she'd conjured up an improved, under-new-management Jimmy Mack. Hat realized sadly that her first clue should have been the mind-blowing sex. It was never like that, Hat thought, as she dropped down from the euphoric state in which the dream had left her.

As she shuffled along the hall into the kitchen she continued checking off the glaring dissimilarities between Dream Jimmy and Disappeared Jimmy. How, for one nano-second, could she have believed it was the man himself? By the time she was drinking her tea a faint voice way in the back of her head was calling to her. But she didn't want to hear what it had to say. Busying herself with making breakfast she did a fantastic job of pretending she couldn't make out the words. It was trying urgently to draw her attention to something alarming. It wanted her to consider the strong possibility that the Jimmy she'd dreamt about was the one she'd really like, *not* the real one she was trying so hard to get back. But despite everything she wasn't ready to give up yet. Although her spirits were low, there was still some fight in her.

Hat got through the remainder of that day without exploding or falling over – in itself quite an achievement bearing in mind the heavy load bearing down on her. But the next day all hell broke loose.

She woke up, opened her eyes and stared, with a fixed, dead-fish glare, at the ceiling. The pressure was mounting. No, she thought, that's an understatement. The pressure has mounted and is in the process of building up a backlog. A sort of dam effect. A dam that at any moment, she strongly suspected, was going to burst in spectacular style and cause irreparable damage to her life. Hat lay completely still, as if under a catatonic spell – actually she was unable to move, she decided. She felt as if she had two hundred thousand tonnes pressing down on her. Indecision was making her inert. She did not know which way to turn. In place of adrenaline hysteria was coursing through every vein at a rate of knots. Instead of snapping her into action, as it had to date, it was rendering her static.

In a gargantuan effort to mobilize herself, she pulled out the pillow from under her head, hoicked it round to the front and held it over her face. 'What the fuck have I done?' she moaned. 'What is the fucking matter with me? Why didn't I just give up like any normal person when he said it was over? Why couldn't I let myself be chucked? What am I? Miss Unchuckable? Who am I? Miss Boomerang? I didn't know what I was doing. How the hell *do* you get off a roller-coaster if you're already whizzing down it at full speed? Worse than that,' she groaned, 'how the hell do you get off once you've insisted on staying on board? Assuring everyone you were fine, could handle everything *and* were the one who made it go faster?'

Events were stampeding towards her from every direction and Hat didn't know what to do. Of course, one event in particular had been advancing inexorably all along, ever since she'd failed to cancel it. Incontrovertibly, it was the one leading the battle charge. The wedding was now only twenty-one days away. At the beginning it had been far enough in the future to seem manageable. Her hopes of getting Jimmy back had seemed realistic. Now it was speeding towards her, careering out of control. Thanks to her antics, it was about as unstoppable as rising vomit and, to Hat, only marginally more attractive. Everything else had been a result of that one huge – she now thought – mistake: her failure to accept the big E Jimmy Mack had given her.

Hat hurled her pillow across the room and sat up. 'I'm going to confess all. I'm going to stop Mum and Dad coming over, sell my wedding dress, apologize to the vicar, pay off the caterers, the hall, send back the presents, give the video-maker his cancellation

fee, and the photographer, drink the booze and whatever else is on that list. I can't take the pressure any
more, I've got to –'

Hat's rant was cut off mid-flow by her bedroom
door swinging open.

'Surprise!'

Her head snapped round. It couldn't be! Her jaw
dropped.

'Close your mouth, sweetheart, that is *not* an attractive expression,' Hat's mother, Margaret, said crisply,
as she picked her way across Hat's clothes-strewn
carpet, arms outstretched. 'Goodness me, this is like
a teenager's bedroom. Aren't you a trifle old to be
living in a pig-sty? How on earth do you ever manage
to find anything? You won't be able to carry on like
this once you're married. Men like order, you know.'

Hat watched her mother making a big performance
of checking where she put her feet down. She
refrained from telling her that she needn't worry –
despite the mess there was no danger of stepping in
any dog shit.

'Hello, my darling pet,' Margaret cooed, reaching
her daughter and wrapping her arms around her neck.

Hat allowed herself to be squeezed for long enough
to avoid the otherwise inevitable and tiresome accusa-
tions of the why-do-my-children-never-let-me-near-
them nature. As she did so she saw, over her mother's
right shoulder, her flatmate appear in the doorway.
By means of a crap mime that wouldn't have earned
her even sympathy money had she been busking in a
tube station, Mish made it clear to Hat that her mother

had turned up out of the blue. With the addition of a vivid facial expression, she conveyed that, no matter what had gone before, she understood that her pal really was in big trouble now.

'So I thought, My littlest is getting married in three weeks' time. I'm thousands of miles away, twiddling my fingers, and I can't wait a moment longer. I told your father, "We're not waiting until next week, we're going over there right now. I don't care how independent she is," I said, "a girl needs her mother at this time more than at any other." As much fun as organizing a wedding can be, it's no picnic, I know that. So, we upped sticks and flew over without a moment's delay and here I am.' She gave Hat's hand a reassuring pat.

Hat knew that a joyful reply, filled with gratitude and surprise, was now expected. It was her duty to declare how incredibly lucky she was to have such a wonderful mother. So, it was probably not the absolutely tip-top moment to tell her that it was all off.

'Yeah, that's great, Mum. Thanks a lot,' she mumbled weakly.

'It's the least I could do, darling,' Margaret replied, satisfied – to Hat's amazement – with her daughter's response. She stood up and smoothed the front of her deep orange frock.

As always, Hat's mother was wearing an outfit that looked like something a geography teacher might pick to go to see Trooping the Colour or some other tedious royal event. Hat knew she'd have chosen it under the delusion that it was similar to something the Queen might wear. Actually, it was.

'Where's Dad?' she asked.

'Would you believe he headed straight for his old golf course after dropping me off here? You'll see him later. He knew we'd have girls' stuff to discuss and he didn't want to get in the way.'

I'll bet he didn't, Hat thought. Her father would do anything to avoid emotional scenes and even more to get in a round of golf.

'Mrs Grant? Shall I make you a cup of tea while Hat gets dressed?' Mish piped up. Hat, in need of a couple of minutes to compose herself, shot her a look of appreciation.

'Yes, that's a good idea. And when you've got yourself together, Harriet, you can take me through everything you've done so far and we can draw up a plan of action, OK?'

'Well, for starters she could give you a hand finding Jimmy, couldn't she?' Mish whispered out of the corner of her mouth as she ushered Margaret into the hall.

'You can't possibly have the groom's mother seated anywhere other than on the bride's father's left,' Margaret howled, as she ran her ever-critical eye over the provisional seating plan her daughter had drawn up. Hat had intended to break the news before they'd got into anything remotely weddingy but she'd been railroaded into handing over the plan. She was regretting it now.

'You'll have to let me redo this completely, darling.

There is a certain etiquette that, no matter how trendy and do-it-yourself a wedding is, must be adhered to. I'll sort this out,' Margaret said, folding Hat's plan and popping it into her handbag.

Hat couldn't take much more of this. It's now or never, she thought, and steeled herself. 'Mum, I've got something to tell you.'

'Don't worry, I already know,' Margaret said, with a heavily sympathetic look.

Hat was astonished. '*What?*'

'I know.'

'How come? Did Mish tell you?' Hat barked, annoyed yet relieved that her flatmate had pipped her to the post.

'No. I can't imagine *she*'d care one way or the other,' Margaret replied.

'Of course she cares when something's made me miserable,' Hat replied hotly. Although she and Mish had not been seeing eye to eye recently, her loyalty towards her best friend was unshaken and she resented her mother's tone.

'Well, if it's making you miserable, why are you marrying him, then?'

Hat was perplexed by this. 'What are you talking about?'

'If him being a motorcycle messenger makes you miserable, and I can tell you it doesn't exactly fill my heart with the joys of spring, then why are you marrying him?'

Hat saw that she and her mother had been talking at cross-purposes.

'Your sister broke the news — told me that your fiancé is a motorcycle messenger. And I'm fine about it now. Obviously, at first, I wasn't best pleased but when I called Priscilla to ask her opinion, she told me he has plans to start a hire business or something. I'm sure that once he's settled down, and with you behind him, he'll make something of himself. Added to that, I'm aware, as I said to your father, that girls of a certain age have to realize that there aren't as many buses approaching the bus stop as, perhaps, there might once have been. So, when all's said and done, there's nothing for it but to hop on to the first that turns up, even if it might not appear to be going in the right direction.'

Hat thought she was going to explode with rage. 'You might as well have said beggars can't be choosers, Mum!' she choked out.

'Oh, don't be silly, darling. I'm just being practical. All I'm saying is that if a girl finds herself still unmarried in her early thirties she can't afford to be too choosy and I'm glad you didn't fall into that trap.'

'Well, that *isn't* what I was going to tell you.' Hat gathered herself to make her declaration, dread welling inside her. She was about to announce that the 'bus' had emptied itself of its passenger and gone back to the depot. And clearly, Hat deduced, it had been the last one on the timetable. No other buses, not even night ones, were headed towards this stop. That was it.

Just as Hat was about to launch into her confession her mother started up again: 'Well, thank goodness you're having a lower-key affair than your sister. *One* of those huge weddings in a lifetime is more than enough for a mother to face. Penny had her heart set on doing every single thing just right.'

'Whereas mine is more like a right old bunfight in a pub, I suppose?'

'Not at all. Really, darling, don't be like this. Penny *had* to have a grander affair, considering who she was marrying. I'm not suggesting that your wedding is any less special. In its own way, of course, it's just as important. The sort of thing you're doing is much more in keeping with your personality anyway.'

That was the final straw. All the fury and feelings of injustice Hat had felt throughout her childhood came crashing into the forefront of her mind. She lost all sense of proportion and erupted.

'Well, as you'll see when we go through the whole itinerary, I *am* having a big-production wedding. Maybe not one to rival Penny's perfect day but pretty lavish all the same.' Hat produced the personalized checklist that had come free with her trusty *Your Very Special Day* pamphlet. The fury had erased from her mind, albeit temporarily, the fact that she wasn't having any day at all, special or otherwise.

Margaret leant forward and took the hallowed sheet out of her hand. Hat could tell that she was making a superhuman effort to stop herself challenging her daughter's wishes. 'Well, that's marvellous, darling. Good for you. And how clever of you to have managed all this,' she waved the piece of paper, 'on your own. Isn't it lucky I turned up just in time to help you make sure everything goes like clockwork?'

Hat allowed herself a childish huh-told-you-so smile, which went, as intended, unseen by her mother. She felt as if she'd won a major battle in the fight towards getting her mother to see her as equal to her sister and she was thrilled. A few minutes later, once she'd calmed down, Hat grasped that she had dug herself into a much deeper hole. The same hole that forty or so minutes earlier, she had just begun to pull herself out of.

15. Mish Finally Gets Involved

Mish caught Hat alone in the kitchen just before she left for work. 'Have you told her? Are you going to tell her?' she hissed, as Hat made her mother a cup of coffee.

'Oh, God, I tried, but she wound me up so much I ended up making it worse. It felt like she was expecting it to have gone bad so I *couldn't* admit it had.'

'I don't blame you. Look, don't worry, we'll sort something out.'

'Like what?'

Mish gave her a hug. 'Don't know yet but we'll handle it, OK?'

Mish left the flat filled with horror. She'd met Hat's mum a couple of times before, but only briefly on both occasions. Until now, she'd thought of her as a distant woman who didn't go out of her way to hide her preference for her elder daughter. Since she'd arrived, everything about her manner had made it plain that she had turned up so suddenly for her own greater good not Hat's. Mish was over-whelmed with feelings of protectiveness for Hat. She couldn't bear to think of the hoops her friend was probably jumping through right now to avoid telling her mother the truth. She had to come to Hat's rescue somehow.

'Aat was the catewews,' Margaret said, addressing her daughter's reflection in the mirror as Hat walked into the living room. Her mother had suggested they go shopping and then to lunch. Hat, banking on her mother enjoying a lunchtime glass of wine, was planning to confess when it had taken the sharp edge off her. She was aware that she'd invested rather too heavily in the possible effect of one unit of fermented grapes.

'What was the caterers?' Hat asked, with a feeling of impending doom.

'The catewews just wung . . .' Margaret continued. Her speech was rendered peculiar because her lips were stretched across her teeth as she applied her lipstick. They were so extended they looked as if they might snap.

'Your answering machine went off and when I heard who it was I picked it up. Hope you don't mind. Weally, darling, you hadn't even organized a tasting! Goodness me, that's absolutely vital. I mean, what if they were to pwoduce pig swill on the day? You'd be sowwy then, wouldn't you? Anyway, I've sorted it out. We're going there a couple of days before the wedding to sample a few of their dishes and finalize the menu. They wanted to know when they could, as the woman elegantly put it, "look forward to receiving the balance of their payment". I said we'd settle the bill there and then, assuming all was satisfactory. That

OK with you, darling?' Margaret pressed her lips together to ensure an even spread of lipstick.

Hat was struck dumb with amazement at the incredible bad luck that had beset her from the moment she'd decided to give up the fight. She wondered whether it was simply that Fate had a personal vendetta against her or whether Sod's Law had decided it was high time for *it* to get involved too. But whether it was Sod's Law or some other life-trueism – she gave a heavy sigh – there could only ever have been one moment for the caterers to call and that was, naturally, at the very second when her mother was hovering over the phone.

Mish had left the flat earlier than she'd needed to, having decided that Hat might want some time alone with her mum to break the news – although she knew that her friend was unlikely to do it. In truth, her principal reason for leaving when she did had been to get away from Hat's mother. Margaret made Mish feel tense and edgy, as if she'd done something naughty and was trying not to get caught. She had the same effect on a lot of people. Her vision of herself was as a helpful, organized, retired lady with an abundance of energy and flair, which she was willing to apply to others' problems in a selfless effort to ease their lives. But most people saw her in a different light, as a domineering, interfering, social-climber who made them feel as if everything they did was wrong.

She wasn't deliberately unkind, she was simply woefully insensitive. Hat's father had opted a long time ago for the line of least resistance, having realized that it was the quickest way to a quiet life. And, for him, it had worked like a charm. Of her two children Penny, having turned out exactly as Margaret had envisaged a model daughter, found that her path had always run smooth, while Hat had had a rougher ride. And she had never learnt the knack of handling her mother. Her dad had often urged her not to engage in head-to-head battles with Margaret over every little issue, but Hat couldn't stop herself. She felt that her mother had never stopped trying to change her into someone other than who she was.

Having witnessed Margaret and Hat in each other's presence, Mish hadn't failed to notice her friend's change of mood. She had to help her out, no matter what, and with that loyal and courageous thought in mind, she resolved to seek out Jimmy Mack.

'No, Ah'm afraid he's away home just the now,' the adolescent boy explained politely.

Mish cursed herself: she'd gone round to Jimmy's flat having forgotten that he'd gone back to Scotland. Then she smiled: this must be the hapless lad who'd stumbled upon Hat in all her near-naked glory.

'Do you know where he is? Have you got a phone number for him?' she asked. She resisted the temptation to ask the boy if he'd fully recovered from his recent shock.

'Ah don't know where he's gone but Ah can give you his ma's number. If he's no there, she might know where he is.'

'Thanks, that'd be great.'

While he shuffled off to get a pen and paper Mish glanced at the hall cupboard, whose door was ajar, and thought of Hat holed up in there.

'Here it is. Is that everythin'?'

'Yeah, that's fine, thanks a lot,' Mish said, turning to go. She toyed with the idea of asking the boy not to tell Jimmy she'd called round but decided against it. The poor lad's already overloaded with things he can't ever divulge to anyone, she thought.

Mish settled herself in a quiet corner of a coffee bar, got out her mobile and dialled the number the boy had given her.

'Hullo.'

'Jimmy, is that you?' She was astonished that she'd got through to him so effortlessly.

'Aye. Who's this?'

'Jimmy, hi, it's Mish.'

She was feeling a bit tentative now that she'd got hold of him – so easily. She'd hoped to prepare herself during the detective work she'd expected to do with his mother.

'Oh, hullo, Mish. You awright?'

'Fine. How are you?'

'Ah, you know . . .'

No, I don't fucking know, you div, Mish thought crossly. If I knew, I might have been able to help my pal make sense of this whole balls-up. But she decided wisely that tearing Jimmy off a strip wouldn't get her anywhere.

'So how long are you going to be up in Scotland, then?' she chirped, wondering how much more inane chit-chat she was going to have to make before she could cut to the chase.

'Don't really know . . . huvnae decided yet. Ah don't really know what Ah'm doing . . . er . . . at the moment.'

Right, Mish thought. That's my in. 'Look, Jimmy, the reason I'm ringing is – and by the way Hat doesn't know I am, it was my idea – er . . . why have you called it all off?'

'Oh, Mish, Ah don't really know. Ah thought Ah needed some space, some time away from everythin' an' that . . .'

Mish wanted to strangle him. She wondered how much more of this woe-is-me stuff she could take.

'Ah do love her an' that. It's no that Ah don't care aboot her. She's like my best mate and everythin', it's just that Ah found myself thinkin' shouldn't there be mair? Shouldn't Ah get a funny feeling in ma tummy when Ah think aboot her? Shouldn't my hairt do a flip every time Ah see her an' that? Shouldn't people gettin' married be head over heels in love, you know?'

Mish thought Jimmy sounded like a lovelorn, virgin teenager who'd got his template of love from some sloppy sentimental movie like *Sleepless in Seattle*. She understood only too well the kind of thrilling sensation he was talking about but she'd been under the impression that grown-ups who decided to join their lives together in holy matrimony had already kissed goodbye for ever to that kind of carry-on.

'I do know what you're talking about, Jimmy, but

doesn't that sort of thing wear out quite quickly? Aren't really good marriages based on friendship and deep love?'

Mish was painfully aware that she was the worst person in the world to be putting up a good defence for the cosy-and-safe argument. From the moment she'd started dating she had changed her partners almost as frequently as she'd changed her knickers – precisely because the incumbent had ceased to excite her in the very way that Jimmy had described. She knew she was flighty but as it had never made her unhappy she saw no reason to change.

'Yeah, Ah s'pose. Funny, cos Hat's steadfastness was one of the things that made me want tae marry her in the first place.'

If you thought she was steadfast *before* you should see her now, Mish thought.

'She's great an' all. It's no her, it's me. Ah wish Ah knew what Ah was doing,' Jimmy continued, uncharacteristically verbose. Evidently he was seizing the opportunity to get it all off his chest. 'But Ah just cannae get rid of this feelin' that there's somethin' missin', that there should be mair, you know?'

'Yes, I understand what you're saying, Jimmy, but Hat is desperate, she really wants you back. She . . .' Mish hesitated, not knowing how much information to give away. She didn't want to scare him off with full reports of Hat's latest antics. 'She'd do anything to be married to you.'

'Oh, don't, Mish, you're makin' me feel terrible,' Jimmy moaned.

Yeah, and not a moment too soon, you wanker. Mish marvelled at yet another example of the generic male ability to imagine that how bad *they* feel about a situation *they*'ve created takes precedence over everything else.

'Well, Hat's not feeling that great either,' Mish replied crisply, complimenting herself on what she felt was admirable restraint.

'Oh, Ah wish Ah knew *whit* Ah was doing.'

Just pull your fucking finger out, you twat! Mish wanted to yell, but avoided such a rash course of action.

'Listen, I'm not having a go at you, Jimmy. I'm just asking you to give it some thought. Think about what you're giving up, think about what you're doing to Hat. Will you?' she said, in a tone that made it clear she was bringing the call to an end.

'Yeah, Ah will, you're right, Ah will. Thanks for ringin' an' that. Cheers.'

16. When the Going Gets Tough

Just as Hat and her mother were leaving the flat, the phone rang. Hat opted quickly not to answer it. She was desperate to get her mother out of the front door before she hijacked another call and ended up pushing Hat into even deeper shit.

Half-way out, Margaret came to an abrupt halt, digging her heels into the carpet like an obstinate mule. 'Aren't you going to answer that?'

'No, Mum, the machine will get it. Come on, let's go.'

Hat recalled, with irritation, the long drawn-out argument she and Mish had had about where to put the snazzy new phone-and-answering-machine they'd bought, just before Hat and Jimmy had decided to get married. Mish had wanted it to go in the kitchen ('Where, funnily enough, you spend most of your time,' Hat had remarked). Ever practical, Hat had worried about steam and other kitcheny vapours mucking up its workings. She now regretted winning the argument: it had been she who had suggested the hall.

'It might be something important.'

'Yeah, well, fine, they'll leave a message.'

As it turned out Margaret was right. It was something important – well, some*body* important.

'Ah, hello, erm, Hat, it's me . . . er . . . Jimmy. Look, Ah'm glad you're no there, cos Ah just wanted tae leave a message, really, lettin' you know that Ah'm sorry an' that . . . but Ah am thinkin' aboot you. Ah still wish Ah knew whit Ah was doing. Ah think this time off is helpin', though. Ah hope you're OK and gettin' on awright an' that . . . erm . . .'

Hat, a hop, skip and jump away from the machine, stood frozen stiff to the spot, as a wild mix of terror, indecision and joy coursed through her.

'Harriet, dear, that's your Jimmy, isn't it? I'm sure he said his name was Jimmy. For goodness sake, aren't you going to talk to him? What's he sorry about? Have you two had a row? Why is he glad you're not here?'

Ignoring her mother's barrage of questions and throwing caution to the wind, Hat leapt for the phone, rugby-tackling the handset off the cradle. She picked it up just in time to hear the click of the receiver being put down at the other end and the dialling tone. 'Shit! Shit! Shit! Fucking bollocks, bollocks, bolluuuuurks!' Hat cursed, gripping the phone so hard her knuckles turned white. Oblivious of all else, she banged 1471 into the phone's keypad.

'You were called today at ten thirty-seven a.m. We do not have the caller's number to return the call,' Hat heard the BT android announce.

'Fuck, fuck, fuck!' she said, slamming the phone down so hard she nearly cracked it.

'Harriet Grant! There's no call for language like that. What on earth is the matter?'

Ignoring her, Hat dialled Jimmy's mobile. Another

android announced that the phone was switched off. Hat thought her head was going to burst. Before she had a moment to think, the phone rang again. She answered it so quickly that the first ring hadn't even finished. 'Hello, Jimmy?'

'No, it's me. Christ, I wouldn't sound so keen if I were you, Hat. It'll make him relax and think he doesn't have to try too hard. Men are awful when they think they don't have to make an effort.'

'Penny,' Hat replied, crestfallen.

'And a cheery hello to you, too! God, you sound like someone's died. Is Mum there? She left me a message saying she was coming over early as a surprise for you. I'll bet it was.' Penny sniggered.

'Yeah, I'll pass you over,' and Hat handed the phone to her mother.

As Margaret chatted to her elder daughter Hat tried to calm down. Despite having failed to speak to Jimmy she had quickly moved through utter desolation at missing his call to elation. She felt as light as a feather. She felt as if she could soar. She was walking on clouds. In a very short space of time, she had convinced herself that Jimmy's call meant far more than met the eye – or ear, in this case. She tried to keep herself grounded while she struggled against the impulse to jump for joy. There were only twenty-one days left until her wedding, and the first sign of life from Jimmy had come just in the nick of time. Hat was sure that his call had been motivated by an attack of nerves that he'd done the wrong thing, rather than an onslaught of please-don't-hate-me guilt. It meant the beginning of the end of his resistance. It heralded his sure-fire appearance on the crucial day. He may not know it yet, Hat thought, but he'd never have called unless he was going to come back.

That night, to her amazement, she got no opposition to the notion from Mish.

'So what *was* James on about, then?' Margaret asked her when Penny had gone off to the loo.

The three Grant women were having lunch in a fake Frenchy cafe in town. It had been Penny's choice, naturally, and Margaret seemed happy with it. Flirty foreign waiters and lots of squishy, doughy baguettes – who could ask for more? Hat hadn't taken in her surroundings: she was preoccupied by the recent development.

'I didn't say anything in front of Penelope because I didn't want to embarrass you, but I would like an explanation, if you'd be so kind. I think I have a right to know if there's something amiss between you and James.'

'Mum, first of all no one calls him James. Second, there's nothing wrong. It was just an argument.'

'What was?' Penny said, plonking herself back into her chair.

Hat grimaced. She hadn't seen her coming. 'It's nothing. Mum heard a message from Jimmy on the answering-machine, apologizing for a fight we'd had. Can we drop the subject now?'

'What was it about?'

'Nothing.'

'Must have been about something. He sounded very down in the dumps,' Margaret piped up.

'It's none of your business, all right?' Hat hadn't meant to sound quite so fierce, but she couldn't think of something minor that they might have rowed about. She ignored her mother's shuddering shoulders and bosom – her tried and tested method for showing how grievously hurt she felt.

'God, there's no need to be so touchy. Guy and I rowed night and day during the lead-up to our wedding. Mind you, it's good practice for married life!' Penny guffawed, and knocked back the last of her wine. She and her mother had downed an entire bottle.

'Penelope, don't say things like that! Harriet will think you're serious.'

Hat was surprised to see her sister roll her eyes.

'Sorry, Mum. No, Hat, married life is a bed of roses, believe me. Every day is a singular joy. Each morning I leap out of bed, impatient to see what the day has to offer.'

Margaret smiled graciously, satisfied that all was well with her elder daughter's marriage to a knight's son. Unlike Hat, she had not picked up the heavy sarcasm in Penny's tone.

'Is everything all right now, though?' Penny asked, with what Hat detected was real concern.

For a second, she wished she could confide in her sister. She suspected it would be an intense relief to have an ally within the family, but it was too risky. Anyway, Penny wouldn't understand. 'Yeah, it's fine.

You know what it's like,' Hat replied, letting out a little sigh. To her relief, that seemed to draw an end to the inquisition on the state of affairs between herself and Jimmy.

As predicted, after lunch, Margaret wanted to go on a trawl of the shops in search of the perfect hat to wear on the big day. Hat cited an ailing orchid in dire need of attention and left her mother and sister to debate the millinery merits of Knightsbridge over Oxford Street.

In fact, having first gone home to pick up her car/van and equipment, Hat did drop in on one of her clients, a particularly tetchy TV presenter who was a bit of a know-it-all when it came to greenery. Unfortunately for Hat, Andrea Garrett also had a passing acquaintance with Alan Titchmarsh, which she clearly imagined should impress her gardener *and* intimidate her. Although Hat never detected any evidence of the famous green-fingered television personality's interference in Andrea's garden she never liked to leave it too long. She was only contracted to appear once a week, but Andrea was one of those people who always presented anyone working for them with a list of Things That Must Be Done – Now. It never bore any relation to how much time Hat was paid for, and Andrea always complained if Hat left before every task was completed. This week she had insisted Hat re-root two fairly hefty saplings. That evening Hat returned home exhausted by the day's events: her mother's arrival, the emotional upheaval of Jimmy's message and her physical exertion at Andrea's had conspired to knock her for six. All the same, she was delighted to find Mish waiting for her.

'Mish, great! I'm so glad you're here. You'll never guess what?'

'What?' Mish was on tenterhooks.

'Jimmy called. He left a really nice message on the machine. Don't have a go at me but he sounded odd, sort of sad. He said that he thought the "space" he was getting was doing him some good. I think he's going to come back.'

'What else did he say?' Mish asked. After much thought she'd decided not to tell Hat about her conversation with Jimmy, and now that he had called, she knew it was right to keep shtum. She didn't want Hat to doubt his sincerity or motives. Even so, she was convinced that her call had prompted him to phone Hat and she was pleased she'd intervened.

'Well, not much,' Hat said pensively.

'Go on,' Mish encouraged.

'He just sounded really sorry and, oh, it's hard to describe but sort of as if he'd done some thinking and wasn't so sure of what he was doing any more. But the "space" thing was making him feel better, he said, which has got to be a good sign, no? Or do you think I'm mad to draw something positive from it?' She sounded less confident than when she'd come in.

'No, I think it sounds very positive. Maybe he's coming to his senses. I mean, why else would he call?'

'Do you think? I'm not just clutching at straws, then? You think it might mean he's coming back?'

'Yeah, I do,' Mish replied confidently. She didn't feel she was setting Hat up for a fall. By her reckoning Jimmy's call was rock-solid evidence that she'd set the cat among the pigeons. She'd made him realize some of what Hat was going through. Surely, Mish thought, if he's half-way decent, he'll do the right thing. She was beginning to think Priscilla might have been right all along – that Jimmy was simply suffering from a bad dose of pre-wedding nerves and that she could now support Hat without being hypocritical or encouraging her friend in false beliefs. At the back of her mind, she was aware that she might be going out on a limb, but she put her doubts on the back-burner.

'The thing is I don't know where he is. He didn't call from his flat – I checked. I think he's probably still away.'

'Yes, I bet he is.' Mish hoped she didn't sound too knowing.

'But where does that leave me with Penny's bleeding dinner party? Unless he makes a magical reappearance within the next five days, I'm fucked. Even if he's going to turn up in time for the wedding how can I explain his absence at that dinner?'

Mish and Hat sat and pondered the dilemma in silence. After a while Mish said, 'Use that bloke, Sean, Stan, whatever his name is – the guy staying at Priscilla's!'

'You mean Sam.'

'Yeah, get him to pretend to be Jimmy at the dinner.'

'I can't. Somebody'll rumble him. Anyway, he's married.'

'What's that got to do with the price of eggs? I'm not suggesting you have an affair with him! In fact, it's better that he's married because it means he won't get any funny ideas.'

'You needn't worry about that. You should see his wife – she's major-league gorgeous.'

'It makes him doubly perfect.'

'I can't. It's just too mad.'

'Oh, yeah? As opposed to chaining yourself naked to Jimmy's bed or boiling toy bunnies in his best pan? I suppose that's all perfectly sane behaviour.'

'I wasn't naked.'

'You're splitting hairs – or pubes. It's no more mad than anything else you've done so far. Priscilla said he had the same sort of colouring and build as Jimmy.'

'Yes, sort of, but my family are bound to notice it's not the same guy on the wedding day . . . assuming Jimmy turns up.'

'Not necessarily. You know what people are like. No one ever remembers what anyone looks like, particularly if they've had a drink. God, I don't recognize half the blokes I've slept with. They're only going to meet him this once. There'll be such complete pandemonium on the wedding day that no one will have time to stop and scrutinize Jimmy's features. Also he'll be wearing all that get-up, won't he? I'm not sure even *I*'d recognize him in that gear. You're focusing on minor details instead of the whole effect. If you *say* it's Jimmy then people will *believe* it's Jimmy.

The power of suggestion and all that. You'll just have to present him with total conviction.'

Even though Mish spoke with passion, Hat didn't look convinced.

'Look, I've got it! Get Sam to wear a moustache! Men look *completely* different when they grow moustaches. Then, on the day, Jimmy won't have one and you can say he shaved it off and that'll be that! It's brilliant!' Mish yelled, certain the idea was a winner.

Hat didn't reply. She was evidently thinking hard. Mish knew that she and Jimmy had had a bit of a tussle about him wearing the full Scottish regalia, that in fact he'd refused point-blank to don it, claiming that only Highlanders were entitled to wear it and that he'd feel like a prat. Either way, she was encouraging Hat to stake a lot on the ability of a Prince Charlie outfit (the correct name for a kilt and all the trimmings, Jimmy had informed her) to cover the massive gap between making two separate individuals look like the same person.

'Or perhaps we should go round to your sister's now and tell your mum everything. Would you prefer that?' Mish drawled.

'No! God, are you mad?' Hat snapped, and lapsed back into silence. 'Do you really think it could work?' she eventually asked her flatmate.

'I wouldn't say I did if I didn't. What with the excitement of your parents meeting him for the first time and your sister in competitive overdrive, and Guy, who couldn't care less what Jimmy's like, seeing as he doesn't belong to his special high-earning toss-pot brigade, yes, I think you could get away with it. But he'd need to have a moustache or something like that, definitely. When blokes shave them off they look like entirely different men, trust me.'

Eventually Hat came round to Mish's position. Her change of heart was partly due to her friend's persuasive line of attack but also, and mainly, thanks to the dread inside her that she would have to tell her mother the truth. In that punch-drunk state, she was unable to see the plan for the folly it was.

17. Meet the Parents

Hat and Sam drove along in her car/van towards Penny's. At first, neither of them spoke. From the moment they had met up that night, Hat had been putting off mentioning Sam's contribution to the deception. Now she couldn't bear the strain a minute longer. She simply had to say something about the 'thing' he was wearing. 'You're OK in that, not too hot or anything?' she asked, nodding nervously in the direction of his last-minute-brainwave disguise. She was aiming to sound both casual and uncritical, and hoped that either excessive warmth might force him to abandon it or he might realize somehow that it was a mistake. She had asked him to wear a fake moustache but Sam had taken it upon himself to go a teeny bit further. Without consulting her, he had donned a full-blown beard. The overall, and arresting, effect was of a makeshift yashmak made of matted pubic hair. Given his blondness he now bore a striking resemblance to Captain Birds Eye. She thanked her lucky stars he wasn't wearing a sailor's cap too.

Having made the nerve-racking call to Sam to ask if, after all, she could take him up on his offer, Hat had arranged to pick him up on the night in question. Her heart had plummeted into the soles of her shoes as she'd seen him walk down the stairs all spruced up for their evening of skulduggery. From the second he'd berthed into view she hadn't known whether to double up in hysterical laughter or fall to her knees weeping at the hopelessness of it all. In the end she'd done neither. Sam was doing her an enormous favour and she could hardly start picking apart his efforts to move the deception along. She had resolved to make the best of a bad job, something at which, unwittingly, she'd been getting pretty good. As she drove along, trying to ignore Sam's appendage flapping in the breeze, she wished she'd never embarked on the whole crazy scheme.

'Well, I wouldn't want to wear it in a Turkish bath, but if it does the job I can manage it for one night,' Sam replied cheerily.

Hat smiled wanly, her gaze fixed on the road ahead. She didn't want to look at the thing more often than she had to.

A few minutes later, it dawned on her that she was just going to have to get on with it, beard and all. 'OK, things you need to know . . . Look, I can't thank you enough for doing this, it's really, really kind of you. Anyway, my dad's one of those silent types, he doesn't say much but when he does speak everyone is supposed to listen.'

'Uh, like most dads.' Sam nodded.

'Is yours like that?'

'Isn't everybody's? They don't make great role models for us guys. No wonder girls usually go for the silent, moody types – reminds them of their fathers. After all, they do say that, subconsciously, every woman is trying to find a man like her father, don't they?'

Hat didn't reply. Sam's observation had made her stop to think. For the first time she wondered if she'd put up with Jimmy Mack's habitual silence because that was what she'd been brought up with – her dad was like that. The idea of being attracted to someone for his similarity to her father made her feel uncomfortable. But, worse than that, as far as she was concerned, it sowed a seed of doubt in her mind as to Jimmy's suitability, and that was the last thing she needed. Well, actually it was the *first* thing she needed so late in the game but the last thing she *wanted*.

Hat banished the queasy thought from her mind and reapplied herself to running Sam through the safety instructions she felt it vital he had grasped before being presented to her family.

'OK, right, my mum. Well, she's sort of snippy and judgemental and a bit of a snob but otherwise she's all right. She already thinks you're marvellous for marrying me and saving me from standing at the bus stop all night long waiting for a bus that was never going to turn up anyway.'

'Sorry?'

'According to my mother, there's a massive queue of women over thirty, metaphorically speaking, all standing about aimlessly at a bus stop even though we all know there's a drastic shortage of buses. She reckons that we have to jump on whichever comes first, no questions asked. Even if it's a number forty-seven and not going anywhere near where you want to go.'

'Oh, I see. I can't imagine you getting on the wrong bus.' Sam smiled at her. She smiled back and decided he was a really nice person and not at all geeky, as she'd originally thought. In fact, she thought, he was damn near perfect, considering what he'd taken on tonight.

'Anyway, my mum and dad weren't supposed to come over until yesterday by which time I was hoping to have got Jimmy back. But they came early to help out and I sort of regressed to a sulky teenager the moment my mum appeared. I didn't tell her it was all off, as I'd planned, and now I'm up to my neck in it and –'

'Look, it's all right, I do understand. That's why I agreed to help out. Weddings are like runaway trains.'

'Exactly! That's just what I said to Mish. So was your wedding like that too?'

'Er, no, not really. They do things differently in Colombia. Anyway, tell me more about your family.'

As Sam clearly wasn't keen to talk about his wedding, Hat carried on with her family resume. 'OK, Mum, Dad, done them. My sister, Penny – don't, whatever you do, call her Plopie. She'll hate you for ever if you call her that.'

'It would never have occurred to me. But "Plopie"? As nicknames go, I can see why she might not love it.'

'She's three years older than me, perfect in every way and married to Guy, who's one of those something-in-the-City types. He works for his dad's company and he thinks he knows everything, which I'm not convinced he does, but he earns a lot of money, which apparently means everybody has to think he knows everything. By the way, my mother will probably only mention this about seven million times tonight so, in case you miss it, Guy's dad is a Sir. He was knighted by Thatcher's lot for services to greed and the exploitation of underpaid workers or something equally worthy. But he might as well be next in line to the throne, as far as my mum's concerned. Both my parents think he's a real catch. Oh, yeah, and, here's another thing that might pass you by, Penny and Guy are incredibly happily married, or so I keep being told.'

'By Penny, I suppose?'

'How did you know?'

'Just a guess. I often find myself wondering what's really going on when people constantly go on about how fantastic their lives are.'

'Well, I'm sure they *are* ecstatically happy,' Hat replied, instinctively contradicting him, although she did wonder if he might have a point, given the weird things Penny had been saying recently.

'Anyway, don't worry, it'll be fine,' Sam said. 'I'll just take your family as I find them. I'm sure they're perfectly normal people.'

'I wouldn't say that.' Hat laughed.

'Erm, shouldn't I know something about *us*, though?' Sam asked. It was a good point that Hat seemed to have forgotten.

'Eh?'

'Something about you and me, I mean, you and

Jimmy Mack. How did we meet? How long have we known each other? That sort of thing.'

'Oh, God! Sorry, I was worrying so much about my family I forgot about all that. OK, we've known each other thirteen months and been engaged for eight. You came into Gerry's office to deliver something, we had a bit of a chat and then a week later you waited outside for me with a pair of gardening gloves and that was it, really.'

'How romantic.'

'Yeah, you'd think so.'

'What do you mean?'

'Well, that *was* a romantic gesture but as it turns out you're not very romantic.'

'I am.'

'You're not.'

'I am.'

'No, you're not, trust me, you're not. You did ask me to marry you and stuff, but that seemed to be an idea rather than a passionate declaration of your undying desperation to be with me every single day for the rest of your life.'

'Oh, right. Well, I *am* very romantic but, as Jimmy Mack, I'm not. OK, got it. But you agreed to marry him all the same?'

'Yeah, because we really love each other. I'm not big on all that swept-off-your-feet stuff – don't trust it, really,' Hat said breezily. She had no desire to focus on the missing elements in Jimmy's proposal, or, indeed, her own acceptance.

She couldn't think of anything else vital that Sam

needed to know. As tonight's dinner was the only time anybody was ever going to clap eyes on him before the real one came back she decided that there was no point in bogging him down with too much information. After all, his main job was to act as her stool pigeon. He just needed to be there, behave properly and keep his head down. She'd do the rest. Now they were nearing Guy and Penny's home and neither spoke again.

'Psst, Hat, you didn't tell me he had a beard,' Penny hissed into her sister's ear. Guy was handing round the drinks and describing, with complete seriousness, the precise age of the Scotch and its ancestry to Philip, his father-in-law.

'Why would I mention it?' Hat replied, feigning casual disinterest.

'Because you just would. That is definitely the sort of thing a woman would mention,' Penny insisted.

'Why?'

'Because it just is! It's the sort of thing you tell people. You definitely mention things like that, like he's got a tattoo, pierced ears, nose, lip, whatever, a *beard*. Christ, especially a beard like that. Those are the sort of things you inevitably use to describe someone. They are what's known as distinguishing features.'

'Only if I was reporting him to the police or filling in his passport application. Anyway, why does it matter how well I described him? I didn't think you'd be trying to pick him out of a line-up. The beard's a recent thing, he hasn't had it for that long,' Hat replied, looking across the room at the clump of miniature dreadlocks hanging from the lower half of Sam's face. She wondered forlornly if he'd hand-woven the thing from the innards of an old mattress.

'Well, I don't think it suits him. I'm sure he'd look better if he shaved it off. Why don't you make him?'

'Well, actually, he *is* shaving it off, ah, just before the wedding. He will definitely not have a beard on our wedding day, OK?' Hat replied hotly. She was keen to get her sister off the awful topic of Sam's beard, which, to her, was looking increasingly absurd.

'Darling, you never mentioned Jimmy had a beard.' Their mother had sidled up to them. No doubt she fancied she'd spoken discreetly, but to Hat she sounded like a public-safety announcement booming out of a shopping-centre Tannoy.

'What's with the beard? Will everyone give it a rest with the beard? It's not like he's got a wooden leg and I forgot to mention it! It's a beard, a bit of facial fluff, no more, no less. It does not say anything about his personality like he's a serial killer or a VAT inspector, OK?'

'Goodness me! Temper, temper,' Margaret said, shaking her shoulders and bosom in that notice-how-your-rudeness-has-actually-made-me-shudder way that only mums seem to manage. Having composed herself after the hideous shock, she continued, 'I disagree. I think a beard denotes something *very* particular about a man's personality. A man with a beard has authority, gravitas. He isn't afraid to stand out in a crowd.'

'And with a beard like that he'd better not be,' Penny added, bursting into giggles, and against her better judgement, Hat couldn't help joining in.

'Harriet Grant, I think it ill becomes you to laugh at the man you are to share your life with.' Margaret was clearly shocked at Hat's disloyalty.

Hat pulled herself together. Her mum was right, she wouldn't be encouraging Penny's teasing if Sam really had been Jimmy. Added to that, like most girls, Hat recoiled instinctively from the slightest whiff of her mum taking the you'd-better-shape-up-if-you-want-to-hang-on-to-that-man line. There's nothing like having a mother take up a boyfriend's case to make her daughter go right off him.

'Yeah, well, he's all right,' Hat said casually.

'*All right? All right?*' The shuddering bosom was in action again. 'He needs to be a little more than "all right" if you want this marriage to work.'

Hat would have liked to kick herself. She had been referring to Sam when she had damned him with that faintest of praise. I've got to get a grip, she chided herself. I'm letting the whole fucking false-facial-hair issue affect my we-are-so-in-love-don't-anyone-go-thinking-anything's-wrong performance. 'I didn't mean "all right" in that way,' she said quickly. 'I meant he's all right, in that really enthusiastic way – like all right, *woo!*' Hat whooped – rather unsuccessfully. She'd been trying for the hysterical exclamatory ejaculation usually heard at country and western concerts.

Mercifully, salvation arrived in the shape of two men.

'What's going on in this witches' coven, hey?' Philip said, with the man he believed to be his future son-in-law at his side. 'Got to keep your eye on them at all times, James, my lad, otherwise they'll plot your downfall, hey?' he said conspiratorially, and nudged him in the ribs in a chummy we're-all-lads-together style.

Hat was mortified. Although she was glad Jimmy wasn't present to witness her dad's attempt at male bonding she wasn't much happier that poor old Sam was having to endure it.

'Shall we eat?' Penny asked, in a brisk tone that clearly meant 'We are going to eat.'

For once, Hat was grateful that her sister ran such a tight ship.

'You don't have nearly such a strong accent in person as you do on the phone,' Hat heard her mother saying to Sam.

'Sorry, my "accent"?' she heard him reply, as the world slipped out of her arse.

'Oh, don't be embarrassed. I heard that message you left Harriet a few days ago, after the row, and your accent was really quite distinctive. It's funny how those machines distort one's voice so.'

'My – my accent?'

The first course had gone without a hitch and Hat's concentration had lapsed. Sam shot her a pleading look, and she realized she'd failed to tell him that Jimmy hailed from Scotland. She needed to think fast. 'He *does* have a *Scottish* accent,' Hat said, widening her eyes meaningfully at Sam. 'I mean *I* can hear it. It's just that he's been in London for so long he's sort of lost it now, haven't you, darling?'

'Aye, that's rrrrright enuff,' Sam said. His version of a Scottish lilt put in the shade Dick Van Dyke's legendary attempt at Cockney in *Mary Poppins*. Hat thought she was going to pass out.

'Oh, yes, I can hear it now,' Margaret said encouragingly.

'Well, it sorrrrt a cummes a cummes and gooes, unless Ah'm wi' maaa ain folk,' Sam continued. It was like listening to Jerry Hall having a bash at doing Billy Connolly.

Hat had heard enough. She glared at him, willing him to whoa up on his Scottification, but he was throwing himself into it with such gusto she feared that at any minute now he was going to break into a Highland fling and start och-aye-the-noo-ing all over the shop. She looked at his wine glass, concerned that he was drunk, but it was still half full. She wondered if perhaps he'd necked some Dutch courage before she'd picked him up to help him get through this night of pretending to be someone else.

'It's a lovely brogue, though. We're friendly with a Scottish couple back home in Canada. You sound just like them – they've pretty much lost their accents too, but it still comes through now and again,' Margaret said.

Hat was astounded. She'd never had occasion to test her mother's ear for accents before but she had just discovered that it was very poor.

*

'Bloody hell! How did you come up with all that stuff about motorbikes? I nearly died when I heard Guy mention them to you,' Hat whispered, as she and Sam climbed into her car/van. Apart from one other hairy moment when Guy had quizzed Sam about the Norton Commando he was building the evening had gone, incredibly, without a hitch.

Hat, who didn't dare touch a drop of alcohol, was now high as a kite with relief. Apparently Penny had given her husband a few conversation starter tips, one of which had been the collector's bike Jimmy was currently rebuilding, from scratch, piece by piece.

'Just as well, seeing as you forgot to tell me that he, er, I was into motorbikes. It's quite a universal blokes' thing. I used to have a couple of old bikes but I sold them when I went to South America – didn't have anywhere to keep them.'

'That's a coincidence, and bloody lucky for me. Well, if this all ends well you should meet Jimmy one day. He'd love to meet someone else who knows about old bikes.'

Sam didn't say anything for a moment. When he did, Hat was surprised by his tone. 'I don't think I'd want to. To be honest, he doesn't sound like a very nice bloke.'

Hat was taken aback – she'd never thought of how other people might interpret what Jimmy had done. 'Oh, no, he is. All this isn't his fault, he's just scared, you know, he got cold feet . . . I think.' She couldn't write Jimmy off as a villain. If anything, she thought, he's more of a lost soul than a prick. To Hat, his calm, low-key, slightly lost quality had always been part of the attraction.

'And as for your Scottish accent! Thank God, my mum hasn't seen *Trainspotting*. She probably thinks anyone who sounds like Mel Gibson in *Braveheart* has a heavy Scottish accent. God, yours was so bad you even managed to make *him* sound like Robbie Col-trane!' she said, changing the subject.

Sam started laughing. 'I never said I was a good actor. You might have told me he was Scottish beforehand.'

'Yeah, I'm really sorry about that. I didn't think. When – if – I get Jimmy back, I'll have to tell him to tone his accent down around my mum . . . God, that means I'll have to tell him what I did.' Hat had suddenly grasped the full ramifications of having got someone to impersonate him.

'Look, if he loves you like he ought to, he'll under-stand everything you did to get him back. For crying out loud, he should think himself lucky that somebody wants him enough to make this kind of effort!'

Hat was embarrassed by Sam's heated reply, the indirect compliment and, oddly, his reference to the strength of her love.

'Yeah, well, all things considered you did really well and I can't thank you enough. Even with that thing wafting around your chin!' She gestured with her elbow at Sam's beard, and the car/van swerved.

'Well, at least it didn't come off! Actually, I had a good time, it was a laugh,' Sam said, grinning broadly.

'Thank Gloria for me as well, will you?' Hat said, as she drew up outside Priscilla's house.

'Oh, she doesn't mind. You can borrow me anytime as far as she's concerned,' Sam said good-humouredly, as he grappled with the passenger door's stiff handle.

Hat thought that that was a really weird thing to say, but she didn't want to get into Sam and Gloria's troubles, assuming they had any – which given their collective perfectness she strongly doubted: she had enough of her own.

18. Penny Has a Few Choice Words for Hat

With the dreaded dinner party safely behind her, Hat heaved a deep sigh of relief and allowed herself to relax for the first time in aeons. Laughable as Sam's sorry excuse for a beard had been, she thought that there was now a strong possibility that the real clean-shaven Jimmy might be mistaken for the hairy Sam. She didn't know how she would explain everything to Jimmy but Sam's words kept ringing in her ears: 'If he loves you like he ought to, he'll understand everything you did to get him back.' She found them a source of great comfort and inspiration. Sam was right, Hat decided. If Jimmy was half the man she thought he was then he'd understand. He'd see how she'd got to such a fever pitch. He'd have to come to terms with the effect on her of his walking out like that. He'd just have to. Her main worry was that he wouldn't see the funny side of it. He had a good sense of humour, but Hat thought that spotting the humour in what she'd done might stretch anybody's imagination.

She was curled up in the living-room armchair still wearing her pyjamas. It was noon on a cold, rainy English autumn day, exactly ten days before her wedding. A mere two hundred and forty hours to go. A trifling fourteen thousand, four hundred minutes between now and D-day. It was six episodes of *East-Enders* away or, for the daytime viewer, eight bursts of *Home and Away*. She had worked out every conceivable configuration of the time remaining. Unlike most brides in the run-up to their weddings, she wasn't counting off the seconds one by one in the overexcited way of a pre-pubescent teenager awaiting a Steps concert: her calculations were more similar to those made by someone awaiting execution. She knew that when the day finally arrived it would be a tremendous release, just like death, and also completely terrifying, just like death. So, today, for what felt like the squillionth time since she'd embarked on this venture, she was in a quandary. She had a mammoth decision to make and she didn't know what to do.

She had called Jimmy's mobile several times over the last few days but it was constantly switched off. Oddly, Hat had taken comfort from this. Secretly she didn't really want to talk to him in case he said something she didn't want to hear. She decided that as he was out of contact with everyone he was wavering. She reasoned that he didn't want to be disturbed as he prepared himself to climb down from the massive boo-boo he'd made.

Today was the day when everything – flowers, cars, reception arrangements, photographer, video-maker – had to be confirmed. And Hat was terrified. Had she been at work the terror wouldn't have got quite such a grip on her, but it was tearing down outside and she didn't work on really rainy days, except at Priscilla's; she didn't get fussy about mud like other clients did. If she went ahead and confirmed them all, Hat was sure that it would be tantamount to yelling in Fate's face, 'Come and have a go if you think you're hard enough!' She was sure it would be asking for it. She reckoned it would be the equivalent of inviting Destiny to shit on her from a great height ensuring that Jimmy did not appear at the eleventh hour. Yet, on the other hand, she was horribly aware that if she *didn't* confirm anything there was going to be no wedding of any description, not so much as a dry vol-au-vent.

Hat was in a right dither. She wished her best friend was there to give her some guidance, but Mish had left early for yet another magazine shoot and wasn't going to be back until later on that evening. Hat went through the people she could ask for advice, and ruled out Priscilla: she knew what Priscilla would say, and Hat wanted to talk to someone who was capable of being rational and level-headed. Gerry was no good either: he'd just flap and tell her to ask Priscilla.

Drawing a blank, Hat felt the full weight of all that she'd taken on flop on to her. A cast of thousands had to be brought into play and she felt weak at the prospect. It was all very well having nurtured her own belief that Jimmy Mack would come back, but showing the green light to a host of strangers, based on nothing other than fervent hope, suddenly seemed ludicrous. Her private belief now needed to be secure enough to launch itself publicly, and Hat wasn't sure that it was. However, as it turned out, she needn't have wasted time worrying because Fate had planned a little surprise of its own.

'Hello, darling,' Margaret chirped down the phone into Hat's ear. 'How are you feeling this morning?'

Hat assumed her mother was suspicious. 'Why do you want to know?'

'What an odd thing to say. I just asked how you were. A perfectly normal question I would have thought,' Margaret replied, not unreasonably.

Hat saw she was reading too much into her mother's inquiry. 'Sorry, Mum, I'm fine. Everything's fine.'

'Well, that's good. Only ten days to go, eh? Are you excited?'

'Mmmmm, kind of,' Hat answered truthfully.

'Darling, I've got something to tell you,' Margaret continued portentously, her daughter's lacklustre reply not registering with her. 'I know you're going to think we're a pair of interfering old so-and-sos but you've seemed so tense recently and I talked it over with your father and he thought it was a good idea.'

'What was a good idea?'

'I just wanted to be of some real help. It's very hard for a mother to sit back and not get involved in her daughter's wedding, you know. Actually, it's not normal so I decided I'd just do the whole lot in one fell swoop, then you'd be free to enjoy yourself a little more. You were like a cat on a hot tin roof the other night and this is *supposed* to be a fun time in your life, you know?'

'Mum, will you just tell me what you've done, please?' Hat could feel anxiety gnawing at the pit of her stomach.

'Very well, darling. I've been to see all the people on your list and confirmed every last man jack of them. Although, I must say, the cost of the disco seemed a little steep. Still, what do I know about discos?'

'What *have* you *done*?' Hat cried. Her voice came out like the agonized squeak of a mouse in the middle of being strangled.

'I've sorted out everything for your wedding. All confirmed and paid for. Done and dusted. Now, isn't that a big help? Aren't you secretly relieved? I've dealt with everyone. And I've sorted out the seating plan too. It's much better now.'

Hat didn't know whether to laugh or cry.

'Well, I'm glad you're not cross. I *knew* it was the right thing to do. Your father was against it, naturally, said if you'd wanted my help you'd have asked for it. But I was sure you'd appreciate me stepping in. Call it a mother's instinct, if you will. Things were clearly getting on top of you. We'll have to have that money back we gave you but that can wait. Anyway, a small word of thanks wouldn't go amiss.'

Hat's mumbled thanks seemed to satisfy her mother.

'Oh, and your sister's here. She wants to know if it's all right for her to come over to see you. Is that OK?'

'Yeah, whatever,' Hat replied weakly. She couldn't

see the point in putting up resistance to any proposal now, however unwelcome. She wondered how her parents were going to react to having shelled out eight thousand quid for something that might turn out to be nothing more than a big knees-up.

'OK, I'll tell her. Dad and I are going to have lunch with Guy in the City. He's going to show us his new office.'

'That should be a riot,' Hat muttered. She wondered how it was possible that she was a full blood relation to a woman who had married a man whose idea of entertainment was showing off his desk.

Once she had put down the phone she slumped back into the armchair, flummoxed. A little bit of her wondered why Penny was coming round and hoped to God it wasn't because she'd smelt a rat. But most of her was consumed by flummoxdom.

As Hat waited for her sister she tried to get the situation clear in her head. She began by contemplating the ramifications of what her mother had done. Some of her – most, if she was honest – was intensely relieved that her mother had steamed in regardless of anybody else's wishes. In ordinary circumstances, Hat would have hit the roof, but in this case her mother had unwittingly relieved her of the gut-wrenching shall-I, shan't-I choice of whether to make that final huge leap of faith. Hat felt that, by accident, her mother had now taken on at least some of the responsibility for the outcome. She reckoned that Margaret could share some of the blame, should it all go pear-shaped. She knew somewhere that there was no basis for this daft notion, but for now she was comforted that everything was going ahead without her having had to pick up the hammer and drive in the nail.

Suspecting that she might incite a lecture from Penny about not taking care of herself if her sister found her still undressed, Hat threw on some clothes. When her sister appeared, though, she wished she'd put a bit more thought into it. Penny swanned in wearing a loose cashmere sweater over a beautifully cut pair of fine wool trousers. Hat looked down at the nondescript fleece she'd pulled on over some favourite old jeans. Physically there wasn't much difference between the two sisters: it was their respective attitudes to appearance that defined the vast difference in their looks. Hat only thought about clothes when she was with her sister, while they seemed to be the reason for Penny's existence.

'Look, I've come over because I need to talk to you,' Penny said, settling herself nervously on one of the wobbly kitchen chairs.

Hat hoped a stray splinter wouldn't snag her sister's perfect, and undoubtedly expensive, trousers.

'Oh, God, this is hard and I really, really don't want you to think I'm interfering.'

Christ, Hat thought, this is all I need, after Mum's momentous news.

'I know we've never been that close, Hat, and I'm sorry about that, particularly now. I'm sure it's partly my fault. We've got such different lives, though. All the same I do wish we were better friends because it would make this so much easier to say. God, I might not be saying it at all.'

Hat could feel a heap of old emotions rising up inside her: jealousy, competitiveness and anger were swooshing into her veins. She was having difficulty remaining calm, but she decided to sit and wait for Penny to spit out whatever it was she was trying to say.

'OK, here goes. Hat, I think you're getting married for the wrong reasons,' Penny blurted out. She stared at her sister, with a mixture of defiance and anxious anticipation.

Hat was torn between fury at her sister's temerity and fear that she knew something. She needed to find out more before she spoke and possibly incriminated herself.

'I don't think he's the love of your life. You are clearly the love of *his* life, anyone can see that, but I don't think he's yours. I think you're getting married for the sake of getting married. Maybe, and please don't take this the wrong way, to be like me – but it's a huge mistake. You *have* to marry for love – trust me – and absolutely not because you want a wedding or to please Mum and Dad –'

'How the hell can you possibly think you know how I feel about Jimmy? You've only met him once!' Hat screamed, incensed.

'Please don't be angry. I'm trying to stop you making the biggest mistake of your life. I'm not doing this to be mean.'

'Yes, you are! You just can't bear the idea that I might be happy. That I'm going to stop being the sad, unmarried sister. That I might get some of what you've got!'

'It isn't that. Christ, I'd love it if you *were* happily married. I've just got this awful feeling, maybe it's a sisterly thing, that you're marrying him for the wrong reasons. And, believe me, I know what I'm talking about.'

'What's that supposed to mean?'

Penny gave her sister a long, considered look. 'It doesn't matter. I didn't mean anything in particular by it. I'm just begging you to think about this. It's not too late, I'll help you get out of it, if you want.'

'Oh, yeah, I bet you will. I cannot believe you came round here only a few days before my fucking wedding to give me this arsing holier-than-thou speech! Maybe it's not going to be as perfect as your oh-so-marvellous-marriage-made-in-heaven but that's OK by me. Maybe Jimmy doesn't compare to the fabulous Guy but I wouldn't marry a twat like him if he was the last bloke on earth!' Hat splurted out, and bit her tongue. She'd gone too far.

To her amazement, Penny didn't throw some horrible retort about Jimmy's deficiencies straight back in her face. Instead she stood up. 'Look, I'm going to leave. This was a mistake. I should have known you wouldn't take it from me.'

'I wouldn't take it from anyone. I bloody well *do* know what I'm doing and I wish everyone could see that!' Hat yelled.

She made no attempt to stop Penny leaving and sat fuming like a sulky child as she closed the front door behind her. Hat was enraged at what she saw as Penny's deliberate attempt to ensure that she alone occupied the special-happily-married-daughter's slot. She was filled with indignation that her sister had dared to advise her on exactly what the correct amount of in-loveness-to-get-married was.

She didn't stop to think that her sister might have had a point, nor to ponder on the meaning behind her words. Her response had been triggered by the way in which she had always felt sidelined by her parents in favour of Penny. Every pretty dress given to Penny when Hat received dungarees or books had fuelled the fury that now raged inside her. As far as she was concerned, the episode had been kindled exclusively by her older sister's determination to hold on to the number-one position in their parents' eyes.

Penny's visit generated in Hat the obverse of its intention. Instead of making her think hard about what she was doing, it reignited the fire of her faith in Jimmy Mack's return.

Even so, after a while, she was feeling edgy and pacing around her flat like a caged tiger. She could not get over Penny's arrogance but her sister's words niggled at her. She was desperate to talk to Mish and tried her mobile a few times but, as always when she was working, it was switched off. Hat really wanted to talk to someone. She ended up ringing Priscilla.

19. Hat Gets More Mixed Up

'Can I speak to Priscilla, please?'

'Hat, is that you? It's Sam.'

'Oh, hi. I should have said hello. Sorry, I wasn't thinking. I'm a bit distracted.'

'So you're not ringing to thank me for the marvellous job I did the other night?'

'No, I'm not,' Hat replied, without thinking. 'God, I'm sorry, that sounded awful. I mean, thank you very, very much, you were great. Sorry, I'm really preoccupied.'

'I was joking. You don't need to thank me, it was a laugh.'

'Yeah it was, in a way . . . except that –' Hat stopped short of divulging the latest developments. 'Just got to wait and see what happens now. Anyway, is Priscilla there?'

'Oh, I should have said. She's out. I've a feeling she's meeting your mother after lunch, don't know where, though. I know she wanted to avoid her coming here, what with me lurking about and all.'

'Tsk, damn.'

'Are you all right? Is something the matter?'

'No. Well, yes, sort of. I'm a bit pissed off about something and I wanted to talk to Priscilla, but it doesn't matter. Will you tell her I rang, please?'

'Yes, of course.'

'Thanks. 'Bye, then, and thanks again for the other night.'

Hat was about to put the phone down when Sam made a last-minute suggestion: 'Look, why don't you come over here and wait for Priscilla? That way you won't have to go over and over whatever it is on your own. If you like you can tell me about it. I'm a good listener.'

Hat paused. A breath of fresh air and a change of scenery were exactly what she needed. She wondered if Gloria knew how lucky she was to have found someone as sensitive and practical as Sam. She hesitated before agreeing – she didn't want to overstep the mark with him. 'Yeah, OK, if you're sure I won't be in the way.'

'It'll be fine. There's just Gloria and me kicking round the house.'

As Hat made her way over to Priscilla's house, she tried to forget about the disappointment that had assaulted her when she'd heard that Gloria was in. It had bewildered her and she had no intention of delving into where it might have come from.

'What do you fancy, then?' Sam said, wandering through to the kitchen once he'd let Hat in.

'God, I wish I knew!'

'I meant by way of refreshment.'

'Oh, that. God, I wish I knew.'

Hat sat down at the kitchen table. She was pleased she'd taken Sam up on his offer to come round. It felt much better to be out of the house, away from the phone, her mother, her sister – her life. She felt relaxed around him and put this down to his detachment from her dilemmas. She liked the way he treated her as if she were normal. Especially as she hadn't been a normal person since the day she'd embarked on planning a wedding, never mind since Jimmy had left.

'A coffee would be great. Where's Gloria?' Hat asked, looking around the room as if she might discover her hiding under the table or in the pantry.

'Upstairs, I think. I told her you were coming over. She'll be down soon enough, I'm sure,' Sam said, putting on the kettle and getting cups out.

Despite that little moment of disappointment Hat now, conversely, very much wanted Gloria to join them. She felt that her presence would instantly wipe out whatever had led to the earlier unexpected feeling. Hat trusted herself around Sam: she knew she wasn't likely, or even tempted, to leap headlong into his arms and beg him to run away with her. She just felt that Gloria's presence would balance things out.

'So, go on. What's got your goat, then?' Sam asked, propping himself against the counter while he waited for the kettle to boil.

Hat wasn't sure she wanted to give him the full, unedited version of the row. It involved too many personal issues, some of which might prove more than slightly embarrassing.

Sam misinterpreted her silence. 'Sorry, you probably don't want to talk to me about it. I'll make your coffee and bugger off. I didn't mean to pry.'

Instantly Hat regretted the silence: she'd humiliated

him. 'No, no. It's fine. I don't mind telling you, although I should warn you it's all a bit silly. You see my sister Penny came –'

Gloria burst into the room, cutting off Hat mid-sentence. She looked as if she was in a bit of a mood but even so Hat was astounded once again by her beauty. Everything about her exuded exotic mystery. Although Hat had begun to appreciate Sam's solid qualities she still had difficulty in imagining how he had won over someone like Gloria. She was the sort of woman usually seen on catwalks and in movies, not pushing a shopping trolley around Sainsbury's with an ordinary, if lovely, man who worked for Voluntary Services Overseas. She threw Hat a per-functory smile and launched into a breakneck-speed conversation in Spanish with Sam.

After a few rapid exchanges, accompanied by a lot of arm-waving, she left the room – in a huff, Hat was fairly sure.

'Is something the matter? Should I go?'

'No, absolutely not. It's nothing.' Sam shrugged his shoulders. Hat couldn't tell if he was really bothered or not. Given Gloria's natural flamboyance it was impossible to tell if she'd just announced to Sam that their marriage was over or asked him where to find the spare loo rolls.

'Gloria seemed a bit pissed off. Is it anything to do with the other night?'

'No, no, really. It's not a big deal. Anyway, what were you saying?' Sam said, carrying over the cups and plonking himself down opposite Hat.

After a moment's thought, Hat decided that whatever was going on between Sam and his wife couldn't possibly have anything to do with her. It was absurd to imagine that someone like Gloria might be jealous of her. 'Where was I? Oh, yeah, Penny came round this morning to tell me I was making the biggest mistake of my life and I lost my rag with her.'

'Is that what she said?'

'Not exactly. She said that it was clear that you, er, Jimmy, as it were, weren't the love of my life and that I shouldn't marry except for love.'

'And aren't I? I mean, isn't he?'

Hat looked at Sam. He was smiling and she couldn't detect any malice in his question. 'I don't know! Don't you start! It's gone way beyond the love-of-your-life department. You, of all people, should know what it's like.'

'What do you mean?' Sam asked, puzzled.

'Oh, you know. Remember what we said about it being like a runaway train? Planning a wedding catapults you out of what was a perfectly normal relationship and into uncharted waters. Forget about the sea of love, it's more like a shark-infested paddling pool. Anyway, of course he is. I'm just furious that Penny thinks she can give *me* lectures. I don't need her pissing on my shoes and telling me it's raining, as if she lives in some lofty state of untouchable perfection. I've got enough trouble pulling this whole thing off without other people chipping in.'

Sam didn't reply immediately, and Hat worried that he might be judging her. At last he said, 'Maybe that's not what she was doing. Maybe she really was trying to establish what your feelings for me – er, Jimmy are. Sorry, I keep doing that. Isn't that possible?'

'No!' Hat cried, exasperated that he should be taking her sister's side. 'Look, she obviously doesn't know top from bottom. She started off by saying that it was clear that I was the love of *your* life, would you believe? I mean, that proves she doesn't know what she's talking about if she thinks you're madly in love with me!'

'It also proves I'm not such a bad actor, after all.' Sam grinned broadly.

For the second time that day Hat was astonished to feel a stab of disappointment. 'My sister and I have always been competitive with each other. Mum made us like that, always preferring dainty Penny over me. Mind you, we're so different we'd probably have ended up like that anyway. I think Penny's trying to stop me from muscling in on what she sees as a special world that belongs to her.'

'Maybe that's exactly what she's doing.'

'What do you mean?' Hat asked nervously, guessing that Sam had a wildly different interpretation from hers. She was beginning to feel quite uncomfortable: talking about the fracas with him was bringing up much deeper issues than she had bargained for.

'Maybe she isn't that happily married, maybe she *didn't* marry for love, despite the press release. Guy did seem like a bit of a . . . twit, if you don't mind me saying so. Maybe she *really* doesn't want you to make the same mistake.'

Hat found she couldn't compute what he seemed to be saying. Eventually, correct or not, she wasn't prepared to accept such a radical analysis of Penny's possible motives. She could not get her head round the notion that her much envied older sister had really been talking about something profound – and personally revealing to boot. Added to that, she was resisting the idea that her sister had come to save her. Hat decided that it was sweetly characteristic of Sam to interpret her sister's actions so benignly. However, it didn't change how she saw things. 'No. We don't have that kind of relationship. She wouldn't come round out of goodness of heart to stop me dropping myself in it. And, more importantly, she would *never* admit to it all not being a bed of roses with the fabulous Guy, that's for sure.'

'Well, she's your sister, you know her best . . .'

'But?' she prompted, sensing he had something else to say.

'Nothing, really. Just that things aren't always as they seem. Don't take everything at face value.'

Something about his tone gave Hat a fleeting sensation that he wasn't referring exclusively to the state of Penny's marriage.

'I don't – or, rather, I'll try not to. But I still think you're wrong about my sister.'

'Well, I was just trying to put a different perspective on it. Hope I haven't made it worse.'

'No, not at all. It was good to talk about it with someone. I probably shouldn't have gone mad at her. I'm just getting so sick of everyone else knowing

179

what's best for me when they don't even know the half of it.'

'Well, maybe *not* knowing the truth means they're able to see the wood for the trees.'

Hat had a creeping feeling that Sam was now trying to get her to do what Penny had failed with earlier. Eventually she looked up at him and saw his expression change. Something about his manner, Hat thought, indicated that he wanted to steer the conversation from the dodgy direction it was beginning to take. He probably hadn't intended to get so involved. Now she regretted having been so frank with him. An awkward silence fell between them.

'Look, we need to put this behind us for a bit. Why don't we go out?' Sam burst out in a jolly let's-move-right-away-from-sensitive-subjects voice.

'You and me?' Hat asked incredulously. Was he asking her out on a date?

'No, all of us. Poor old Gloria, she's been cooped up in the house all day. I think she's got cabin fever. That's probably why she seems a bit grumpy. Why don't we go dancing later on? Gloria loves dancing and there's a fantastic salsa place I know.'

'Just the three of us – you, me and Gloria?' Hat asked, in a way that made it clear she thought he'd gone off his head.

'No!' Sam laughed. 'We'll invite Gerry along too. He'll love it. Why don't you give him a ring at work? He's always telling me what a great dancer he is. I just want to get out and have some fun ... I want to forget about everything,' he added, snappishly.

He was irritated and Hat hoped that it wasn't her problems that had caused his change of mood. She wasn't very keen on a night's dancing but she didn't see how she could turn him down after what he'd put himself through on her behalf. Added to that, she felt she owed both him and Gloria a big favour.

She called Gerry, who was right up for it, then returned home, having made an arrangement to meet them all later that night at the Bar Rocca in King's Cross.

20. Dancing Queen

Hat felt mighty peculiar as she set off for the evening's entertainment. She had the same over-excited, sick-to-the-stomach, nervy feeling she'd had whenever she'd bunked off school or skipped a day's work for no good reason. She was not given to self-indulgent flights of fancy, and now she was doing something new and different but vaguely taboo. And Hat didn't usually do things like that.

Over the last four weeks, her entire life, indeed her every waking moment, had been held hostage by a pile of problems, yet she was trotting off for a night of enjoyment as if she didn't have a care in the world. It just didn't feel right: it didn't sit well with Hat's belt-and-braces personality. Her instincts were encouraging her to stay at home and put in a few more hours of major panicking. Going out was possibly the greatest Fate-tempting-move she'd made so far. When Hat had wavered Mish had finally persuaded her to go.

'Come on, it'll be good for you,' she'd said over the phone, having called to let Hat know she was going to be later than expected.

'But it feels so weird, going out ten days before blast-off to do something that's got nothing to do with it.'

'That's exactly why you should go! Christ, what's the alternative? Another night jumping through hoops with your parents? A fight with your sister? Or staying in alone picking fluff out of your belly button waiting for the phone to ring. I know which I'd plump for.'

'You're probably right.'

'Go. You might actually have some fun for a change. Even if you don't dance you can always enjoy the show Gerry will put on. You know what a brilliant dancer he is. Actually, come to think of it, he dances a bit like Ricky Martin. I thought Gerry said straight men can't dance.'

'Oh, fancy him as well, do you? Blimey, the list is endless,' Hat teased.

'Listen, looking like that he could have two left feet and it wouldn't matter.'

When Hat arrived at the club, which was a short walk west of King's Cross station, she wasn't sure at first if she'd got the right place. Although music could be heard from the street there were no other clues to indicate that a salsa bar was in the vicinity: there were no bouncers, no neon signs, no queues of spotty teenagers waiting nervously to see if they'd pass muster. The only hint was the music emerging from below Hat's feet.

The club was reached by a few steps descending into a kind of half-basement below a Spanish delicatessen. A large darkened window with the remains of the words Bar Rocca stencilled in an arc looked out on to a couple of feet of concrete where some overflowing bins lived. Hat walked down the steps, uncertain of what might lie ahead. She pushed open the heavy wooden door and was confronted by a smoky room packed to the rafters with people. Holding the door open, which gave her the option to flee if necessary, Hat peered around trying to pick out her crew.

She was relieved to make out Sam, Gloria and Gerry sitting at a table half-way down the right-hand side of the room. As she made her way towards them, Sam spotted her and waved. The room wasn't large but it took her some time to squeeze through the throbbing crowd to her friends. Almost everybody in there was Hispanic, and the atmosphere was completely unEnglish – wild, noisy and flamboyant. Virtually every person standing, including the bartenders, was moving to the music. Hat felt like she'd walked into a Cuban movie. A small area in the middle of the room was devoted to more committed dancing than that performed by the general crowd, and those occupying it were gyrating energetically in an amorphous mass.

Once Hat had reached them, Sam offered to get in a round of drinks and pushed his way over to the bar while Hat settled herself at the table. In contrast to her earlier mood Gloria was happy now. Hat guessed that being in a familiar environment surrounded by people who spoke her own language probably helped.

'I've been picking up some Spanish,' Gerry yelled, over the music.

'Spanish men?' Hat yelled back.

'Very funny. No, language. *Te quiero mucho.*'

'*Te quiero mucho*,' Gloria repeated, laughing.

'What does that mean?'

'I love you very much, or I want you very much. Either, apparently, depending on the situation.' Gerry arched his eyebrows suggestively.

'Could be handy tonight,' Hat observed.

'*Quiere bailar conmigo?*' Gloria said suddenly, leaning over to Gerry.

Hat had no idea what she'd said, but to her amazement Gerry did.

'*Sí, gracias,*' Gerry replied, standing up and leading the Colombian beauty on to the dance floor. Hat watched as the pair fell instantly into a particularly fruity version of the saucy lambada.

'Quite a spectacle, eh?' Sam said, as he came back to the table, clutching four bottles of beer and jerking his head in the direction of his wife and her dancing partner.

'Yeah.'

Even given Gerry's sexuality, Hat marvelled at Sam's casual attitude towards the lewd dancing his bride was doing with another man. If I didn't know better, I might mistake it for indifference, she thought, as she picked up her beer. They must be so secure in each other, she concluded enviously. She had imagined that someone with Gloria's looks would elicit a lot of attention and therefore a lot of jealousy.

'I'm really glad Gerry's come,' Sam bellowed above the noise in the club. 'I'm not that great at dancing. Too English for all this explicit physical expression!' He clinked his beer bottle against Hat's.

She was comforted to hear this. From the moment she'd walked in, she'd dreaded being asked to dance. She knew she'd make an arse of herself, attempting the lithe movements required to blend in with the house style. The universally accepted arm-flailing and hip-shaking known as disco was about all she could manage. And she wouldn't dream of having a stab at that without a few more drinks inside her.

Sam shouted something else but Hat couldn't hear him above the din and shrugged her shoulders apologetically.

After a few more failed attempts, they gave up trying to make coherent conversation. Instead they turned to watch the dancing. Gerry and Gloria were moving as one elastic, symbiotic body and made a spectacular couple. They looked like Siamese twins joined at the hip. Suddenly, the sight of them as they ground into each other's groins made Hat laugh. Would tonight's experience turn Gerry into one of his own much-criticized greedy poofs?

'What?' Sam shouted.

'What, what?' Hat mouthed back.

'What made you laugh?'

'I just wondered if Gerry was on the turn,' she yelled, nodding towards the erotic display being put on by his wife and their friend.

'Doubt it somehow. Anyway, gay men are always the best dancers.'

'And Colombian women by the look of it.'

'Yeah, they're not bad,' Sam said, smiling.

For a split second, Hat thought she detected the

same detached tone she'd heard him use before when speaking about his wife and it puzzled her.

'Bloody hell! Any more of that and I'll be challenging you to a duel for your wife's hand. I never realized women could be so sexy,' Gerry said breathlessly, and sat down at their table. Sam grinned. 'Yeah, she's good, isn't she?' He leant over to his wife, who'd sat down next to him. '*El dice que pelees conmigo por ti por que tu bailas maravillosamente,*' he explained. She giggled, and gave Gerry a playful slap on the shoulder.

Much later that night, the three housemates walked Hat home – there were no cabs in sight. From a grey, drizzly day it had turned, unusually for late September, into a warm, dry night. They fell quickly into two pairs, Sam and Hat in one, Gloria and Gerry in the other. The latter were several yards ahead and as they walked along they broke into bursts of salsa. A delight to behold, Hat thought.

'Thanks for coming tonight. I needed that. It's been really great to get out of the house, not having to worry about who's watching,' Sam said suddenly.

She was puzzled. Who would be watching them? He surely couldn't mean Priscilla – she was hardly the nosy-landlady type. He didn't elaborate further, and she decided not to ask – she didn't want to pry. All the same, she had an increasingly strong feeling that all was not as it seemed between Sam and his stunning wife.

'And Gloria seems to have had a good time too,' she said eventually, nodding at the pair dancing away up the street.

'Yeah, she really has. I have too.'

'And me.'

Hat felt a desperate urge to hold Sam's hand. She couldn't remember ever feeling so close to someone without wanting to sleep with them. In fact, she couldn't remember ever having felt so close to someone she *had* slept with. The thought crossed her mind that this must be how it felt to have a lovely, protective big brother. Except that, somehow, Sam didn't feel like a brother. To her, he felt like someone who genuinely cared about her without having an agenda of his own. She resisted the temptation to show her affection – a move like that would be wide open to misinterpretation, but as she walked along Hat felt a pleasing glow. And it was particularly welcome in the midst of her current travails. She was glad that she'd made a friend like Sam.

21. Drawing a Veil

The following day Hat felt strangely detached, and padded about the flat in a kind of dreamy trance, which was surprising, given that she was slipping ever nearer to what might be a bottomless abyss. She was now nine days, or two hundred and sixteen hours, from the moment of truth yet felt less electrified by panic than she had for ages. It freaked her out a bit. She'd become so accustomed to adrenaline charging around her body, making every minute seem like the night before a big exam, that it was odd to feel almost normal again. She had no idea where the calm had come from but she was enjoying it. She guessed that, in her present predicament, it was not likely to hang around for long.

Indeed, the phenomenon was short-lived. The phone rang and, as ever these days, foretold more doom.

'Hello, darling. Today I thought we'd pick up your dress and do all the little last-minute things. The dress must be ready by now but even so I thought we'd take along your shoes. It's vital to try them on with it before you take it away from the dressmaker's. That way, last-minute alterations can be made before it's too late. You have bought them, haven't you?'

'Yes,' Hat replied gloomily. The calm had been

sucked out of her body with turbo-charged speed as her mother rattled off her plans for the day.

'That's a relief. Right, so I thought dress first, shoes, organize veil, tiara, et cetera.'

Hat made a snap decision. 'I'm not wearing a veil.'

'*Not wearing a veil!*' Margaret screeched, as if Hat had said she wasn't going to be wearing pants. 'You have to wear a veil! It's a church wedding, for heaven's sake.'

'I do not have to wear a veil. I am not walking up the aisle peeping out from behind a net curtain like Dot Cotton, OK?'

'Who's Dot Cotton?'

'Never mind.' Hat had forgotten they didn't get *EastEnders* in Canada and that, even if they did, her parents were hardly likely to watch it. 'Anyway, I'm not wearing a veil.'

'Don't be ridiculous, of course you're wearing a veil. It's traditional.'

'Yeah, and so's being a virgin until you're married but guess what?' Hat laid on a meaningful pause. She was being deliberately coarse.

'That's enough, thank you very much,' Margaret snapped. While she was more than happy to pontificate night and day about the role of 'relations' within a marriage, she preferred the abstract to the specific. She was not the kind of mother who sat around chatting with her kids about their sexual antics. In fact, she was the kind of mother who preferred to remain in blissful ignorance of that area in her children's lives. The little sex education Hat and Penny had received at home had been of the birds and bees variety, and Hat had picked up most of what she knew along the way, as it were.

'Then we'll have lunch. I'd like to go through the invitations again because although most people have replied, there are some yawning gaps. For example, you can't possibly not have your second cousin Celia.'

'Who?'

'Celia Wood. Come on, you remember, poor old Celia, lives in Bournemouth. Sad girl, frightfully lonely, I'm pretty sure. She does something tragic like professional cat-sitting. She was your father's cousin Ian's daughter by his second marriage to that awful, tarty girl Sandra. Funny that her daughter should have turned out so dowdy and spinsterish.'

'Mum, what *are* you talking about? I've never heard of this woman, let alone met her.'

'Probably not, come to think of it, but she's all alone in the world and you can't begrudge a lonely old maid a day out, can you?'

'I don't want a load of old people I don't know at my wedding. It isn't a funeral. Just how old is she?'

'Oh, I think she'll be a good forty by now.'

Hat rolled her eyes. From the description she'd imagined a ninety-year-old. 'God, she might as well hang herself right away, then.'

'Well, that might be a *bit* drastic but I take your point, which is one of the reasons I'm so pleased that you're getting married,' Margaret replied, having missed Hat's sarcasm.

Hat heaved a loud, exasperated sigh.

'Anyway, we can discuss all this over lunch,' Margaret continued, oblivious to her daughter's mounting rage. 'I'll make my way over to you now and we can go straight to the dressmaker's from there, OK?' she added, in a tone that made it clear to Hat that it wasn't a question at all.

Hat put down the phone and marvelled at the memory, only a few minutes old, of the calm she'd been enjoying. Perhaps she'd dreamt it. The runaway train was evidently still careering wildly along the track, gathering speed all the time. The only thing that had changed was that her mother had pushed her out of the driving seat and taken over the controls. Hat was just a helpless passenger now, like everybody else. Of course, she *could* yank on the brakes by coming clean but that had long ceased to be an option. She had elected to go with the flow of her mother's intervention. Except, she thought, as she prepared herself for another fun-filled, action-packed day, it had turned out to be more of a torrent than a flow.

The phone rang again. As Hat shuffled towards it she wondered wearily what delights this call would hold. If I carry on like this, there's every chance I'll die of emotional exhaustion before the day, so that'd be a result, she groaned inwardly.

'God, you sound awful. Has something happened?' Gerry chirped.

'No. Well, not really, just your average impending disaster, wholesale humiliation or, possibly, wholesale success, depending on how the dice fall, eh? So, just another ordinary day in the life of a woman on the edge of a self-propelled nervous breakdown.'

'It's going to be fine, I know it is. I can feel it in me waters.'

Hat smiled at Gerry's poor imitation of *Coronation Street*'s Bet Gilroy. She knew he had no foundation for being so positive but she appreciated his support.

'What are you doing?' he asked.

'Waiting for my nemesis in the shape of my mum. She wants to see my dress before I pick it up to see if she can add anything I've missed – i.e. ruin it completely.'

'Oh, come on Hat, she won't,' Gerry said, unconvincingly.

'We'll see.'

'Wasn't last night fun?' Gerry evidently felt a change of topic was required.

'Yeah, it was, actually. You and Gloria make quite a pair. Pity you're not one of those greedy poofs.'

'Isn't it? She's fabulous, though, isn't she, so sexy, don't you think?'

Hat was shocked to feel a stab of jealousy pierce her heart.

'But, you know, there's something about her I can't put my finger on. She's sort of different . . .' he continued.

'Maybe it's because she's foreign . . .' Hat suggested, dismissing the sensation that had just assaulted her.

'No, no, that's not it. I feel a real connection with her. I wish I could describe it. There's something about her that speaks to me – she's like a kindred spirit, you know.'

'Ooh, Gerry, better watch yourself, she's a married woman. If you're going to go bi don't fall for a lady who's not available.'

'No, I don't mean that sort of connection, it's something else.'

'I think I hear greedy poofery beckoning. Don't fight it,' she teased.

'I don't think I'll be going down that road just yet, do you?'

'Who knows?' Hat laughed. Suddenly she realized the time and began to gabble: 'Look, I've got to go, I'm not even dressed yet and Mum'll be here any minute now. Thanks for coming last night. It was fun.'

'OK, 'bye. But listen, before you go, I wanted to say – don't be so down on the whole thing. It's going to work out, I am absolutely sure of it. There's no point in being miserable, it'll only make the whole thing even more stressful. Believe he's coming back and try to enjoy this time. Trust me.'

Hat was touched that Gerry was making such an effort to be upbeat and loyal to her cause. 'Thanks, I'll try,' she said. 'See you later.'

She hung up but didn't move. She was confused by that smidgen of jealousy she'd felt. Although she didn't know Gloria well, she'd liked her better after their night out than she had before. Until last night she had seemed a little aloof, and Hat, understandably, had put it down to the confidence afforded her by her beauty. Now that she had seen her in her own environment she had appreciated the misery of Gloria's position. It couldn't be much fun living in a country so completely different from her own, no matter how much in love she was. Hat, who was keen to find an uncomplicated motive for the jealousy, decided that it came from envy of Gloria's relationship with Sam. She also knew that Gerry was right about putting a brave face on it. If she went around looking like death warmed up, her mother might suspect something. Worse, the negativity might affect, in some karmic way, the eventual outcome. Once again, she decided to stride forward with zeal.

'You see, it's crying out for a veil,' Margaret pronounced, waving her arm majestically towards her daughter's beveiled head. She had taken up a position on the seat next to the mirror, facing Hat.

'No, it isn't.'

'Yes, it is, darling. The veil makes the whole thing just perfect.'

'It's perfect as it is. I am *not* walking up the aisle suffocating behind a net curtain, OK?' Hat said, pulling it off.

As Hat had predicted, her mother, unaware that her daughter had already bought and rejected one, had urged her to try on one of the veils Mrs Kostas had lying around for just such an occasion.

'Don't you agree, it needs a veil?' Margaret asked Mrs Kostas, articulating each word as if she was talking to someone hard of hearing.

Hat wanted to die of embarrassment. Since Mrs Kostas was foreign Margaret had assumed she couldn't speak English very well. Luckily the dressmaker was kneeling on the floor with a mouthful of pins, seeing to the dress's hem. She was clearly accustomed to being caught in the middle of such disagreements. She mumbled something and shrugged her shoulders nonchalantly. Hat suspected that even though Mrs Kostas was a veil advocate too, she wouldn't betray this in front of Margaret. She also noted that the pins would have hampered her speech anyway.

'See, Harriet? Mrs Kostas agrees with me,' Margaret cried.

Hat gritted her teeth, silently cursing her mother's acute nose for support, even if it was unspoken.

'That dress *needs* a veil. Whoever heard of a bride being married in a church without one?'

'Mum, Mrs Kostas did not agree with you. She didn't say anything. I am not wearing a veil and that is the end of it!' Hat barked.

Margaret's bosom shuddered again, and she gave Hat a thunderous look that said she did not appreciate being shouted at in front of the dressmaker.

'Darlin', I fink you look an assolute picksha,' Mrs Kostas said, as she stood up and admired her client in her handiwork.

Hat looked in the mirror and was entranced by the image she saw. She had never before seen herself look anything like this. The long, flowing style of the dress made her look tall and elegant, and the deep, mossy green of her suede shoes set off the colour beautifully. Hat was delighted.

Eventually Margaret, having got nowhere with her ostentatious sulking, gave her verdict. 'Yes, darling, I must say you do look very pretty.'

Hat wasn't sure that her mother had ever paid her a compliment before, least of all on her physical appearance, and in spite of herself she was thrilled. The dress was everything she'd hoped it would be. She just prayed she'd have the opportunity to wear it.

'I won't say another word about the veil, although I do think it would be the icing on the cake. I'm prepared to draw a veil over the whole episode, ha, ha,' Margaret announced, shortly after they had left Mrs Kostas' tiny workshop. 'Now, let's go and have some lunch. Any chance of your James joining us? I'd like to get to know him a little better. Could you call him?'

'No, no, no,' Hat said, rather more aggressively than she intended.

'Goodness, why ever not? He's surely keen to get to know his future mother-in-law a little better. Go on, give him a call.'

'No. I – I can't.'

'Can't? Why can't you?'

'Because he's – he's . . .' Hat was grappling for a feasible explanation. She was flying by the seat of her pants. Having got away scot-free, it would seem, with the substitution of Sam for Jimmy at the dinner, she had not made provision for any eventuality that might crop up thereafter. Suddenly she lit upon a copper-bottomed excuse – and it was true. 'He's gone up to Scotland for a few days.'

'When did he leave?'

'This – yester – this –' Hat tried hastily to work out which day sounded more convincing '– this morning.'

'This morning,' Margaret repeated.

'Yes, *this* morning,' Hat repeated.

'Right, I see. And why, might I ask?'

'Why what?' Hat asked innocently. She was playing for time.

'Why has he gone up there?' Margaret asked impatiently.

'Because – because his mother isn't very well. In fact, she may end up not being able to come to the wedding at all,' Hat replied, seizing another golden opportunity. In for a penny, in for a pound, was her thinking. This way I'm covered if Jimmy does turn up but none of his family do because he'd already told them it was off.

'He didn't mention it when we met the other night.'

'She wasn't ill then and now she is, OK?'

'Nothing serious, I hope. It would be a terrible shame to miss her son's wedding.'

'It's a – a –' Hat couldn't believe she was trying to drum up yet another fantasy affliction – this time one that would incapacitate Jimmy's mother without actually putting her at death's door.

'A what?'

'A – a – skin disease,' was what Hat eventually plumped for.

'Oh, poor woman. What kind?'

'Ah – one that's on your skin.'

'As you might imagine, if it's a skin disease,' Margaret replied tartly. 'Psoriasis, eczema, impetigo?'

Hat had no idea which of these ailments was most likely to cause confinement. However, she guessed her mother might and she didn't want to land herself in it. 'Erm, not absolutely sure.'

'Darling, I think you should show a little more interest in your future mother-in-law's health, don't you?'

If I carry on with this disease lark much longer, Hat moaned silently, I'll have to take a medical degree.

'So, when will he be back?'

'He won't be back till – till the night before the wedding,' Hat blurted out, without thinking.

She was amazed to find that her excuse turned out to be an approximation of the truth – well, the truth as she hoped it would pan out. She noticed that it felt wonderful to say something that wasn't entirely made up – well, she hoped not.

'The night before the wedding? What about the rehearsal? What on earth is he doing going all that way so soon before your wedding? Of course, if his mother was seriously ill that would be another matter, but really! He *must* be at the rehearsal, it's vital. You'll have to ring him and get him back down. This is unheard-of!'

Shit, Hat thought, bollocking, arsing, fucking shit. She'd forgotten about the rehearsal. I'm just not cut out for major lying and deception, she surmised, as she stood there searching for another excuse.

'Oh, yeah, I meant to tell you,' she stammered eventually, 'we've decided not to bother with a rehearsal.'

'Not to bother with a rehearsal?'

'Mum, will you stop repeating everything I say? It's like listening to someone learning English off one of those stupid tapes! We are not having a rehearsal, we don't need one. How hard can it be? He walks into the church, up the big space between the pews and stands in front of the only person wearing a sheet. He won't need a map, he's not blind. Then Dad and I arrive and we head straight for him! That's about the long and short of it, isn't it?'

'It's a cassock, not a sheet, dear,' Margaret retorted, and sniffed theatrically. That was her second-favourite technique for displaying hurt at an insult, or disapproval of bad behaviour.

'Whatever. Mum, please, don't make this any harder than it is for me already.'

'What on earth do you mean "harder than it already is"?'

'Nothing, nothing,' Hat replied – her outburst had revealed a lot more than she'd meant it to. 'I'm just exhausted with everything, you know.'

'Yes, actually, I do, darling, which is why I'm so glad I came when I did and that I took control. I don't know how you'd have coped without me. I don't think you'd quite realized what you'd taken on.'

Hat rolled her eyes to the heavens and muttered, under her breath, 'If only you knew how true that is.'

22. It's Mish's Turn to Panic

While Hat was being put through her paces by her mother, Mish was finally getting up. A painful awareness hovered over her of just how close her friend's wedding day was getting, and there was still no sign of Jimmy. Mish had half expected him to telephone within a few days of her call to announce his return, but she'd been over-confident. It came to her that she was faced with two choices: she could admit failure, thereby heaping yet more misery on her best friend's already heaving pile or she could crank up her efforts on Hat's behalf a notch. Being an optimistic girl, she opted for the latter. And not just for Hat's sake. It was now a personal mission to get Jimmy back – to save her best friend from bitter disappointment and public humiliation, and because Mish would not accept defeat. And she felt responsible and guilty for having encouraged Hat to steam ahead regardless. Mish had originally been the voice of dissension, until suddenly, without reason as far as her friend was aware, she'd had a change of heart. For all she knew, if she had maintained her earlier position Hat might have given up. Mish determined that another talk with Jimmy was required, in which she would attempt to impress upon him that he *had* to pitch up. And if that didn't work she'd threaten to kill him. Given the deadly cocktail of dread, hysteria and rage rising inside her right now, she didn't think it would be too hard to do either.

'Hello,' a cheery Scottish voice sang – Mish thought she sounded like someone right out of a Baxter's soup commercial. She was thrown off course. She'd not banked on anyone other than Jimmy picking up the phone.

'Hello, who is this?'

'I'm sorry. Hello, this is Michelle, a friend of Jimmy's. Is he there, please?'

'No, I'm sorry, he's not. He left a few days ago.'

Mish wondered if he'd done a bunk after she'd called. If so it wasn't a good sign. 'Do you know where he went?' she asked, trying to sound nonchalant.

'I'm not sure, pet. He said he was going off round the Highlands on his bike for a while then possibly back to London.'

'Oh,' Mish replied lamely. She didn't want to end the call without getting as much information as possible, but she didn't want to arouse Jimmy's mother's suspicions. However, it turned out that she was ahead of Mish.

'Are you a friend of my son's and Harriet's?'

'Yes, yes, I am,' she said quickly.

'Well, I think this whole business has knocked him for six a bit. What he wants is time on his own. I can't be sure, but I wouldn't expect him back in London for a while yet. I think he needs to take stock.'

What the fuck's that supposed to mean? Mish howled inside her head. Take stock? He's not a bleeding shopkeeper! He's my pal's fiancé and he's gone AWOL – simple as that! Take stock, my arse!

She composed herself. She guessed, from the woman's tone, that Jimmy's mother was of the indulging-their-children's-every-trial-and-tribulation ilk of parents – painfully unlike Hat's. She wasn't a hundred per cent sure but it seemed pretty clear that Jimmy's mother knew what had happened and, even worse, that as far as she was concerned the wedding was well and truly off. Mish wondered what to do next. She decided to end the call as casually as she could.

'Oh, well, never mind. If he calls you, would you ask him to give me, Mish, a ring on my mobile, not at home,' Mish asked. She reckoned it was worth leaving the number – just in case.

Mish hung up and wondered what to do. Did she confess all to Hat? Did she say nothing and just pray that he'd turn up? Did she fly up to the Highlands and search for Jimmy? At that point needles and haystacks sprang to her mind. Then it dawned on her that the way she was feeling right now must be exactly how Hat had felt after Jimmy had made his announcement. Although Mish had been sympathetic to Hat's plight, she hadn't fully appreciated until now the mania that had been driving her. Now that *her* body was alive with frenzy, Mish understood why Hat had allowed herself to run away with the whole saga. This revelation made her see that confessing to Hat was not even remotely an option. How could Mish expect her to accept defeat now, after all she'd been through? Freshly emboldened by opposition and adversity,

Mish decided she was going to see it through to the bitter end with Hat. It was better for her pal, she decided, to drive the whole thing through to a conclusion – whatever form that might take. For all her refreshed solidarity Mish knew she had to come up with something – fast. Sensibly she recognized that this was not a job that could be done single-handedly. A summit meeting was urgently required and she called for back-up.

'So, wait a minute, let me get this straight. You actually spoke to him, in person?' Gerry asked Mish, for the third time.

'Yes,' Mish replied, impatiently. She wanted to get on with the urgent business of hatching a recovery plan, not waste time going over what had already happened.

'And you think he sounded like he might come back?'

'Yes – how many times am I going to have to explain?'

'Don't get out of your tree, my little lady. I'm just trying to establish the facts.'

'It's just as I said,' Priscilla chipped in, 'he's got pre-wedding nerves. He'll be back.'

Hat's three closest friends were huddled round Priscilla's kitchen table.

'Yes, well, I hope so, Priscilla. The thing is, I spoke to his mum and it sounded like he might have gone off on some sort of balls-aching journey of self-discovery. It didn't sound much like he was headed for London. Lost up his own arsehole, if you ask me.'

'Ooooh, sounds fun,' Gerry piped up, putting on a ridiculously camp voice.

Neither Mish nor Gerry watched their language around Priscilla as they would around other people in their sixties – no one did. Nothing about her made people feel that they need behave other than naturally. Everyone felt at ease with her.

'No, rest assured, he'll be back. It's a jolly good thing you called him, though. It's exactly what he needed, someone to talk some sense into him. Stuff and nonsense, all this pussy-footing around. I've never heard the like ... Actually that's not quite true. In fact, when this first happened I told Hat about a girl I once knew, Grizzle –'

'Ah, Priscilla?' Gerry interrupted.

'Yes?'

'Can we concentrate on the matter in hand?'

'Yes, absolutely. Gerry, you can do nights and, Mish, seeing as you work off and on, you can do days.'

'What?' Gerry and Mish cried out.

'Keeping watch outside Jimmy's flat, of course. What else?' Priscilla replied.

'Are you serious?' Gerry had not warmed to the plan.

'Yes.'

'And what if he turns up? What do we do then? Jump him, stuff him into a potato sack and hold him hostage until the morning of the wedding?' Gerry inquired.

'Not a bad idea, if a little far-fetched. No, you talk to him, make him understand the situation. It shouldn't be too hard. He's on the verge of coming back as it is. I can feel it.'

Mish and Gerry exchanged looks of incredulity – they both thought Priscilla's plan was completely mad. She caught them. 'Do either of you have a better idea?'

Her question was met with shamefaced silence.

'Very well, unless you can come up with something better, then staking out Jimmy's flat it is. Good God, it's only for eight days, you needn't look quite so woebegone. You should thank your lucky stars we're having such mild weather for the time of year.'

Gerry looked at Mish and shrugged his shoulders. 'I suppose there's nothing for it.'

'Guess not.'

'So you'd better start tonight. No need to get there too early, though, you don't want to be seen and arouse suspicion.'

'God, no! We wouldn't want to do anything like that,' Mish exclaimed, ironically. Gerry was about to put up another protest when the doorbell rang.

'Get that, will you, Gerry? I'll open a bottle of champagne – well, sparkling wine, but who's counting? I think we deserve a drink,' Priscilla announced, and walked over to her fridge. It was a massive pre-war thing that had stood in the same place since the day Priscilla's mother's cook had taken proud possession of it. It usually housed nothing more than mouldy cheese, a variety of expensive jams in varying states of decay and, on a good day, some just about usable milk. Luckily it was always home, too, to a bottle of champagne or, failing that, a close relation. Priscilla's family had once been very grand, but the glory days had ended in the early sixties when her father had gambled away the remainder of his fortune. Her parents had never quite got used to living as normal people – and neither had Priscilla, whose mindset and demeanour were still those of a duchess.

'So, look who it isn't!' Gerry announced, with forced cheeriness, as he walked back into the room, Hat following him.

'Hello, everyone. Blimey, what are you three up to? It's not often I catch you together.'

'Nothing. Nothing at all!' Gerry and Mish said in unison.

Despite having been mistress to a number of married men during her sexual career, Priscilla had never behaved once as if she was guilty of anything. At the sound of their flannelling she rolled her eyes and stepped in with an effortlessly plausible explanation. 'We were trying to come up with something for your hen night, if you must know. What do you fancy?'

'Oh, God, that. I really don't want to do anything – it seems a bit farcical to have one as we don't know what's going to happen on the day,' Hat said, sinking wearily into a chair.

'No more farcical than anything else that's happened so far,' Gerry said.

'I thought you were on my side.'

'I am. I just think we should have a hen night. What harm could it do?' Gerry regretted having been so sharp. He was torn between wanting to shake some sense into Hat and wanting to make sure everything turned out all right for her.

'No, I don't want to tempt Fate any more than I already have. Anyway, I'm exhausted. I've had another fabulous day with Mum, arguing the toss over veils and the like. One good thing, though, I've managed to get out of the rehearsal.'

'How did you pull that off?' Mish asked.

'I told Mum that Jimmy had gone back up to Scotland for a bit. Erm . . . actually, I said he was away until the night before the wedding,' Hat muttered.

Mish and Gerry threw each other a look. If only she knew how close to the truth she was!

'What about Sam? He could do the rehearsal,' Priscilla piped up.

'I didn't think it was fair to ask him again and, anyway, that would have been pushing my luck, such as it is, just a bit too far.'

'I'm sure he wouldn't have minded, but at least you've bought yourself a little more time,' Priscilla said.

'Yes, I guess so. Are he and Gloria around?'

'No, no need to worry. He's taken Gloria down to meet his parents. They're spending the night there.'

'Oh,' Hat replied, disappointed. She'd been aware of a vague desire to see Sam – he made her feel safe.

'Here, have a drink. Let's all get sloshed and forget about everything for an entire evening, OK?' Priscilla commanded, and handed Hat a glass of Asti Spumante.

'Done. Cheers!' Hat raised her glass. She felt in dire need of a night of oblivion.

23. Gerry Does a Columbo

Later that night, leaving Hat all cosy and warm, near comatose, but blissfully ignorant of what he was off to do, Gerry made his way over to Jimmy's flat.

That evening Hat and Mish had got spectacularly drunk, rendering a homeward journey impossible. Mish had conked out on the sofa, and Gerry, who had shown remarkable restraint with the alcohol, mindful of his impending nocturnal duty, had tucked Hat up in his bed.

To speed up his journey he had borrowed Priscilla's old bicycle, which lived in the garden shed. It was an old-fashioned thing, referred to by its owner as a butcher's bike, although, as he frequently pointed out, Gerry had never seen a butcher on anything like it. It had huge unwieldy wheels, a wicker basket on the front and unnecessarily long handlebars. The design not only forced the rider to sit as if they had a poker up their bum but made reaching the handlebars extremely difficult – unless, Gerry mused, you were blessed with arms so long your knuckles scraped on the ground when you walked. It was an excruciatingly uncomfortable ride. He was sure he looked like a camp old librarian from an Agatha Christie story, and felt very foolish as he pedalled along. He avoided passing any of his usual haunts. As he approached

Jimmy's flat and dismounted, he briefly contemplated leaving the bike there, once his duty was done, and making the return journey on public transport.

Handily, the nasty sixties block that housed Jimmy's flat was opposite a small park, and a clump of trees near its entrance provided Gerry with exactly the sort of cover he was looking for. He looked up at Jimmy's living-room window and saw that there was no light on. It was eleven o'clock. Gerry rarely smoked and when he did it was only because he was pissed. All the same, he'd brought along some fags, figuring that they'd give him something to do to while away the hours. He lit a cigarette and wondered what the fuck he was doing. He didn't often hang around strange places in the middle of the night, but when he did it usually led to a more interesting result than the one he was hoping for tonight. All the same, if this was going to make Hat happy then it was worth it.

As he lit his sixth cigarette in twenty fruitless minutes Gerry wondered grumpily if this was stretching the bounds of friendship just a tad too far. He had never taken to Jimmy. He hadn't actively disliked him, he just didn't think the man was good enough for Hat.

Another interminable ten minutes passed during which Gerry, whose feet were cold, entertained himself by starting to panic about frostbite. He dimly recalled seeing a documentary about it, and he was sure they'd said you couldn't walk if you had no toes. Gerry tended to be histrionic about the most minor things and always flew straight to the worst-case scenario. If he had a headache then it was an unde-tected brain tumour. If his knee hurt it was cancer of the cartilage. If a hair wafted on to his shoulder he was facing overnight baldness.

When a full hour had passed Gerry had had enough. He was too cold, he thought, to act sensibly in the event of Jimmy turning up. Added to that, a policeman doing his rounds had given him a funny look, which had not been one of sexual interest. Any minute now, he feared, he was going to be arrested.

Just as he was settling himself gingerly on to the bike, he caught sight of a figure approaching Jimmy's building. He leapt to attention, stopped breathing and stood stock-still. He didn't want to draw attention to himself. Through the darkness he made out a man of, he reckoned, about Jimmy's height. He seemed to have the same sort of colouring, too, though it was hard to be sure in the dark. The man let himself into the block of flats and disappeared. Ever optimistic and spurred on by the passionate desire to go home and get warm, Gerry decided that it was probably Jimmy he'd seen, and then that he was not the best person to tackle him, that that was best left to Mish.

'Was this bloke on a motorbike?' Mish asked groggily, propping herself up on one elbow. Gerry had found her snoring loudly on the sofa and shaken her awake. He had seen no reason why she should enjoy a night's undisturbed sleep after the torture he'd endured.

'Erm, no, he wasn't, come to think of it. But I'm sure it was him.'

Keen to be the bearer of glad tidings and, moreover, to establish a *bona fide* excuse for leaving his post while on duty, Gerry had allowed himself to move swiftly from not-at-all-sure to absolutely confident that he'd espied Hat's errant fiancé.

'I doubt it. Jimmy never goes anywhere without his motorbike.' Mish slumped down again, like a dead dog.

'Well, maybe it's broken down or something. What if it was him?'

'I'll go round tomorrow, OK? Now please let me go back to sleep, my brain is splitting in half.' She pulled the thick blanket Priscilla had provided over her head.

'My, my! Some of us have been out all night in the snow and sleet, enduring all kinds of discomfort, selflessly looking out for our friend's interest without so much as a murmur of complaint,' Gerry grumbled huffily.

'Go to bed. It's not snowing and you only left just after ten – it's not even one o'clock yet, so you've hardly been out all night,' Mish moaned.

Gerry pursed his lips and flounced out of the room. As he crawled into bed beside Hat, he concluded that he'd done a sterling piece of detective work for which he'd reap his reward later. He fell asleep humming the theme tune to his favourite cop show – *Cagney and Lacey*.

The next morning, feeling very much the worse for wear, Hat and Mish staggered back to their own flat.

They would have lounged around, quite happily, at Priscilla's all day, had the atmosphere been remotely conducive to what they required: nursing sore heads. It had appealed particularly to Hat as she would have been able to avoid her mother's calls or unexpected visits for an entire day. But Priscilla's loud renditions of a selection of arias from her favourite operas had driven them homeward. True to her hearty form, Priscilla never got a hangover, although she drank like a trooper.

Once safely inside their own four walls, Mish made her way straight into the living room where she stretched out on the sofa. She was planning to enjoy an uninterrupted fest of daytime television. The perfect hangover cure. Meanwhile, Hat slipped off to her bedroom. It wasn't until she walked back into the room wearing her wedding outfit that Mish recalled, with hysterical panic, what she was supposed to be doing.

'What do you think?' Hat asked, in a weak voice.

Mish sat bolt upright. 'You look fabulous. Completely and utterly fabulous. Oh, Hat, you look so pretty.'

Hat smiled half-heartedly. 'As every hour passes taking me closer to the moment of truth, I am more and more sure I've lost my mind. This plan is doomed. What the hell am I doing? I can't believe it's got this far.' She groaned.

'Come on, sit down. It's going to be all right.'

'I can't, I'll crush the dress,' Hat wailed.

Mish laughed. 'It is beautiful. You look stunning, amazing, wonderful, honestly.'

'*You* don't think it needs a veil, do you?' As ever, Margaret had sown a seed of doubt in her daughter's mind, which had sprouted into a full-grown lawn.

'No, definitely not. It's perfect just as it is.'

'Oh, God, I feel like Miss Havisham. I'll probably be wearing this dress until the day I die. A withered old bag with bits of green silk hanging off me. Someone will eventually find me and think I've gone mouldy.'

'You are *not* going to be Miss Havisham,' Mish said firmly, and stood up. 'Hat, get changed, do something completely unconnected with the wedding. I've got to go out for a bit,' she continued, in as casual a fashion as she could muster.

But it didn't wash with her friend. 'Out? Why are you going out?'

'I've just got to do something. I won't be that long.'

'What have you got to do? Don't go out. I don't feel like being on my own right now.'

'I have to, Hat.'

'Why?'

'Because I've just got to. It's important, please don't ask. Trust me, all right? I'll see you later.' Mish left the room. She felt awful leaving Hat in such a desperate mood but she had to do her shift on the stake-out: it might be the only way this whole thing would come to fruition. Much as it pained her to leave Hat in the lurch, and without an explanation, she was not going to let her go down without putting up a fight on her behalf.

*

Hat removed her wedding gear with the same care that a nurse might use when handing over a replacement heart to a transplant surgeon. She felt as if her entire future, and the direction it would take, lay in every stitch, every seam, every thread of that dress. The feeling didn't come from the fear that she couldn't live without Jimmy. Its source was an enormous melee of aspiration, pride, independence, defiance, yearning and dogged determination. As she hung the dress on the beautiful padded hanger Mrs Kostas had supplied she smoothed down the front with her palm then gave it a little shake to ease out any creases. She stood back and gave it a long, hard look. 'I am putting that on and walking up that aisle, no matter what!' she said. It was not so much a battle-cry as an incantation.

While Hat was conjuring up the spirits that oversee beleaguered brides, Mish was approaching Jimmy's flat. She was fuming: she resented having to drag herself out, particularly in her weakened condition, and even more so because, from her point of view, Jimmy was responsible. Jimmy and his pathetic fantasies about love. If all else fails, she thought, I'm going to give him a piece of my mind – and he won't forget that in a hurry!

She stomped round the corner and, as Jimmy's block came into view, she saw the boy who had given her the phone number enter the building. Her heart sank: it was him Gerry must have seen. She leant up against a wall, trying to decide what her next move should be. Her head was still throbbing and she didn't fancy skulking around in the street all day. At that moment, she heard the roar of a motorbike and she knew, as sure as eggs is eggs, that it was Jimmy. She nipped into a nearby doorway and from this vantage-point she watched as the motorbike drew up outside the flats. Then Mish saw something she had never, ever anticipated. Jimmy had a woman on the back of his bike. She watched, stunned, as the pair dismounted and took off their helmets.

'Fucking arsehole,' she muttered, under her breath. Of all the things in the world that had made Jimmy do a runner, neither Mish nor Hat had ever considered that it might have been another woman. Mish found it hard enough to believe that he'd got hold of her fabulous friend, never mind another woman. She felt like marching straight over and hurling abuse at him but the couple disappeared into the flats as she emerged from her hideaway.

Mish stood on the pavement, wondering if anything would be gained in going up to his flat to confront him. She wasn't worried about making a fool of herself, she just wanted to be sure it was the right thing to do for Hat. After much deliberation, she decided to go home. She'd established what she needed to know. Jimmy was back, but there was a spanner in the works: an unpredicted eventuality had emerged and she didn't have a clue what to do.

On arriving home, she was relieved to discover that Hat wasn't in. She needed time to think. She wanted to prepare yet another contingency plan. Her first move towards clear thinking was to take some painkillers – her head was pounding.

Almost immediately the phone rang. It was Penny, announcing a surprise for Hat. And Mish was sure that Hat wasn't going to like it.

24. Countdown

After Mish had gone out on her mysterious mission, Hat had paced around the flat amazed that even though her wedding was now only one hundred and sixty-eight hours away she had nothing to do. She realized, with discomfort, that one of the up-sides of being at the helm of her own nuptials was that she'd had nine million things to occupy her thoughts all day long. She hadn't had any spare time to worry about her problem. But now that her mother had commandeered the arrangements Hat was redundant. She felt as if she was watching someone else operate her limbs. Eventually, in order to con herself that she had some role to play, however, minor, she decided to check off her wedding-present list – names against presents. It was hardly necessary but it was something to do, even though it had been done a zillion times already.

She settled herself down with the list in front of the mountain of John Lewis boxes that dominated the living room. Small boxes held up bigger boxes, long boxes propped up oblong boxes, like rudimentary pillars, teeny boxes nestled between medium-sized boxes. It looked like something for which the Tate Gallery had paid some installation artist twenty thousand quid, earning themselves a lot of flak along the way. The pile had grown inexorably – like rubbish during a binmen's strike – and now extended from corner to corner along the back wall. In some places it was so high it nearly reached the ceiling.

Mish was constantly terrified the whole thing would come crashing down one night in the middle of *Coronation Street* and cave her skull in. On more than one occasion she'd warned Hat that she didn't fancy meeting her maker at the hands of a matching set of coffee spoons.

Hat, however, found it strangely comforting. Here was tangible proof that things were still marching on, that the machine was still chugging away. The presents had kept coming, of course, because no one knew the wedding was in severe danger of not taking place. Still, Hat thought, it's not like I'm going to *keep* them if I don't get married.

Hat sped through the catalogue of names and found herself at the Ns in no time. Her mother had rearranged the list, putting all the guests into alphabetical order, and Hat admitted grudgingly that this had turned out to be quite handy. Just as she started on the Os the doorbell rang. As always, Hat's heart did an optimistic little leap. Since Jimmy had left, she had never once heard the phone or doorbell go, nor indeed the roar of a motorbike, without feeling a rush of expectation. Jimmy's bike, a Triumph Bonneville, had a very distinctive sound, yet all motorbike engines had the same effect on Hat – even though she'd have been able to pick out his from a hundred others. How odd, Hat mused, as she went to answer the door. I never felt anything like this when we were together.

'Hello, Harriet, it's Dad.'

Hat was astonished. Her father was the last person she'd have expected to pitch up unannounced at her house. She couldn't recall the last time they'd been alone together. 'Oh, hi. Come up.' She buzzed him in and waited on the landing.

'Hello, darling. Hope it's OK me dropping in like this,' Philip said, as he climbed the stairs towards her.

Hat wondered what he was up to. He was not given to acts of spontaneous affection, and he certainly wasn't the sort of father who volunteered intimate chats.

'Yeah, it's fine. Is everything all right?' Hat asked, suddenly worried he'd come round to break bad news.

'Yes, yes. I just thought you might like to go out for a cup of tea and a walk or something.'

Hat looked out of the window at the grey autumn day. Why would anyone want to go for a walk in that? 'Erm, it's a bit grim for a walk, Dad.'

'Very well, let's just go out and have a nice tea together somewhere,' he replied – slightly impatiently, Hat noted. He obviously had a reason for wanting to talk to her, she concluded, and was intrigued.

'All right, I'll get my coat,' she said.

The two hours and forty minutes that Hat and her dad spent together were, as far as she was concerned, painfully stilted. They chatted about this and that – her work, how he spent his days in Canada, the paucity of golf courses over there – and Hat kept expecting him to get to the point, to make some announcement. But the time dragged by and he didn't reveal anything. So desperate was she to keep the conversation going that at one point she even found herself asking about Guy's new office. She had one false alarm when he made an allusion to his intended speech. So this is what he wants to talk to me about, she thought, and toyed momentarily with the idea of telling him not to bother as it might all be a waste of time. But she knew she couldn't as it would let the cat right out of the bag.

At last Philip looked at his watch, stood up and said it was time he was getting her home. As they reached her house, he kissed her goodbye, declined her offer to come up and went on his way, leaving Hat bewildered as to what the whole palaver had been about. Until she opened her front door.

'Surprise!' A collective, high-pitched yell burst forth as Hat walked into her living room. Her heart raced with shock as she tried to work out what was going on. From her immediate right, going clockwise, were four beaming faces, well, three beaming faces and one that conveyed total panic. That face belonged to Mish. The others belonged to Gerry, Penny and Margaret. Hat wondered how this unlikely group had got together and what the hell they were doing in her flat. She didn't have to wait long to find out.

'I heard you weren't having a hen party so I decided to throw one for you!' Penny said.

Hat forced a smile, then glared at Mish. Maybe she could shed some light on how the fuck this had been allowed to happen. Mish gave Hat a tiny it's-not-my-fault shrug, accompanied by an I-couldn't-get-you-out-of-it sympathetic half-smile-cum-half-grimace.

'Come on, have a drink,' Penny commanded, and handed her sister a glass of champagne. Hat took the glass and squinted at her sister quizzically. She looked like she might have had quite a few already.

'Relax, you look like you've seen a ghost. It's only a hen party. I wanted to make sure you walked out to face the firing squad in style!' Penny brayed, as she turned back to refill her mother's glass.

As soon as the focus was off her, Hat sidled up to Mish. 'What the fuck is going on?' she hissed into her ear.

'Look, it's nearly as much a surprise to me as it is to you. I had no idea Penny was cooking this up until I came in about an hour ago. She rang up and just sort of announced it was happening and that was that,' Mish replied, out of the corner of her mouth.

'Well, if you've got nothing to do with this why did you go out all secretively, refusing to tell me what you were doing?'

'I just went out, OK? I swear I didn't know about this. I'm allowed to go out without your permission, aren't I?' Mish replied hotly.

'Well, I'm not talking to my sister at the moment, remember?'

'I know. I think that's why she did it – she wanted to make up for having a go at you,' Mish muttered.

'Couldn't you have put them off?' Hat asked.

'I tried. I said it wasn't your style and that you didn't want one anyway, but Penny insisted. You know what she's like. She reckons you need cheering up. Give her a chance, I think she's really sorry about sticking her nose in before. Anyway, you've been out, so how could I have warned you? Where have you been?'

'My dad turned up wanting to take me out. Now I know why. That'll have been Mum's brilliant idea. No wonder he was like a cat on a hot tin roof all afternoon.'

'Well, if you ever switched your arsing mobile on I could have warned you. I don't know why you bother to have the thing! What was I supposed to do? Paint a warning on a sheet and hang it out of the front window?' Mish retorted, again out of the corner of her mouth.

'The pair of you look extremely conspicuous, talking like that – as if you've both had strokes,' Gerry remarked, as he joined them. 'I can guess what the problem is but it's a little late to start worrying about that now. Just enjoy yourself, Hat, and in the words of the great Doris Day, "*que sera, sera*". Your man will be there on the day, just wait and see.'

Mish glared at him, and raised her eyebrows, but he didn't seem to notice.

'Let your hair down for once and stop trying to control the outcome of every little thing. Life is full of surprises,' he continued, then returned to Margaret and Penny with whom he'd been chatting.

Hat gave his back a surly look, which, as he didn't have eyes in the back of his head, was wasted. He'd stung her with his comment about trying to control everything but she wondered if he might be right. And she was grateful to him for flirting with her mother. Gerry was always a star with the older ladies.

'He's right, we might as well have a laugh. We are kind of stuck for the night now, aren't we?' Mish said to her pal.

'I guess.' Hat paused. 'Anyway I think Gerry's right,' she continued. 'He *is* coming back. I'm sure of it now.'

'You know what? He's going to bloody well come if I have to drag him there by the scruff of the neck!' Mish snarled, and knocked back her entire glass of champagne in one gulp.

25. And the Surprises Just Keep Coming . . .

'What the hell are we doing here?!' Hat hissed, when she realized, too late, that they were approaching Priscilla's house. Although Penny had announced excitedly that the evening held more surprises, Hat had assumed they were headed for a restaurant.

'Don't worry, I made sure that Priscilla had warned Sam. He's gone out for the night,' Gerry mumbled.

'All the same, it's a bit risky, isn't it? Why here?'

'It was your mum's idea, don't ask us. Those two set the whole thing up.' Mish contorted her face grotesquely and jutted her chin towards Hat's mum and sister.

The trio was squished up together in the back of Penny's swanky car. It was one of those cars that appears to be huge and roomy but only proves to be so for those who paid for it, namely the driver and his or her companion. The back seats were really designed for Harvey Nichols' bags, not human beings who hoped to use their limbs after a journey. Margaret sat proudly in the front passenger seat while her elder daughter manoeuvred her status symbol expertly through London's damp streets. Hat was surprised that her sister's driving betrayed no sign that she had drunk too much to be legally at the wheel. She wondered how often Penny did this kind of thing.

She was pretty sure that, officially, Penny and her mother had come up with this 'surprise' in an attempt to be nice and supportive. However, she also knew that they wouldn't have done it for entirely selfless motives. She couldn't help feeling like the victim of a plot: she felt out of sorts and irritable. The only thing that provided any solace was her conviction that Margaret had not begun to suspect that things had gone wrong.

On entering Priscilla's living room Hat was pleased to see that someone, she presumed Penny, had invited two of her old friends from college – Alison and Kath. It's going to be a relief to chat to people who know nothing about what's been going on, she thought, as she walked towards them.

Almost as soon as the greetings were done and they'd embarked on a bit of catching up, Hat heard her mother welcoming another guest. 'Hello, I'm so glad you could come. Let me introduce you to a few people.'

She looked over her shoulder and almost fainted. It was the vicar. Hat despaired. She wondered crossly how many brides could expect to see their vicar pitch up at their sodding hen nights. She made her excuses to Alison and Kath and marched over to Priscilla. 'What on earth is *she* doing here?' Hat demanded, between the gritted teeth of a false smile.

'Oh, that was your mother's idea. She was convinced it would make things easier on the day, given that there's not going to be a rehearsal. Ever wedded to convention, your mother. She simply would not be persuaded otherwise. This whole affair was sprung on me only a few hours ago, long after you two had left this morning.'

'You should have put your foot down. You don't usually let anyone get one over on you.'

'Hat, my dear, I did my best but I could hardly put up too much resistance. After all, if there were nothing awry, there'd be no reason *not* to allow your mother and Penny to throw you a surprise party. And, as for banning the vicar, why shouldn't the poor old cow pop in for a drink? Look at her, I'm sure she hardly ever gets invited out. Extremely unlikely with that hair, I would imagine. How is it that every single female member of the church sports such a truly dreadful haircut? I assume the Archbishop of Canterbury hasn't issued an edict forbidding any of his female clergy to visit a decent hairdresser. And as for her skirt! Well, there's no excuse for that!' She raised her eyes to heaven before she swept off with characteristic flamboyance.

Hat watched her walk away with a mixture of despair and admiration. Despite her years Priscilla was as impeccably stylish as she'd been in her youth. She was wearing the same black silk jersey cocktail dress she'd had for years and even though, as ever when she was at home, she was barefoot, she still looked incredibly elegant. She couldn't abide with frumpiness. She admired women who made no effort with their appearance much more than those who did but, in her eyes, got it spectacularly wrong. Summoning all her courage, Hat shot another glance at the vicar, who smiled and gave her a cheery wave, blissfully ignorant of the scorn her outfit and hairdo had engendered in her hostess. Hat made a little pointing, hopping gesture to indicate that she'd be over to talk to her shortly, although she didn't want to talk to her at all. She took in the skirt upon which such scorn had been poured. It was a deep brown and burgundy dirndl affair that hung at a most unflattering length, smack-bang between the ankle and the knee. Priscilla was right, as usual, Hat thought. Just because a person devotes their life to Christ, it doesn't follow that they should dress badly. Hat, however, wasn't going to waste time worrying about the vicar's crimes against fashion. That was the least of her worries right now.

'Hello, it's . . . nice to see you,' Hat said bravely, as she approached the woman who, in theory, was going to marry her to Jimmy in seven days' time.

'It's lovely to have been asked. I hardly ever get out.'

Hat groaned internally. Typical of Priscilla to have been right on the money yet again.

'Well, thank you for coming,' Margaret chipped in.

'No, thank *you* for asking me,' the vicar replied, laughing.

Oh, Christ, thought Hat, how long's this exchange going to go on?

'Has your fiance's gout cleared up? I was worried that he might still have it on the big day.'

Fuck, fuck, fuck, Hat thought. She'd created a minefield for herself by lying left, right and centre and, what was more, telling different lies to different people.

'Gout?' Margaret barked, her face a picture of astonishment.

'Didn't you know?' the vicar asked innocently.

'I had no idea. James suffers from gout?' Margaret asked, turning to her daughter. 'Dear me, poor chap. He's very young for that. He seemed perfectly healthy the other night.'

'Oh, you've met him, then? I have yet to have the privilege. He hasn't been well enough to come to any of my services so far, has he, Hat?'

Hat summoned a weak smile, which was quite an effort since the world seemed to be falling out of her arse.

'He's *more* than well enough now. My husband and I met him for the first time the other night at a lovely dinner party organized by my elder daughter, Penny. She's over there – you must meet her. She's married to the financier Sir Terence Gray's son.'

Hat's guts contracted as they always did when her mother made unnecessary mention of her son-in-law's father's title. She was always embarrassed by this naff habit. It wasn't like Guy's dad had discovered a cure for cancer. He was simply a businessman who'd donated a shedload of cash to the Tory party in order to secure himself a knighthood.

'I'd love to, in a moment,' the vicar replied politely. Hat suspected she'd never heard of Sir Terence Gray and was not much given to investing importance in people's titles.

Margaret smiled grandly and returned to the subject that was working like an enema on Hat. 'It's a terrible shame about the rehearsal, don't you think? Honestly, young people don't seem to have any idea these days, do they?'

Hat sighed with relief. At least she'd remembered to tell the vicar the rehearsal was off.

'Well, it is a little unusual not to have one but I'm sure it'll be fine on the day. There's not really that much to it.'

'Goodness, I've just realized! That means you'll be meeting James for the first time on the day you marry him to my daughter, doesn't it?' Margaret declared, aghast.

'I've known worse!' the vicar replied, and laughed heartily. Margaret joined in with the hilarious joke.

Bloody side-splitter, Hat thought. Soon she might *have* to tell her mum the truth, before things got any further out of hand.

At that moment, Gloria entered the room and approached the group, beaming beatifically. Margaret took advantage of the interruption to whisk the vicar off to meet her elder daughter, and Hat was left with the ravishing Colombian. Gloria looked like she had something particular to say. Hat's heart sank: she wasn't in the right mood for a conversation made up of improvised sign language punctuated with a few 'jesses' and 'stops'.

'*Es muy importante para mi que entiendas que yo no quiero a Sam. Le quiero mucho pero como un hermano,*' Gloria said, slowly, perhaps hoping that this would overcome

Hat's lack of Spanish. Hat smiled and shrugged her shoulders to show that she had no idea what Gloria was talking about. She wondered why people all over the world thought that if they talked slowly enough a person who didn't speak their language had a better chance of understanding.

Gloria had another stab. 'Sam *es solamente como un hermano, para mi. Es mi amigo.*'

'Oh, right, yes. *Amigo*, good, yes.' Hat jumped eagerly on the word. She was pretty sure that it meant 'friend'. Still, she had no idea why Gloria should need to share this piece of information with her: it was pretty obvious that someone's new husband would also be their friend. They bloody well ought to be at any rate, Hat concluded.

'*Vale, entiendalo*, Sam *es mi amigo.*'

'Yes, great, I've got it. *Amigo*, yes, Sam is your friend, OK, understood,' Hat replied pleasantly, attempting to hide her bemusement.

'Jess! My freend,' Gloria repeated, clearly convinced that she had got her message across. Then the pair stood in silence. Hat wasn't sure how to advance the conversation. Eventually she performed the internationally recognized mime of tipping a glass to her lips, accompanied by raised eyebrows.

'Jess,' was Gloria's reply.

Hat returned a moment later with the wine. As she did so, a horrible thought popped into her head. What if Gloria hadn't been trying to tell her that Sam was her friend? she panicked. What if she had been telling her to keep away from Sam, that he was *her* friend?

Maybe, Hat thought, *amigo* means something more than friend in South America. After all, the people in those Almodovar films are always up to no good with everyone else and they're only supposed to be 'friends'! Maybe, Gloria's staking her claim and telling me that I'm not to use him as my beard again. She studied Gloria's expression intently as she handed over the glass, but Gloria, as usual, wore a look of serene beauty from which nothing, not even misery or joy, could be deduced. Gerry might be right, Hat thought. Maybe there was something different about this woman.

26. One More Surprise

'Look who I found, everybody! Naughty boy, I caught him creeping in at the back door. I must say, he frightened the life out of me,' Margaret sang out, in a sickly isn't-it-sweet voice, as she burst into the room grasping Sam's elbow.

Hat nearly collapsed. This was a most unwelcome bolt from the blue that she had *not* reckoned on.

'At first I didn't recognize him without his beard. He's shaved it off. Pity, I thought it very distinctive. Do you know everyone?' Margaret asked. She didn't wait for an answer. 'Everyone, this is James, Harriet's fiancé. He's hoicked himself all the way back from Scotland, only went up a couple of days ago, poor chap. Evidently couldn't keep away from his love.' Hat's mother beamed and squeezed Sam's arm. He glanced around the room sheepishly. 'Isn't this marvellous? Now you'll be able to have the rehearsal, after all!' Margaret went on, directing her proclamation towards the vicar and Hat.

The vicar nodded sagely. Hat had turned to ice.

'But, first of all, how's your mother?' Margaret asked, turning back to Sam solicitously.

'My mother?' Sam replied, nervously. He was trying not to drop Hat in it.

'Yes, Harriet told me she was unwell. How is she?'

'Oh, you know, erm, sort of up and down, rrreally . . .' Sam stuttered, remembering his Scottish accent half-way through.

'Is there any sign of it clearing up?'

'Clearing up? Erm, well, it's harrrd to tell with that kind of . . .' He threw Hat a desperate silent plea.

Without stopping to think Hat jumped in. 'What the hell are *you* doing here?' she cried.

All heads turned to look at her, and she realized quickly from the expressions of horror that her outcry had not been the most loving welcome and that it was hardly the way she'd be likely to greet her husband-to-be.

'My word! That was uncalled-for, Harriet. You can at least give him a kiss before you tick him off for bursting in on your hen party,' Margaret said, jumping to Sam/Jimmy's defence.

Hat looked around, and noticed that Gloria's expression was the only one not to have changed: she seemed barely to have registered that her husband had arrived. Then Hat saw Mish, who looked as panic-stricken as she felt.

'Yes, come on, Hat, don't be horrid. Give him a kiss,' Priscilla barked from the other side of the room.

Hat made a mental note to throttle her later. She decided she'd better get it over and done with before the whole room started chanting, 'Kiss him, kiss him.'

After all, she reasoned, I guess it's what a woman in these circumstances *would* do.

She shuffled towards Sam, threw a furtive apologetic look at Gloria and planted a perfunctory kiss on his cheek. As her lips met his face, she heard him mutter 'Sorry.' Despite her own feelings of utter desperation, she felt badly for him. It wasn't his fault he'd got caught up in this mess. However, she did wonder why he'd come back when he knew what was going on.

Suddenly she heard Margaret's voice. She'd lit upon a very good, and obvious, point: 'I don't know how you knew that Hat's hen party was here. It was a surprise. Penny only cooked it up today.'

Sam looked as if he'd been electrocuted.

'I told him!' Mish called cheerily.

'But you didn't know about it either, until I called you at your flat a few hours ago,' Penny chipped in.

Hat wasn't sure whether she was suspicious or simply bemused, but either way she herself wasn't enjoying this. This was what it must have been like to be cross-questioned by the Gestapo when one didn't know anything.

'I got the plane down as soon as Mish called me. I couldn't wait a moment longer to see my love.' Sam grasped Hat's hand in his.

Hat nearly jumped out of her skin. She threw a desperate look at Gloria, imploring her not to blow her top.

'Well, now that you're here, you scamp, you might as well come and say hello to Miss Henson. She's been dying to meet you.' Margaret led Sam towards the vicar.

Freed from his clutches, Hat raced over to Gloria, frantic to smooth things over. 'Gloria, I'm so sorry. I am really sorry, I didn't mean it to go this far . . .' Hat faltered. She realized she was guilty of doing exactly the same thing she'd thought so odd earlier – she was drawing out each word and sounding like some wonky old cassette tape.

'Hello, girls,' Gerry twittered, bounding up to them like a puppy. 'Well, this is a turn-up for the books, isn't it?'

Hat scowled at him.

'Personally I think your young man's lovely, much nicer than the real one.'

'Thanks a lot.'

'So you got him to shave it off, then?' Penny said, skipping up to them, evidently buoyed up by the considerable amount of booze she'd had.

'Shave what off?' Gerry said, without thinking.

'His *beard*, remember?' Hat hissed.

'Oh, that, of course, silly me. Yes there's nothing Sa – Jimmy wouldn't do for Hat,' Gerry said, keen to defend his friend against her sister's criticism.

'Well, I must say, he looks a million times better without it.'

Penny turned to Gloria and gave her a quizzical look. Hat wondered if she could get away without doing an introduction. Apparently not.

'Hat, aren't you going to introduce me to your friend?' Penny asked.

237

'Ah, yes, of course. This is Gloria she is . . . she is . . . she is . . .'

'Freend of heez,' the Colombian beauty piped up, pointing at Sam.

Hat shot her a look and caught a surreptitious wink. She let out a massive sigh of relief. Clearly Gloria had not forgotten the purpose for which she had loaned Hat her husband.

'Oh, right. Jimmy's friend,' Penny said, looking over at Sam with what Hat feared was a suspicious eye. 'And here he comes – your friend, and your fiance,' Penny continued. She had put an unnecessarily lewd emphasis on 'friend'.

Hat looked over her shoulder and saw her mother with Sam again, arm linked chummily through his. They were headed towards her group.

'I think young James should be rewarded for his ardour,' Margaret announced, as she slid into their midst. 'You two go off and have a lovely time all alone, never mind about us. It's the very least James deserves, having tramped all the way down from Scotland, in the howling wind and rain, just to catch a glimpse of you, Harriet, don't you think?'

Hat glanced at the window. It was barely drizzling outside.

'Yeah, come on, Hat, don't let me down,' Sam said, widening his eyes in a meaningful way.

Hat couldn't think what plan he might have afoot, and quickly agreed. Anything was preferable to another evening of knife-edge tension waiting for someone to rumble them, all the while having to listen to Sam's excruciating Scottish accent. And I'll find out what the fuck he's doing here, she thought, as they made their farewells.

'See you at the rehearsal, then. And take care of that gout. Cheerio!' Miss Henson called, from the other side of the room where she was flanked by a forbidding-looking Priscilla. No doubt, she's about to talk her through her fashion *faux pas*, Hat surmised.

Sam and she slipped out of the room, the picture of young love stealing a few moments together. Once in the hall, the living-room door closed safely behind them, they stood in awkward silence, neither knowing what to do or say next.

'Shall we go to the pub then?' Hat asked eventually. She was aware that if anyone came out and found them still standing there it might look very odd indeed. 'I can't,' Sam said. 'That's why I came back.' He stopped and glanced around, as if he was searching for something. 'Let's go and hide out in that room over there until things calm down and I'll explain.'

Intrigued, Hat agreed and followed him to the tiny little room next to the door leading down to the cellar. It was a proper old-fashioned boxroom with floor to ceiling shelves running along both walls making the remaining space very narrow. Each shelf was piled high with boxes of every imaginable size and shape – dusty old hat-boxes that had once contained the very last word in *haute-couture* head apparel, long thin flat boxes in which Priscilla's debutante gowns had been delivered, glove boxes, shoe boxes, tiny boxes for jewellery, corsage boxes, handbag boxes. Each was emblazoned with the logo of the top couture houses of the period.

Sam closed the door quietly. There was limited floor space and the only seat was the tiny set of steps built for reaching the upper shelves. He offered it to Hat, who settled herself on it while he made himself comfortable on the floor. He leant against the door – just in case.

'I'm *so* sorry about tonight. I had no idea your mother would catch me. Priscilla had warned me about the party and everything but when I went out I realized I was being followed, so I had to come back. I tried to creep in through the back and that was when your mum caught me.'

'Followed?' Hat repeated.

'Yeah. Listen, you've got to promise not to tell anyone this, OK, absolutely no one? I may be over-reacting. After all, I'm allowed out on my own. It's just that I panicked when I saw that I was being followed by a bloke from Immigration.'

'Why would a man from Immigration be following you?'

'Because I'm married to Gloria.'

'But she's all right, isn't she?'

'Yes. But you see sometimes when a British person goes abroad to work and gets married, erm, very quickly to a foreigner the immigration authorities get a bit funny. If they think something's up they investigate the couple to make sure the marriage is for real. You know, to make sure that people aren't just marrying the foreigners to get them into this country – or out of their own, for whatever reason.'

'Oh, well, they'd only have to take one look at Gloria to know that that wasn't the case.'

'Yeah,' Sam agreed. 'The thing is, Gloria is a political hot potato in Colombia. The immigration authorities are bound to know that. And what with us getting married so soon before I came back it might have aroused their suspicions.'

'But it is a real marriage, isn't it?'

'Oh, God, yes, completely, absolutely, totally, but these days you just can't be too careful. If she *was* deported she'd almost certainly go to prison for life – or, more likely, much, much worse. She'd probably just disappear, like so many others have.'

'Blimey! Is it that bad over there?'

'Yeah, the government, such as it is, is totally corrupt. The drug barons run virtually everything. Gloria's a journalist and she wrote a lot of articles exposing some very powerful people. She had been threatened just before I was coming home. That's why we got married so quickly, so that she could come back with me.'

'And also because you were in love, surely?' Hat asked, hopefully. Sam had sounded almost clinical. She wanted to believe that the concept of marriage was desirable to and attainable by everyone, not just something she was currently pursuing like a woman possessed.

'Oh, yeah, and that, of course,' Sam replied. 'So, anyway, what they do is set a particular immigration team on to your case and if they're keen enough one of them will follow you to see if you're leading separate lives, or seeing other people –' Sam broke off and gave his companion a guilty look.

'Oh, God! Do you think they might have seen you with me the other night?'

'I don't know, but there's a chance. At any rate we've got to be very careful.'

'Fuck.'

It was dark in the boxroom. Sam had wisely not switched on the light as the door's top half was made of mottled glass panelling through which it would have been detected. Neither spoke for a few minutes. They sat huddled up, with only the light from the hall. Had things been different, the setting would have been rather romantic.

'And now I've got to do the rehearsal as well,' Sam said, without a hint of blame or resentment.

Hat was overcome by his generosity: he hadn't considered bowing out of his commitment to pretend to be her fiance. 'No, no, you can't risk it. I'll have to tell my mum. I'm going to tell her at least a version of the truth sooner or later anyway. It's just that every time I think I'm going to get it out, something happens and I end up putting it off again.'

Sam smiled at her. 'Somehow I don't think your mum is going to understand.'

'Unlikely, I agree. But I'll have to find some excuse for why you're – er, Jimmy's not at the rehearsal. If it's as bad as you're saying we can't put Gloria in more danger.'

'Well, we would have had to come up with some pretty good reason for her to be there, I admit. I could always say she was my best man!'

Hat laughed, assuming he was joking. She couldn't contemplate the deception going so far. Nor could she imagine Gloria's generosity extending to that.

'You know what?' she said. 'I still believe Jimmy's going to come back. In my heart of hearts I'm convinced he's going to turn up. He left a message the other day. He sounded miserable and unsure of himself. You see, he's really a decent bloke. He's honourable. My friends all think he's another Pet Rescue, loser type but he's not, he's just a bit quiet. Deep down, I think, he knows we have to go through with it, having made the decision together.'

'And because you're in love, surely?' Sam asked, using the exact words and tone with which Hat had posed the question to him a few minutes earlier.

Hat laughed. 'Oh, yeah and that, of course.'

Suddenly they heard the door of the living room open and Margaret calling, 'Don't worry, I'll find it. Goodness, it isn't *that* long since I was here.'

Hat and Sam froze as they strained their ears to decipher in which direction Margaret was headed. They stared at each other, transfixed by horror, as they heard her approach the very room in which they were holed up. Stunned into paralysis, they watched the door handle turn like zombies.

Sam wasn't prepared for Margaret's strength and

he lurched forward as she forced open the door. He threw himself into Hat's arms and began to kiss her passionately.

'My word! What the devil is going on here?' Margaret exclaimed, as her eyes fell upon the entwined pair. 'I was looking for the loo. I thought you two had gone out.'

Hat broke away from Sam's embrace and fumbled for an excuse. 'Sorry, Mum, we couldn't decide where to go . . . and ended up . . . erm . . . in here.' She was finding it hard to make sense. Sam's kiss had knocked the wind out of her, not only because she had not anticipated it but because, and much more importantly, it had been wonderful. He was one of life's rare great kissers.

'Oh, don't worry about me. You, erm, carry on. I must find the lavvy,' Margaret said, and withdrew with an indignant look.

Hat thought her mother might actually be embarrassed, not a state she remembered having seen her in before.

As soon as they were alone again, Sam laughed. 'Sorry about that, I couldn't think what else to do! It seemed like a good idea at the time.'

'It's OK, don't worry, it's fine, it's . . . don't . . . I . . .' Hat murmured, not daring to look at him. She was terrified that some telltale sign had given away the fact that she'd enjoyed it.

'God, at this rate I'll end up *having* to marry you!' Sam joked.

Hat was relieved that he was making light of it.

'Why that's bigamy!' she replied quickly, remembering the old Groucho Marx joke.

'Big o' you? Big o' you? It's pretty big o' me. Wait till my wife hears about it!'

Hat burst out laughing. She'd never met anyone else who knew that joke off by heart.

27. A Few Days After the Hen Party

On Thursday of that week, Margaret, who was staying at Penny's house for the duration of her visit to England, set off bright and early for her younger daughter's flat. She and Hat were due to visit the caterers and Margaret planned to put them through their paces.

Hat was ready and waiting for her. She'd resolved that today was the day she had to confess all. She couldn't bear the strain of lying so spectacularly to her mum. Mish hadn't surfaced: Hat, who hadn't slept much, had heard her come in late. From a note she had left on the kitchen table Hat had learnt that her flatmate required a long lie-in as she'd been clubbing until the wee small hours.

After the kiss a few days earlier, Hat had snuck out of Priscilla's house leaving Sam in the boxroom waiting for everyone to go. She'd felt bad at deserting him, but the atmosphere in there had become too uncomfortable for her and she'd been keen to extract herself. She'd suspected that Sam, too, had been relieved by her departure. Since then, she had spent most of her time trying not to think about how she'd felt when he'd kissed her. This was not a good moment to start falling for another man, least of all one who was already married, and not just to anyone but to Miss Perfect.

By the time Hat had made her tea she had regained her characteristic practicality. She'd convinced herself that she wasn't about to fall for anybody else, that she had been thrown momentarily off course by a meaningless gesture made by a nice person who had been making a brave attempt to save her bacon. There was nothing more to it than that, Hat concluded briskly.

As Hat sat in her kitchen, waiting for her mother, the tea going cold in front of her, she wondered what the hell had happened to her life in the last five and a half weeks. She felt as if she'd been taken hostage by a madwoman. She hadn't had a moment to think since the whole wedding train had started tearing down the track, despite Jimmy's efforts to derail it. She'd even stopped going to work, having told her clients that she needed time to prepare for the wedding – under normal circumstances, a reasonable excuse. She had planned on doing as little work as possible during the final lead-up to the wedding – in fact, they'd deliberately chosen an autumn date as it was Hat's slow time, when gardens don't do much growing.

Hat sipped her tea. It was high time she faced the music. She would warn her mother gently that there might not be a wedding, as such. Her aim was to alert Margaret to the possibility that she might have ended up paying for a big wedding party after a non-wedding. Another thorny point suddenly occurred to Hat: she would also have to tell her mother that Sam wasn't Jimmy. She winced. Margaret would take a very dim view of *that*. Every explanation Hat tried out sounded completely barmy. She went over and over the conversation in her head, anticipating her mother's barrage of hysterical questions, and realized that if she went ahead with her revelation she would be throwing herself on the mercy of a woman she had rarely found to be merciful. She could not think of the right way to put the whole thing, but how does anyone explain a deep-seated yearning not to let go of a conviction that, in the face of all odds, things are going to work out? She wished her mother could understand complicated emotions, sex – that she was more like Priscilla, for all her eccentricities.

The doorbell rang, then Margaret's voice came over the intercom. 'I'm not coming up,' she barked. 'I've got a taxi waiting. Come straight down.' On her last visit to England Margaret had once accepted a lift in Hat's car/van. What with the plant debris, tools and bumper-car-ride element, she'd refused ever to get into it again.

'Yes, all right.' Hat was instantly infuriated by her mother's presumption that she'd be ready to jump at the very second she pitched up.

Hat climbed into the cab all fired up to come clean, but before she could start, she noticed that her mother was wearing an ostentatiously sour expression. It was a classic rendition of the don't-ask-me-what-the-matter-is-because-you-know-very-well look and well known to anyone who has ever had a mother. Hat paused to appraise the situation. Historically, that look had always meant 'don't ask' but woe betide her if she *didn't* ask. Not asking, as she knew from experience, would inevitably lead on to the if-you-care-so-little-for-my-feelings-then-I-don't-know-why-I-bother face, heavy sighs and tedious lectures.

Weighing up all the options and their ensuing fall-outs, Hat decided to put her confession on hold and ask the expected question. 'Mum, is something the matter?'

'No. Should there be?' her mother replied, quick as a flash, prickling with indignation.

How predictable, Hat thought. 'Are you sure?' she asked, knowing she had no choice.

'Well, as you've pressed me, I will tell you. I wasn't going to say anything but you've forced me to and now I think I *should* say my piece.'

Hat turned away from her mother and rolled her eyes. She was glad to note that the glass divider between the driver's compartment and theirs was closed. She didn't fancy getting her dressing-down in public.

'After the scene I witnessed last night, I am fearful that you are entering into a union based entirely on sex.'

'*What?*'

'The unseemly scene I happened upon last night. It was like a couple of animals on heat. I mean, really! And with that lovely vicar only yards away, not to mention your own mother. What were the pair of you thinking?'

'Mum, it's not what you think. Please, calm down. I swear it's not like that,' Hat cried, trying to suppress a chortle.

'Don't patronize me, young lady. I know what I saw. There's a time and place for that sort of thing and it is *not* in Priscilla's boxroom. What is wrong with James? Does he think of nothing else? No wonder he's only a motorcycle messenger. He obviously can't keep his mind on anything other than sex for more than two minutes!'

'Mum! For crying out loud, don't be so horrible. He's a really, really nice person and not at all like that.'

Hat stopped short. She realized she was talking about Sam, not Jimmy. Luckily for her, however, her mother had plenty to say on the subject, so her confusion went unchallenged.

'That is as may be. But you should think very carefully about how much of your interest in each other is based on sexual attraction. I couldn't bear to think of your father in *that* way before we married, and look at us now, still together after forty years. I'm absolutely sure sex was the very last thing on Penny's mind when she married Guy . . .'

'Yeah, well, look at him. Who could blame her?'

'Harriet! That is exactly the sort of attitude I'm talking about. A silly, childish obsession with sex, elevating it to an importance it simply shouldn't have within a long-term commitment. I appreciate that at your age you don't have much time left and can hardly expect to pick through the cream of the crop but all the same I'd hate to see you marry someone just because you found them physically attractive.'

'That is *not* why I'm marrying Jimmy Mack, thank you very much! He's my friend, he's kind, he's honourable and he's decent, and I don't care if he is a bloody motorcycle messenger. And, seeing as you're so bloody interested, as it happens I don't fancy him that much anyway, OK?'

Hat withdrew into a sulk. She had shocked herself. She couldn't believe what she'd said. She had never admitted to anyone, including herself, that she didn't find Jimmy irresistible – she hadn't dared. Unlike her mother she'd always hidden a sneaking suspicion that if a marriage didn't begin with mad, passionate lust it might end up in a lot more trouble than one that did.

A few minutes later, the taxi drew up outside the caterers' premises. The aggrieved pair, feeling equally entitled to self-righteousness, entered in silence.

Judith, the nice middle-aged woman with whom Hat had dealt from the beginning, was waiting for them. Hat had only met her once, all other conversations having taken place on the phone. Margaret fell in with her straight away and the two were soon chatting like long-lost friends.

As Judith led them from the tiny entrance hall into the kitchen Hat remarked to herself that she bore an unfortunate, given her name, resemblance to the television presenter Judith Chalmers. Hat had liked Judith at their previous meeting but now that she was deferring to her mother, albeit under Margaret's tacit insistence, she wasn't so sure. Despite her mother's domineering air, she felt that Judith should still be deferring to her. It was, after all, she who had hired her. However, after a few moments of watching Margaret in action, Hat conceded that few people, let alone newcomers to the phenomenon, were up to defying her.

The epicentre of the business, named unimaginatively Judith's, was a large room that looked like a cross between a homey school kitchen and a mortuary. Along the back wall ran a work surface made of stainless steel (perfect for dead bodies), while set below and above the counters on the three other walls were a variety of different-sized ovens, grills, microwaves, hobs and blowtorches – Hat wondered what possible culinary use they might have. Three women and one man were rushing around stirring sauces, pulling things out of ovens, laying out pastry cases on trays, piping, and generally creating an atmosphere of controlled chaos.

'You've caught us right in the middle of preparing for a big banquet tonight, a do for a firm of lawyers,' Judith explained.

'Oh, I'm so sorry. We'd have been happy to come at another time if that would have been more convenient,' Margaret lied.

Hat knew that her mother was trying to present the picture of an easygoing mother of the bride.

'It's not a problem. Actually, I'd been a little surprised that nobody had asked for a tasting before now,' Judith said to Margaret, inclining her body slightly towards her.

That did it. Hat went right off her, and even more so when Margaret shot her an I-told-you-so look.

Judith ushered them towards a large catering tray upon which was laid out a miniature assortment of the proposed menu: crostini, vol-au-vents, and satay sticks for nibbles 'to keep the wolf from the door', as she put it, when people first arrived. An asparagus, rocket, sundried tomato and walnut salad for the starter. Salmon *en croute* with baby potatoes and seasonal vegetables for the main course, and *creme brulee* (browned, Hat noticed, by the blowtorch) for pudding. She and her mother tasted tiny mouthfuls of each dish. Everything was utterly delicious. Hat wanted to cry, it was so exquisite.

'This is perfect, just perfect,' Margaret said, daintily wiping her mouth on one of the napkins Judith had thoughtfully provided.

'I'm so glad. I do want Harriet's day to be perfect.' Judith beamed benignly at Hat, as if she was Margaret's idiot child.

'Right, well, that's everything I think. We'll let you get on and look forward to seeing you on the day. Harriet, would you mind popping outside and seeing if you can get a cab? I need the ladies'.'

Hat bade Judith a grumpy farewell and wandered out on to the street in a daze. The caterer had been recommended to her by one of her clients, who'd used her company for her own daughter's wedding, but she hadn't expected her to be so good. Somehow the knowledge that the food would be so glorious upped the ante, and she felt even more panic-stricken.

'That's all sorted out, then,' Margaret said, as she joined Hat. 'Well done for finding such a marvellous caterer, darling. And very reasonably priced too, I thought,' Margaret continued cheerily.

Hat decided to get it out. 'Mum, I need to say something.'

'Don't worry, darling. I've said my piece, there's no need to apologize. What are a few cross words between mother and daughter?'

Hat scowled at the idea of her mother imagining that she was about to beg her forgiveness.

'Let's forget the whole thing and go and get a coffee.'

Hat acquiesced. After all, it had waited this long, it could wait a bit longer. Not *that* much longer, however, as the rehearsal had now been rearranged for tomorrow – the day before the wedding.

28. The Wedding Rehearsal

'What are you doing? You can't have a rehearsal!' Mish wailed, as she followed Hat around their flat while she readied herself to leave for the church. She felt extra guilty because she'd still done nothing since having seen Jimmy and that woman. The only positive action she'd taken was to dissuade Gerry and Priscilla from continuing with the staking-out idea on the grounds that it wasn't the most efficient use of their collective resources. Predictably Gerry had been only too keen to abandon the plan, but so had Priscilla: she was still convinced that it was all going to come good.

'There isn't a groom . . . erm, yet,' Mish went on. 'I mean, he might be there tomorrow. Obviously that's what we're all hoping for here. But today, there will be no, I repeat, no groom. If you do this, it's going to blow everything!'

'No, it isn't. I've already worked it out. I'm going to go, keep Mum happy, make sure everyone knows what they are doing and say that Jimmy's gout has flared up again and he can't walk.'

'Oh, right,' Mish replied, defeated.

'What's the alternative?' Hat snapped. 'Own up now? I can't – I just *can't*! It's too late. I should have done it ages ago, I know, and I cannot believe that I am about to go to a fucking rehearsal for a wedding that doesn't look like it's going to happen! But I've got to. It's all got out of hand, but I've got to keep going!'

'Yeah, s'pose,' Mish replied, meekly. She sat down and watched Hat as she sped round the flat, gathering things up, putting them down again, emptying out her bag, stuffing things back into it. She was flapping and achieving nothing, rather like a headless chicken. Mish knew that the mess her friend had got herself into was completely and utterly preposterous but, like Hat, she didn't see what else could be done.

'So, are you coming or not, bridesmaid?' Hat asked, standing at the front door, which she'd already opened.

'Might as well. I've got nothing else on.' Mish linked her arm through her pal's. They were facing the biggest prat-fall of their lives but they might as well go down laughing and together.

'For the love of God! Have you taken leave of your senses? He *has* to be here! Can't he borrow a cane or a Zimmer frame?' Margaret yelped.

'No, sorry, Mum. He really can't walk at all.'

The pair were standing a few feet away from the small group formed by the others present – Penny, Mish, Philip, Gerry, who was Hat's other bridesmaid, and the vicar. Those not involved in the row were chatting tactfully among themselves, trying to stay out of the way.

'What about a wheelchair, then?'

'Mum, where's he going to get a wheelchair? It'll be fine, I'll tell him everything he needs to know when I see him later. It's no big deal, really.'

'Well, he'd better be on form tomorrow. I'm not having my day ruined by that boy's gout.' Margaret harrumphed and shook her bosom indignantly.

'Erm, it's *my* day, Mum.'

'Oh, you know what I meant,' Hat's mum replied dismissively.

She was right, Hat did know exactly what she meant.

Margaret instructed the vicar to begin the rehearsal and Hat took a deep breath. She was steeling herself to get through this, the last ordeal before her day of reckoning.

'Right-oh. Well, this is all most unorthodox but if you're ready, Harriet, could you and your father make your way towards the vestibule and wait until I say, "Music." Of course, on the day there will be music but for now you should take me saying the word as your cue. When you hear that, will you, Mr Grant, walk your daughter into the church and up the aisle towards me and tomorrow, we hope, the groom, ha, ha?'

Oh, she's a right comedian, Hat thought, as her father took her arm. Just as they were turning to take up their position, the doors of the church flew open with a crash and Sam bounded in panting heavily.

Everyone watched open-mouthed while he gathered his breath. 'Sorrrrry I'm late, I got – held up in – erm – trrrrraffic,' he blurted out, gasping for air. He'd clearly been running for quite a while.

Hat looked at him, wide-eyed, saying nothing. She felt as if she could weep with gratitude. He really is the nicest bloke in the world, she thought.

'What about your gout? Harriet said you couldn't walk,' Margaret bellowed.

'My gout?' Sam hesitated for a minute then remembered Jimmy's supposed affliction. 'Ah, my gout, yes, aye,' he continued, and started to hop about on one foot. 'Ow, ow, God, oh, sorry, Vicar, ow, ow, it's rrrrrreally awfie bad acktually. But I think it might be berginnin' to clear up, ye ken?'

Hat flinched as he held his leg and staggered around. He was the worst actor in the world.

'Well, I must say it's a peculiar type of gout. You ran in here like an Olympic sprinter!' Margaret continued.

Hat cursed: she was like a dog gnawing at a captured rat.

All eyes turned to Sam.

'Well, I couldn't feel the pain because I was thinking of Hat,' he said, turning to the bride-to-be and holding out his hand. For one second, Hat thought he looked as if he really did love her. Maybe he's not such a bad actor after all, she decided, smiled back at him conspiratorially and slipped her hand into his.

'Aaaaaah,' the group cooed.

'Very well. Shall we start again?' the vicar called authoritatively, once the assembled company had had its fill of love's young dream.

'As before, Harriet and Mr Grant, if you would make your way to the entrance. Mrs Grant and Penny, if you would take seats in the first pew on the bride's side. And, James, if you would come to the altar with me. You should stand on my left and your best man – oh, is there no best man?'

'No, he isn't coming, he can't,' Hat called from the other side of the church, and grimaced as she heard her voice booming out. It sounded like a foghorn – a waffling one at that.

'No best man?' Margaret cried. Each outburst sounded more enraged than the last. She was so exasperated at the slapdash, casual manner in which her daughter was undertaking the whole procedure.

'No, he – I –' Sam looked around nervously. His eyes fell upon Gerry. 'I was gonnie ask Gerry if he'd stand in for him.'

Gerry widened his eyes as he stepped forward. 'Really? I'm flattered. I'd be delighted . . .'

Gerry and Sam fell in together and walked up the aisle a few paces behind the vicar.

'What the hell are you doing here?' Gerry whispered.

'Priscilla told me Hat was going ahead with it and I couldn't let her go through this on her own.'

'I see. You're being a really good *friend* to her, I must say,' Gerry replied. He had developed a deep suspicion about why any guy would make such an enormous gesture.

'Well, I like her.'

Gerry decided to be bold. 'Just "like"?'

'Oh, Gerry, don't ask.'

'I see. What about Gloria?'

'Don't ask.'

'Right, OK. Well, you've got a little bit of sorting-out to do, I reckon.'

'You don't know the half of it.' Sam let out a plaintive sigh.

Once the two men were settled in their designated positions the vicar instructed the bride-to-be and her father to make their way in. In a trance Hat walked up the aisle on her father's arm. She was filled with heartaching hope and gut-wrenching fear. Oh, God, oh, God, oh, God, what am I doing? I've got to get out of this. I've got to tell the truth. This cannot be happening. I cannot go on. Yet all the while she kept slowly walking forward, heading towards her fate. As she approached the altar, Sam turned with a warm, bright, heartening smile. It gave her just the lift she needed to get through her current dismay.

'. . . Let no man put asunder what God has joined together. And then I say, "You may kiss the bride."'

On cue, Sam leant forward and gave Hat a sweet but appropriately chaste kiss.

Oh, fuck, Hat thought, as she tried to stop herself melting, this is all I need right now – a reminder of just how fabulous a kisser he is.

'And then you, the newly married couple, follow me through to the vestry to sign the register. After that you go out on to the lawn for photographs. And then it's off to the reception where the fun begins, hah, hah!'

'Now, you're going to have to leave straight away and stay away from Harriet until tomorrow, young man. It's bad luck for the groom to see the bride on the day of her wedding before they meet in church. Off you go!' Margaret said good-naturedly, as she shooed Sam away. With the rehearsal completed her spirits seemed to have lifted a little. The group was hovering in the vestibule, waiting for the rain to subside before making a dash for their respective cars.

'The last thing I'd want is any bad luck tomorrow,' Sam said, staring at Hat as he departed.

He really wants the best for me, I'm sure, Hat thought, as she waved him goodbye. As she watched him begin to walk away, she was overcome suddenly by a wave of childlike need. She took herself, and everyone else, by surprise, as she called, 'You will come tomorrow, won't you?'

Sam stopped in his tracks and spun round. His face betrayed a painful mixture of tenderness, longing and courage. He squared his shoulders and called back, 'Of course. I wouldn't miss it for the world.'

A bewildered silence ensued.

'One would hope not. What a peculiar thing to say.' Margaret sniffed, and buttoned up her coat. Naturally, the significance of his words had eluded her, but Penny shot her sister a look of piercing inquiry.

Hat, thrown by Sam's expression, pretended not to see it.

29. Nineteen Hours and Counting

'And I was,' dramatic pause with punctuating nod of the head, 'only twenty-four hours from St Cuthbert's! Only twenty-four hours from her arms . . .' Gerry sang, using a corkscrew as his microphone to enhance his impressive, if slightly bastardized, impersonation of Gene Pitney. The three were now safely installed in Hat and Mish's flat, armed with enough booze to ensure that the hairy night ahead sped along well oiled.

'It's not twenty-four, actually,' Mish said, looking at her watch. 'It's . . . erm . . . *nineteen* until blast-off.'

'Yes, sweetheart, but I don't think there's an appropriate song including that exact time span, do you? However, if you're going to be a stickler for details, very well . . . "and I was," ' dramatic pause and punctuating nod plus provocative flick of a hip, ' "only nineteen hours from Tulsa! Nineteen hours from her love . . ." Doesn't sound quite the same, does it?'

'Erm, hello? Do you think we could steer clear of the how-many-hours-left-before-Hat's-ha-ha-wedding subject?' Hat interrupted. 'I'd like to think about something else – anything – if you don't mind.'

'Yes, let's,' Gerry replied obediently. 'Instead let us move straight on to the much more fascinating subject of your-beard-is-clearly-in-love-with-you-and-it-looks-like-you-might-be-feeling-the-same-way-what-the-hell-are-you-going-to-do-about-that? Shall we?' he continued, handing round three large glasses of wine.

'Oh, God, yes!' Mish cried. 'When he turned back and said, "I wouldn't miss it for the world," and gave you *that* look, I thought, Hello, what's going on here?'

'Christ, had you not noticed before, then? I mean, why else would he pitch up at the church?' Gerry chipped in.

'I don't know what you two are on about. He did not give me a funny look,' Hat said emphatically, interrupting her friends before they went right off the rails with their new, as they saw it, discovery. 'We are *not* in love, not him with me or me with him. You are both reading things into what happened today that just aren't there. It's a crazy idea. You're just being ridiculous.'

'Oh, yes? Well, while we're at it, what, my lady, were you doing asking him to the wedding? You presumably meant as a guest, no?'

'What else?'

'Yes, indeed, what else? It's just that, if I may remind you, your family believe he's the groom, remember?'

'Fuck, I didn't think of that,' Hat said. Suddenly she was struck by an idea. 'But by tomorrow, with any luck, the real groom will have turned up and everyone will know that it wasn't Sam all along so it won't matter if he's there after all, no?' she asked plaintively. She felt she needed Sam to be there, come what may.

'Bet he'll find a way, after all – love knows no bounds . . .' Gerry crooned.

'You two! Stop this! Sam is not in love with me, and I am not in love with him. How could I be? I'd hardly put myself through this living hell just to go and fall in love with someone else, would I? I am in love with Jimmy. I want to marry Jimmy – OK? Sam is being a fantastic friend – OK? And, on top of that, I'd like to draw your attention to the fact that he is actually *already* married and, what is more, to a drop-dead gorgeous woman. He's not very likely to be falling in love with me when he's already got Miss Perfect, is he?'

'I'd forgotten about her,' Mish admitted.

'And it looks like you're not the only one,' Gerry chipped in.

'And what's that supposed to mean?' Hat demanded.

'Call me crazy but I *do* think Sam's in love with you. Not only that but I don't think he's ever been in love with Gloria, or her with him. I told you before, I think there's more than meets the eye going on between those two. Maybe it's a marriage of convenience – maybe he married her to get her into the country or something.'

Hat jumped in frantically. 'You're mad! Why would he do that? Jesus, where did you get that idea? You wouldn't exactly have to hold a gun to a bloke's head to get him to marry Gloria!'

'All right, keep your hair on. I'm just saying that there's something fishy about that woman and I can't put my finger on it.'

'Play your cards right tomorrow and you just might!' Mish cried out suggestively.

'Sadly, as you know, I'm a man's man so there will be none of that crossing-over carry-on for me, no matter how pissed I get at Hat's reception.'

'Oh, you don't know what you're missing, darling,' Mish said.

'Come on, you two! Sam and Gloria *are* happily married. They're just very confident and relaxed about each other, which is why they've both been able to be so good to me,' Hat said heatedly. She was trying to reassure herself as well as attempting to put an end to their speculation. At this delicate and scary moment in her life, she herself could not fathom the heartfelt depths of meaning she'd detected in Sam's face as he'd left the church. Everything, but everything, was upside down, inside out and arse about tit. She couldn't begin to unravel the whole mess.

With devil-may-care abandon the trio continued drinking into the wee small hours of the morning. Hat knew, in the back of her mind, that she shouldn't really be so wildly incautious but, she reasoned, it was all in the lap of the gods now and nothing she did so late in the game would change the course of events. The plane was on automatic pilot. If it crash-landed, so be it: she'd just have to see how many life-jackets there were to go round. Eventually the three friends crawled into bed, each one as merry as a lord.

After a few fitful hours, Hat woke up at six thirty with a terrifying start. Immediately, she was aware of paralysing fear coursing through her veins. Her stomach was churning and her palms were dripping with sweat. She was out of breath, as if she'd just run up three flights of stairs. The dream that had woken her so abruptly was still playing in her head. She'd been travelling somewhere in a cab. Suddenly the driver, a large, grumpy old man, had slammed the brakes on and told her to get out. Hat told him that they hadn't reached her destination, to which he replied, 'But this is as far as I'm going.' Bewildered and dazed, she'd got out, wondering how on earth she'd complete her journey. Then, without warning, she was in a forest. Her mother and Mrs Kostas, with a mouthful of pins, were pursuing her through densely packed trees. Between them they were dragging a veil so long that the end of it was entwined around the trees in the distance yet it didn't hamper their progress. Finally they caught her, and while Mrs Kostas held her down, her mother tried to wrestle her into the veil. It was during this struggle that Hat had woken up. She was sure the dream was a premonition – she was not going to finish her journey. Oh, Jesus Christ! Her head sank into her hands as she sat up. Jesus Christ! How am I going to get through today? What the fuck have I done? Jimmy's never going to turn up, of course he isn't! Why did I ever think he would? I'm going to make a total arse of myself in front of loads of people! Why, oh, why did I do this? No amount of plotting, blocking, wishing, hoping and praying was going to help her out today.

In an effort to compose herself Hat looked out of the window, in the faint hope that rain might stop play, but the day was shaping up to be bright and crisp. Perfect for an autumn wedding. The weather seemed to have a salutary effect on her and she made a decision. She marched into her flatmate's bedroom, to find both her and Gerry sprawled across the bed in deep slumber.

'Mish, are you awake? I'm going to call it off.'

'Eh? What?' Mish sat bolt upright, blinking and looking round the room frantically.

'I can't do this. It's bonkers. I'm not doing it!' Hat wailed.

Mish came to. 'No, listen, not yet. Wait. Don't give up yet. Make some really strong coffee. I've got to go out.'

'Go out?' Hat howled. 'What for?'

'To get – for – to get – some milk and bread! You must have something to eat. You'll be able to think more clearly when you've got some food down you. I'll be back in a minute and then we'll talk about it. Just don't panic and *don't* do anything.' Mish clambered out of bed and pulled on some clothes. She gave Gerry a hard prod in his back with her foot. 'Oi, sleeping beauty! Get up, will you? Our friend needs some company.'

'What's going on?' Gerry shouted.

'Keep your hair on. I'm nipping out for a minute, you stay with Hat. She's wobbling out,' Mish said.

'Nipping out? What time is it?'

'We need some bits and bobs, OK?' Mish said, and widened her eyes at him.

'Oh, right, whatever. See you in a bit, then.'

Ordinarily Hat would have guessed that Mish was up to something but she was overwhelmed by the horrors that lay in wait for her.

Mish hared out of her bedroom, cast a swift look over her shoulder then grabbed Hat's car/van keys and flew out of the front door. She hadn't done anything about Jimmy since she'd seen him outside his flat with the woman. Out on the street, she ran towards Hat's car/van. Mish had only driven it once before and she'd forgotten just how decrepit and idiosyncratic it was. After a mighty tussle with the driver's door she got herself behind the wheel. She put the key into the ignition and turned it, to be met with a loud spluttering, wheezing sound, like an old man having a coughing fit after his ninety-fifth fag of the day. Mish cursed and tried again but it just wouldn't start. Just before she gave up and ran round to the local minicab office she willed God to give her a hand. She wasn't one jot religious but under the circumstances, she reasoned, He might be prepared to overlook her hypocrisy. He did, and the engine kicked into life.

'Hope you can get me back too!' she implored the car, as she crashed into gear.

She wasn't a great driver at the best of times. As she didn't own a car she rarely drove. Luckily, as it was still early, there were few people on the roads and she soon made it to Jimmy's. She was in no mood for nice manners and pressed the entry bell to his block for far longer than necessary. She was going to give Jimmy one last chance and, failing that, hell.

'Hullo,' a sleepy voice said, into the intercom.

'Jimmy, it's Mish. Let me in, I need to talk to you.'

'Oh, erm, OK, come up.'

Mish was a little thrown that Jimmy had let her in without resistance, but she bounded up the stairs to find him standing at the door of his flat in a T-shirt and jeans, looking somewhat dishevelled.

'Do you know what today is?' she barked, as soon as he'd closed the door behind her.

'How could Ah forget?'

Again, Mish was thrown off course. He wasn't in the defiant mood she'd anticipated. 'Yeah, well, I shouldn't be telling you this but here goes. Hat is going to be there today, in the hope that you'll turn up.'

'What? Where?' Jimmy replied.

'She thinks that, come what may, you'll be there.'

'Be where?'

'At the church for your wedding.'

'But how could Ah? Ah mean, there is no weddin', it's been called off.'

Mish grasped that, of course, Jimmy had no idea that it was still on – ostensibly. 'Ah, no, you see . . . it hasn't.'

'Whit d'you mean, Mish? We broke up weeks ago.'

'Yes, officially, I suppose you did, but . . .' She became aware that there was no way of finishing the sentence without dropping Hat in it. She decided that, even so, there was nothing for it. 'But not as far as Hat is concerned, in terms of the wedding plans and everything.'

'Ah don't understand. Whit are you talkin' aboot?'

'Look, everything's exactly as it was. The dress, the reception, the photographer, *every single thing*. She's gone ahead as if nothing had happened. Hat is going to be there at two o'clock in all her finery with nothing more than a faint hope that you just might do the right thing!'

'Christ almighty!'

Jimmy staggered back a few steps then steadied himself against the door of the hall cupboard. 'Why didnae you tell me this when we spoke before?'

'Cos I was trying to get you to come back to her without using emotional blackmail. I *was* hoping you'd want to go back to her because you cared about her and were upset to hear how devastated she was.

'But . . . but Ah cannae marry someone because Ah feel sorry for them.'

'No, maybe not, but you can because you said you would,' Mish replied tartly.

'Oh, this is terrible, Ah feel terrible. Ah cannae believe she didnae call it off. Ah just cannae believe it,' Jimmy said. He was clearly in a state of tremendous shock.

'Well, if it's any comfort to you neither can she,' Mish said, more sympathetically, remembering that until recently she'd also had trouble coming to terms with Hat's refusal to face facts. 'She didn't *plan* to not call it off, things just overtook her and she kept putting off the shame and humiliation of having to admit her fiance had dumped her.'

'Ah feel absolutely gutted aboot this.'

Infuriated by his constant references to how *he* felt, Mish was spurred on to inject some heavy sarcasm into the proceedings. 'Oh dear, well, perhaps your girlfriend can give you a shoulder to cry on.'

'Ma girlfriend?'

'Yeah, listen, don't try to deny it. I saw her.'

'Who?'

'That red-haired woman – I saw you with her.'

'What red-haired woman?'

'I came round the other day to see if you'd got back from Scotland and you were with some woman, getting off your bike.'

'Oh, that was my auntie Morag, Euan's mum. Ah've got my wee cousin stayin' here the now. He's seventeen, he was only supposed to be here for a bit but he won't go back now. She's come tae get 'im. I gie'd her a lift doon.'

Mish felt as if the stuffing had been knocked out of her. Most of the aggression she'd been directing at Jimmy had been fuelled by the, admittedly weak, conviction that he'd done the dirty on Hat. Then she remembered that, notwithstanding his newly discovered innocence in that department, he was still hardly guilt-free.

'OK, sorry about that, my mistake. But you've got to do something about Hat. If you aren't going to marry her then put things straight, will you? Part of why she's gone off the rails like this is because she reckons you weren't clear about why you were leaving and that led her to believe you might come back!'

Jimmy didn't respond. He stood there gazing

forlornly at his feet. 'Ah'm *still* no sure about what Ah've done.'

'For crying out loud, Jimmy, it's too late for that shit!' Mish yelled at him. 'Listen, I've got to go back, she's going to wonder where I've been. You'd better come round to ours and explain or turn up at the church and bloody well marry her, OK?' Mish pulled open the front door with a passionate tug.

'Yeah, no, Ah will . . . Ah will.'

Mish didn't have time to wait around to see if Jimmy had more to say – she knew from experience that if she did she'd be there all day. She raced down the stairs three at a time then stopped in her tracks to call back, 'Whatever you decide, don't *ever* tell her I was here, will you?'

'No, Ah won't, you're awright there,' Jimmy replied, before closing the door.

Mish zoomed home as fast as the crappy old car/van would take her. She jumped a few red lights *en route*, which made the journey seem even more exciting and daredevil than it already felt, fuelled as it was by her mission to act as Hat's saviour. Just as she was about to let herself in, she remembered in the nick of time what she was supposed to have gone out for, nipped into the local shop and furnished herself with the supplies. As she turned the key in the lock she checked her watch: it was eight forty, she'd been gone for a little over ninety minutes.

'Blimey, you've been gone for hours! What did you do? Bake the bread then milk the cow yourself?' Gerry called from the kitchen, as he heard Mish enter.

She cursed him silently for drawing attention to the length of time she'd been absent. 'God, yeah.' She wrestled herself out of her coat and flung it towards the pegs. 'Nowhere was open. I ended up walking miles until I found a shop.' She frantically picked off the price labels that showed where the stuff had come from. 'And then I realized I didn't have any money, so I ended up having to beg some, would you believe? Where's Hat?'

'I persuaded her to have a bath.'

'Then why did you make me go through all that stupid nonsense about why I was so long?' Mish tutted angrily.

'Because I was wondering why it had taken you so long.'

'You didn't really think I went out at seven a.m. just to get bread and milk, did you?'

'Erm . . . yes, sorry, I did. Didn't you? You seem to be holding some items that strongly resemble that description.'

'That's because I had to cover up where I've really been, you idiot.'

'And where *have* you been?'

'To see Jimmy, of course!' Mish couldn't believe Gerry hadn't guessed.

'Oh, God, of *course*. Well, any success? Did you see him? Is he going to change his mind?' Gerry whispered.

'I did see him and the answer is – I don't know.'

'Oh, fabulous.'

'No, you don't understand, it's going to be OK . . .

sort of. Whatever happens, he's either going to come here and explain, in which case Hat won't have to go through with the whole awful thing, or he's going to be at the church.'

'Did he say that?'

'Not in so many words but that's how we left it. He's not a complete arsehole, he'll do the right thing – for him, I mean, whatever that is. I told him more or less everything she'd done since he'd left. I had to so that he'd know what was at stake here. After all, he does care about her, so he says.'

'But, Christ, Mish, it's a bit of a gamble, isn't it? I hope you're right.'

'Believe me, so do I. But for now we've got to keep Hat occupied and extra-super-positive, OK? We can't let her crumble now.'

'Agreed.' Gerry raised his coffee cup and clinked it with Mish's, affirming their pact.

30. The Heat Is On

It was now ten thirty. There were only two and a half hours to go before they had to set off for the church. Mish and Gerry had managed, with the aid of Saturday-morning mayhem-style television, to keep Hat's mind off quitting. They'd also achieved – amazingly, given the circumstances – to keep her relatively cheerful. They kept reminding her of the monumental effort and will-power she'd shown to get this far. They urged her not to lose faith when she was so close to the finish. They tried to remind her of Jimmy's essentially good nature and his other plus points, which proved a stretch for them both as neither had been enthusiastic about him.

Mish thought that this was what it must be like to coach a cross-Channel swimmer who'd had enough and was trying to get back into the boat just as land came into view. All the while, she was acutely aware that the moment was approaching when she would have to start Hat's makeup and hair, if she was to be ready in time. As the minutes crept by, she decided that the odds on Jimmy turning up at the flat were lengthening, in which case, she reasoned, he was intending to turn up at the church. He had to. Even wishy-washy old Jimmy wouldn't leave Hat high and dry. Nobody would, knowing what he now knew,

Mish assured herself. He was going to take the plunge. He was going to stop dilly-dallying and make that all-forgiving, winning romantic gesture. Nobody could care about someone and let them down like this. As for what he'd do about the doubts he'd expressed to her, well, she mused, he could sort them out after the wedding. They were his problem and he should have done something about them long before now.

Catching Gerry on his own for a split second in the kitchen, Mish seized the opportunity to lay out her plan of action. 'Listen, I'm going to start on Hat's makeup and stuff.'

'What?' Gerry squeaked.

'I've got to. I think he's going to turn up at the church. It's nearly eleven so he's obviously not coming here, is he?'

'Yeah, but what if he's done a bunk again?'

'He won't have. He couldn't.'

'But what if he has?'

'That's a risk we're going to have to take. She'll never be ready if I don't start now. He *is* going to be there, I'm sure!'

'God, I hope you're right,' Gerry replied.

'Right about what?' Hat said, walking in still wearing her dressing-gown.

The pair, who looked as guilty as kids caught with their hands in the cookie jar, stared at their friend.

'About whether Velcro rollers are better than traditional Carmens!' Mish cried gaily, after a moment's pause.

'What's a Velcro roller?' Hat asked, as she poured herself some of the coffee Gerry had made.

'They're what I was going to use on your hair. They're brilliant because they give it body without that awful old ladies' bouffant look you get when you use Carmens,' Mish gabbled, to cover her nerves. They'd so nearly been caught.

'Yeah, well, it hardly matters what my hair looks like now because I'm not going through with it,' Hat replied, dragging out a chair and plonking herself down on it. Her whole body was limp with defeat.

Mish and Gerry exchanged looks. They knew they were both thinking the same thought.

'You are!' they cried in unison.

'Eh?'

'You are. You are going through with it. Come on, Hat, pull yourself together. We've got to get you ready.'

'What's the point?'

'Because you've got this far, you can't turn back,' Mish urged her. 'Do or die. *Carpe diem!* To infinity and beyond!'

'Buy one, get one free!' Gerry piped up enthusiastically.

Despite her despondency a laugh burst out of Hat. 'Do you really think I should?'

'Yes, yes!' her friends cried.

'Why?'

Gerry looked blank. He was happy to be swept up in the current feverish mood but he couldn't think of a sensible answer to Hat's reasonable question. It was

Mish who supplied it: 'Because you've got no choice. You wanted to have your day and here it is! What's the worst that could happen?' she asked.

Gerry grimaced. He had a list as long as his arm of possible answers to that.

And Hat had the first instantly to hand. 'Erm, Jimmy doesn't turn up and I end up as a national joke?'

'No, he *is* going to turn up. I know he is, trust me!' Mish declared, her heart beating wildly. She'd whipped herself into a paroxysm of passionate encouragement. She felt like a cheerleader on speed.

Hat looked at each of her friends. After a moment's contemplation she announced: 'All right, let's do it,' with an uncertain smile.

Just as Mish had finished applying one of the most expensive and luxurious foundations in her kit to Hat's face the doorbell rang. It didn't seem to bother Hat, but Mish nearly jumped out of her skin. Gerry and she exchanged panicked glances – what if it was Jimmy?

As Gerry went to answer it, Mish took a furtive look at her watch. It was eleven thirty, too late, she prayed, for someone, even someone as hopeless as Jimmy, to be calling off the wedding.

'Goodness! Are you only just starting to get ready?' Margaret marched into the living room, trailed by Penny.

'Mum, leave her alone. It'll be fine. After all, Mish

is a professional,' Penny chided. Surprised by this show of solidarity, Hat shot her sister a grateful look.

'Right, well, better get on with it, then. Don't mind us, we won't get in your way. I've only come to steady your nerves and make sure everything's just so. We'll leave with you two, give you a lift if you like . . .' she waved her hand imperiously at Gerry and Mish '. . . and your father will pick you up shortly afterwards as arranged, Harriet.'

'Mum, let's get out from under their feet. Come on, we'll go and have a cup of coffee,' Penny said, easing Margaret determinedly out of the room. As she left, she threw Hat a long-suffering look and raised her eyes to heaven. Hat returned a warm smile. She'd never felt so close to her big sister in all her life. There was something different about Penny today: she seemed more approachable, more human. Hat couldn't think what had changed.

'I'll make sure they stay in there,' Gerry whispered, exiting after them.

'Do you reckon I *am*, maybe, sort of, mad, really and truly round the bend, mentally ill, deranged?' Hat asked, in a hushed tone, as Mish began to put in the famous Velcros.

'Erm, no, funnily enough I don't,' her friend replied, expertly rolling up Hat's hair. 'I think you *did* go a bit mad but never actually certifiable. You just lost the plot.'

'Yeah, but now, today, all this. Going through with it not knowing if Jimmy's going to be there. Come on, that is barmy, isn't it?'

'Not if he does turn up. Which he will,' Mish replied. Her conviction that he was going to do the right thing was growing with every second that ticked by.

'But if he doesn't I might as well be carted off from the spot straight into a loony-bin, yeah?'

'If you like. I'll give you a lift in your van.' Mish laughed. 'But you know what? I've just got this funny feeling he's going to be there.'

'Oh, Hat, you look absolutely gorgeous,' Penny said softly. She had popped her head into the room as Mish was finishing.

'Thanks, Penny, er, thanks very much.' Hat was abashed: not only had she never before worn full makeup, but she'd never, ever been complimented on her appearance by her sister.

'You've done a marvellous job,' Penny said.

There was a brief pause while Mish brushed out Hat's hair, then Penny spoke again. 'Mish, would you mind leaving Hat and me alone for a moment? I'd just like a quick word with my little sister.'

Mish, knowing full well that Penny wasn't the most supportive sister in the world, glanced at Hat to make sure she was OK with the idea, then headed for the kitchen, intending to trap Margaret in there until the sisterly talk was over.

Penny closed the door behind her.

'Hat, I want to apologize for the other day.'

'Oh,' Hat replied, flummoxed. She'd had a vague foreboding that Penny was going to have another go at her.

'I also want to explain why I did what I did,' Penny began, as she paced up and down the room. 'Oh, God, I've never said this aloud before but here goes. Better out than in, as they say.' Hat had never seen her so unsettled. 'I've come to realize that I don't love Guy. Actually, I don't think I ever did. I'm not even sure I like him very much. I married him because, well . . . because he seemed so perfect – rich, handsome, successful . . .'

Before she could stop herself Hat blurted out, 'Knighted Dad.'

Penny turned to her and shrugged her shoulders. 'Yeah, that as well probably, embarrassingly enough. I thought if I married someone who was so perfect on paper I'd be bound to have a perfect life.'

'You have, haven't you?' Hat asked gently.

'In theory, I suppose. But I haven't got any of the things that really count, companionship, friendship, shared interests, kids . . .'

'I always wondered about you and kids,' Hat put in.

'Guy wanted to wait until he'd got his first directorship, would you believe? And now I don't know whether I'd want to have a baby with him at all. Anyway, what I'm trying to say is I got married because of a dream, a fairy-princess fantasy, that being married to someone rich and handsome means that you're always protected from everything that's grubby and ordinary. Well, it doesn't, being married to someone who isn't your soul-mate is about as grubby and ordinary as it gets, Mercedes or no Mercedes.'

'Oh, Penny, I'm really sorry.'

'Hat, I'm so lonely,' Penny said, flopping next to her sister, tears welling up in her eyes. 'And his "suitability" isolates me even more. I keep thinking, Who am I to want ordinary things when I've got all this?'

Without hesitation, even though she couldn't remember the last time she and her sister had shared a moment of physical affection, Hat put her arm round her sister's shoulder. 'Well, he *is* a bit of a jerk,' she teased.

'He is, isn't he?' Penny sniggered through her tears. 'You see, I was worried that you were getting married for the sake of being married, like I did, not because he was Mr Right. But then I saw the two of you together at the church yesterday and I realized that you've got a real bond. You can tell from the way you look at each other that you're soul-mates, all right.' She squeezed Hat's hand, which was still draped over her right shoulder.

Oh, fuck! Hat moaned internally. She means Sam, of course she does. Why does everyone think there's something between us? Can they all see something I can't? In a frantic attempt to heave herself away from this thorny subject, Hat turned her thoughts to Jimmy. Just focus on him and why you want to marry him, she urged herself. She didn't do much better with that either because she knew Jimmy wasn't her soul-mate. I can't deal with this! Hat wailed inside. I wasn't looking for a soul-mate! I've never thought about soul-mates until now! Oh, why did Penny have to mention soul-mates? Jimmy is *not* Guy, he *is* Mr Right and I *am* going to marry him! she ranted silently.

'Are you all right?' Penny said suddenly.

'Yes, sorry. I was just thinking about what you'd said. I'm really, really sorry that you're not happy with Guy. But you know what? You're right. In a way, I have always been a bit jealous of you and your perfect life.'

'Yeah, my "perfect life". Well, now you know the truth. Just goes to show you shouldn't take everything at face value,' Penny said, with a wan smile.

Hat felt as if a bolt of lightning had gone through her. Sam had said exactly the same thing. He'd been right about Penny all along: she hadn't wanted to stop Hat muscling in on her 'special, perfect world', it was quite the reverse. She'd wanted to save her from making the same mistake. Hat was overcome with tender feelings towards her sister and mystifying confusion. She wasn't at all sure now why she'd jumped at the idea of marriage. Maybe Penny was right: maybe all along she'd been after the things she'd imagined her sister had. Hat was more terrified now than she'd ever been at the possibility of Jimmy not turning up. She was losing grip on the lifeline to which she'd clung for dear life, the very thing that had guided her through the last hideous, traumatic weeks. Her rock-solid conviction that she wanted to marry Jimmy Mack – and, what's more, for all the right reasons – was slipping away from her and her blood was turning ice cold.

'What are you two up to in here?' Margaret

said, bursting in just as Hat's head was about to explode.

'Nothing, Mum, just a sisterly heart-to-heart before she goes into the breach,' Penny said, standing up and smoothing down her exquisite chocolate brown silk trouser suit. She stood behind her mother's back and gave her sister a rallying thumbs-up.

Hat stared at her blankly then gathered herself up. 'No, I *do* know what I'm doing. I *do* know what I'm doing. I know what I am doing,' she said firmly.

Penny gave her a quizzical but understanding smile.

'Well, too late if you don't, ha, ha!' Margaret barked.

If only she knew how often she was right, Hat thought.

A little later, to her amazement, Hat stood in the living room ready for the off in all her wedding finery – lingerie, dress, wrap and shoes. She was holding the most beautiful tumbling bouquet of roses, ivy and heavenly scented starburst lilies. Nestling in her long hair was a tiny hoop of matching flowers. As her mother fussed and picked over every inch of her she felt a bit like a shop dummy.

Everybody else was gazing at her in reverence.

'You look utterly breathtaking,' Gerry sighed.

'And so right not to go for a veil with that style of dress,' Mish chipped in innocently.

Margaret treated her to a withering stare.

'You could not look more perfect,' Penny said quietly.

She was right. Between the dress, Mish's makeup and the crown of flowers, Hat looked exactly like herself and yet, just as she should, more beautiful than ever before.

Hat gave her sister an intensely mixed gaze. She wanted Penny to save her from making the biggest mistake of her life and yet also to urge her forward, assuring her that it would all work out fine.

'Your father will be here any second now. He won't be late, I told him I'd skin him alive if he was!' Margaret said good-naturedly, as the group prepared to leave. 'We've got to get a move on, darling, or we'll be late. See you there!'

'OhmyGodohmyGod, I've just remembered, last-minute check!' Penny said suddenly. 'Something old, something new, something borrowed, something blue – got them all?'

Having done everything by the book, Hat had met the requirements. 'Yes, I borrowed the wire for my headdress, there's blue thread in my stockings, this wrap is old and as for new – well, that's everything else.'

'Fine but wear these for good measure.' Penny removed a pair of emerald drops from her earlobes and handed them to her little sister. Hat fought back tears as she took them.

'Come on, quick sticks, we've got to get a move on!' Margaret addressed the dawdling crew.

'Good luck,' Mish whispered meaningfully, as she was bustled out of the room.

'Am I going to need it?' Hat asked.

'You never know...' Mish replied, before she was whisked out of the flat, leaving Hat waiting with more shaky uncertainty than any bride has ever known.

31. Here Comes the Bride

Hat lowered her head as she leant forward. She was trying to make sure that her hair stayed exactly in place. She stepped out of the car, and took her father's outstretched hand. He gave her the warmest, sweetest smile she had ever seen. She thought she detected moisture in his eyes, but she couldn't be sure. Right now, she wasn't sure of anything. Hat had never dabbled with hard drugs but if someone had told her that this was what an acid trip felt like, she'd have asked why on earth anyone would ever take one.

She stood on the pavement, clutching her father's hand, and looked up at the church spire. The warm sun was blazing down on it casting an elongated pyramid-shaped shadow on the lawn that lay between her and the church. It was a beautiful, crisp, clear day, the sort of day Hat had dreamt it might be for her wedding. Adrenaline, stomach-dropping-out-of-her-bum fear, hysteria, excitement, massive regret, dizziness and bowel-twisting nerves were scorching through her body. Each sensation seemed locked in a fierce battle as to which had the strongest hold on her intestines. This was the moment of truth. She knew that the only thing for it was to run for her life, then that, whatever the outcome, she had to face the music. She wanted to crumple into a heap and sob, then to skip into the church and whoop with joy. It was finally over. She felt as if she had floated out of her own body and was now watching herself from above.

Through the murky haze of her trance, Hat heard her father's voice: 'Darling, are you all right?'

She looked at him and nodded.

'You don't have to go through with it, you know. If you're not sure, now's the time to say.'

Hat wanted to give him a hug. She knew he didn't mean it – it was more than his life was worth to encourage her to bolt now: her mother would have his guts for garters if she found out – but she appreciated his uncharacteristic attempt to interpret her feelings.

'No, Dad, I'm fine. It's now or never,' Hat heard herself reply.

She realized that this might sound a bit odd to someone ignorant of the full story but she knew he wouldn't really be listening anyway.

She put one green-suede-shod foot in front of the other, gripping her father's arm with the might of a toddler learning to walk. *He's going to be there. He has to have come. He's going to be there*, Hat chanted to herself, as they walked slowly up the path and into the church.

Once they had arrived in the vestibule, hidden from the main body of the church, Hat faltered. For a split second she was sure she was going to faint. Her head spun and she clutched at her father to stop herself falling over. Then she looked down at the floor, took a deep breath and stepped forward into the church. Right on cue, the music, Rachmaninov's 'Vocalise', a dreamy lyrical song, began to play and, briefly, she felt a surge of ecstasy rush through her. She felt as if she was floating on clouds as free as a bird. A couple of seconds later she crashed back to reality. The pews on Jimmy's side were empty. Not one single person sat in them. Not even a sheltering tramp. Jimmy had told his friends and family that it was off. He wasn't coming. Hat thought she was going to collapse with shock. But somehow she kept walking up the aisle. She glanced to her left and took in the sea of faces. Each wore a wild, confused, concerned expression – what was going on? Where was the groom? Hat wrestled her eyes into focus and looked forward, towards the sanctuary. As she already knew, Jimmy Mack was not there. The vicar stood, a few steps up, facing into the church, holding an open prayer book. She looked stumped. She had instructed the music to begin, having been informed by her curate that the bride was waiting outside. In keeping with the odd things that had occurred in the weeks prior to this peculiar wedding, she'd assumed that the groom was going to come in with Hat.

It was a moment later that Hat's father spotted that something was awry, and when he eventually did, he turned to his daughter – his face as bewildered as that of a lost child. He didn't understand.

But Hat did. The awful truth bore down on her with a resounding thump. She'd always known Jimmy wasn't going to turn up. Why on earth would he? She'd selfishly, madly, insanely pursued her own demented fantasy. And now she was going to pay for it. A sardonic smile played across her lips as she thought, Talk about getting your just deserts. She reached the altar and felt a strange sense of calm wash over her. The worst had happened and it was over. That was it. She had driven this thing through to the bitter end. She was finally going to be able to unburden herself of the truth – what a tremendous relief that would be! Hat gave the vicar a brief nod of acknowledgement, letting her know that she would handle the bizarre situation. She squared her shoulders, raised her head and turned to address the congregation. Every pair of eyes was glued to her face. Hat picked out, in turn, her mother's horrified expression, the pity, sorrow and love in Penny's face, Mish's go-on-girl-willing-her-to-be-brave cast, and finally Gerry and Priscilla's amazement. No matter what they were trying to convey she was on her own, she knew that. She was about to speak when she caught sight of a figure hovering at the back of the church, half hidden by a pillar. It was a beat before she recognized Sam. She gave him a small smile and felt instantly emboldened by his presence. It was as if he was sending her waves of courage.

Hat began to speak, making a valiant attempt to be controlled and precise. 'Erm, hello, everybody. Thank you for coming. I expect you're all wondering where the – gr – gr –' The word 'groom' stuck in her throat. She urged herself to continue. 'Where the groom is . . . Well, he's . . . You see, I . . .'

Suddenly the deafening roar of a motorbike reverberated throughout the timeworn building. The noise filled the church and amplified as it bounced off the beams and pillars. The heads of the entire congregation, in one unified move, spun round just as a man astride an enormous bike bombed in through the doors. He brought it to a screeching halt at the foot of the aisle and turned off the engine. It shuddered to a stop as he jumped off. He tore off his helmet and sprinted up the aisle towards Hat, his kilt flapping.

'Ah'm sorry Ah'm a bit late,' Jimmy whispered into her ear, as if they'd seen each other only ten minutes earlier.

She stared at him in disbelief. This couldn't be happening. How? Why?

Hat heard a strangled yelp from her mother – she'd evidently just clocked that Jimmy wasn't Sam – and steeled herself for a second. Perhaps Margaret was going to charge forth and demand an explanation. Nothing happened. Maybe she's just so relieved to see me get married she won't bother to make a fuss – not here, at any rate, Hat thought.

'Is *this* your intended?' the vicar asked, clearly relieved that the proceedings could now take place.

'Yes, he is,' Hat replied, feeling an enormous wave of gratitude to the vicar for not mentioning his lack of similarity to the man whom she'd previously met.

'Very well, then, I'll begin,' the vicar said. 'We have come together in the presence of God to witness the marriage of James Dougal Mackenzie and Harriet Rosemary Grant, to ask His blessing on them, and to share in their joy. Our Lord . . .'

As the vicar embarked on the ceremony Hat's mind tuned out. She could hear the woman's voice but it had turned into a drone, like the gentle hum of traffic in the distance. It was as if she was listening to a conversation two people were having in the next-door room. Hat couldn't hear the words because she was trying desperately to come to terms with the notion that in a few short minutes she would be married to Jimmy Mack. All her dreams were coming true. It would appear that, after all, she was having her fairy-tale wedding. And it was taking place right now. The person standing on her right was real. He had turned up. And, what's more, he was wearing the kilt, the sporran, the whole Prince Charlie – even, she saw, down to the skean-dhu. Jimmy had rolled up in the very outfit he'd refused point-blank to wear when they'd first discussed getting married.

Here he was. The man she'd last seen walking out on her six weeks ago was alive and kicking and, apparently, more than happy to marry her. Forty-two interminable, desperate, demented days had passed since she'd last clapped eyes on him. And, boy, had she been through the mill. As inexplicably as he'd left, he was back. Every humiliation, degradation and mad act she'd put herself through over the last few weeks had paid off. Every moment of misery, loneliness and despairing bewilderment was now done with. He was back and everything was going to be all right. The sound of Jimmy's voice snapped Hat out of her reverie.

'I do,' she heard him say, loud and clear.

'Harriet Rosemary Grant, do you take James Dougal Mackenzie to be your husband? Do you promise to love him, comfort him, honour and protect him, and, forsaking all others, be faithful to him as long as you both shall live?'

Out of the corner of her eye, Hat had seen the vicar turn slightly, as she addressed her. She was now awaiting the inevitable response. She looked into Jimmy's eyes and saw in them everything she'd always seen. He hadn't changed. He was the same Jimmy Mack she'd always known. Jimmy Mack had come back. And then, as if awakened from a drugged sleep, it came to her and she knew for sure. 'I do—n't.'

A shocked gasp rippled through the congregation. The atmosphere stiffened like quick-setting concrete. The entire place turned rigid with electrified anticipation. They must have misheard.

'I'm s-sorry,' the vicar stuttered.

'I don't,' Hat repeated, this time as clear as a bell.

A stunned silence fell. You could have heard a mouse fart.

'I'm so sorry, Jimmy Mack, but I can't. I just can't. It's not right,' Hat said, squeezing his hand between hers.

With more courage than she had known she had in her, she looked directly into his eyes, willing him to say something, do something, to make it all right.

He simply stared back at her. Hat couldn't imagine what he was feeling or thinking.

Nobody spoke for what felt like the longest time in the world. Then she saw his face break into a mixture of tremendous relief and pitiful sadness.

'No, Ah know,' he replied gently.

32. What You Want and What You Need

'So, erm, here we are . . .' Jimmy said, a small laugh shaking his otherwise steady voice.

Hat didn't say anything. She was thinking about something unrelated to the scene she had just caused: she'd noticed his bony knees underneath his kilt and was wondering if he was wearing any pants. She knew that, traditionally, men didn't with kilts but she wasn't sure how far Jimmy would have gone in the name of custom. She'd never find out now, she realized, and she didn't care.

The pair sat alone in the vestry where, if things had gone to plan, they'd have been signing the register at about now. The vicar had suggested tactfully that they repair to the secluded room to discuss, in private, what she had referred to as the 'hiccup'.

'Jimmy, why *did* you come back?' Hat blurted out.

He looked at her, and she could see that he was weighing up how best to answer her question. She willed him to tell the truth. He might as well: however uncomfortable it was going to be, it would be for the best for them both.

'Cos Ah felt so bad.'

Hat gave him a small smile. She'd guessed as much. 'But not because you're madly in love with me,' she continued boldly, already knowing the answer.

'Ah really do care aboot you. You've been a fantastic friend to me an' all that, you know . . .' Jimmy stumbled. Hat could tell he was balking at saying the thing he feared might hurt her so much she wouldn't recover.

'But you don't love me in the way that you ought to love someone to marry them?' Hat persisted. She was driven to hear the truth.

'No, Ah don't, Hat,' Jimmy replied bravely. He gave her a regretful smile.

'Don't worry, because I don't love you like that either,' Hat said, smiling back at him.

'Do you no?' Jimmy replied, his eyes widening. 'So why all this? Why did you carry on wi' it all? Whit aboot all that carry-on in the hospital an' that? What was all that aboot?'

'I was chasing a dream, a fantasy. I wanted to be madly in love like that, so I made myself believe we loved each other in that way. When you asked me to marry you it seemed possible, even likely. And then once you'd gone I couldn't see the wood for the trees. I just had to get you back, had to make you love me the way I thought I loved you.'

'Christ almighty!' Jimmy said, and let out a huge breath.

'Unfortunately I didn't realize all that until now when you pitched up . . . when it was just a bit too late.'

Jimmy laughed.

'Occasionally I had a sneaking suspicion that maybe I was out of control, that maybe what you'd done was for the best, but I never let myself accept it. I just got whipped up into a frenzy about the whole wedding thing and lost sight of what it was supposed to mean. Then my mother turned up and I lost control completely. With her at the helm it got harder and harder to get out of it. On top of all that I started believing that we were star-crossed lovers, that we *had* to be together, that true love conquers all.'

'An' you're sayin' you don't believe that now?'

'No, I don't – well, not about us, anyway. Don't get me wrong, I was devastated when you left and I missed you and everything. But because I couldn't have you everything blew out of all proportion.'

'Well, they do say you always want what you cannae have, don't they?' Jimmy said, philosophically.

'Yeah, and you want it even more if you've had it and *then* lost it . . .'

The pair paused as the enormity of their individual admissions sank in.

'Oh, Hat,' Jimmy said, 'how did we ever start talkin' aboot marriage?'

'Erm, excuse me, that was your idea to start with, remember?' Hat replied, with a display of mock outrage and indignation.

'Was it?' He guffawed. 'Just goes tae show Ah didnae know whit Ah was doin' either. But it seemed like a good idea at the time.'

Hat looked at her now definitively ex-fiance and was flooded with love for him – the wrong kind of love, though, she reminded herself.

'Whit are we gonnae do now, then?' Jimmy continued, jerking his head towards the door leading into the church. It was the only way out.

'*We* aren't going to do anything. This isn't your fault, after all. I didn't see any of your relatives or pals out there,' Hat replied.

'Erm, well, no you see *Ah* told them it was off.'

'Yes, well, that was one way of dealing with the situation.' Hat sighed. 'Listen, I'm going to go out there and invite everyone to a knees-up – what would have been our reception. Will you come? The grub will be fantastic.'

'Do you want me to? Would that be awright?'

'It'd be more than that, it'd be great. It would also be the right thing,' Hat declared, and stood up.

'I'll pay you back all the money as soon as I can,' Hat said to her father, as he settled himself in the empty chair next to her. Having made sure that Jimmy was happy and safe in the company of Gerry and Priscilla, she'd sneaked off on her own to gather her strength in a dark corner of the hall.

'Oh, darling, don't worry. I don't suppose it makes any difference whether you got married or not. You still had your day. And that seems to be what you wanted more than anything else.'

Hat squeezed his hand affectionately, overwhelmed by his generosity. 'Don't let Mum hear you say that. Actually, where is she? I haven't seen her since we left the church.'

Although they'd failed to tie the knot, Hat had left with the groom in accordance with etiquette. He, thinking that he'd be whisking his bride away with him, had brought a spare helmet, and Hat had chosen to travel with him because she didn't want him to have to face a room packed with people he didn't know.

'She's here somewhere, but be warned, she's on the warpath,' Philip said, and gave his younger daughter a rueful smile.

'Well, for once I don't blame her.' Hat knew that, sooner or later, she was going to have to swallow her medicine and get the dressing-down over and done with.

'Dad, will you give us a mo?' Penny said, as she joined them. She'd been looking for her sister ever since she'd seen her arrive and had discovered her hiding place at last.

'Yes, of course. It's no use now, though, Penny, she's made up her mind,' their father said, as he stood up to leave them to it.

'Hat, I've got to know,' Penny started, 'did all that stuff I told you this morning make you change your mind?'

'Yes . . . partly.'

'Oh, Christ, Hat, I'm so sorry. I should have kept my mouth shut. I genuinely wasn't trying to ruin your day.'

'You didn't, Penny. You saved my life.'

Penny stared at her. 'Sorry?'

'Thanks to everything you said, I realized, a little

late admittedly, that I didn't love Jimmy Mack in the way I should. And that he didn't love me that way either.'

'Bloody hell! Then what was all this about?'

'I think you know the answer to that already,' Hat replied sagely.

Penny shrugged her shoulders and gave her a wry, sad smile. 'I guess I do. Oh, and by the way, that bloke at the altar today, that wasn't the same bloke who came to the rehearsal, the one who came to my house for dinner, was it?'

'Erm, no. The man at dinner was a – a stand-in.'

Penny looked bewildered.

'It's a long story, I'll tell you sometime.'

'You'd better. Anyway, whoever the stand-in is, you watch out, he's got feelings for you. You can tell by the way he looks at you. I'd think about giving him a go if I was you. He seems lovely.'

'He is, but we're just friends. Anyway, he's married.'

'Married?'

'Yes.'

'Who to?'

Hat was about to tell her when she saw Sam and Gloria walk into the reception. Despite all her protestations that she nursed no romantic feelings for him her heart sank. She'd assumed that he'd come alone to the church. 'Her,' Hat said, nodding in the direction of the newly arrived couple.

Penny turned to see who she meant. 'That's the girl from your hen party, isn't it?'

'Yes.'

'But I don't understand, why would – how does she – what was –'

Hat cut her sister off – no one was going to be able to work it out without a blow-by-blow account. 'Like I said, it's a really long story. Let's have a drink this week and I'll explain everything.'

'I'd really like that – just the two of us?'

'Yeah, I'd like that too. Right now, I'm going to mingle. I'd better show my face before people think I'm ashamed of what I did.'

'But you're not, are you?'

'No, funnily enough. I did what I did. A bit stupid, I admit, obsessive, some might say, but at least I didn't spend the rest of my life regretting that I'd married the wrong guy. Oops! Sorry, Penny, that wasn't meant to be a dig.'

'Don't worry. It's just a pity it didn't dawn on you a bit sooner – might have saved everyone a lot of trouble,' Penny said laughingly. 'I'm going to the loo. I'll catch up with you later.'

Hat smoothed the front of her dress and headed towards the drinks table where most of the guests had accumulated. Some people were giving her odd looks – clearly they couldn't imagine what had happened, and the groom's presence at the reception, his apparent happiness to be there, despite having been jilted right at the altar, was making it even harder.

Hat made straight for the least threatening group, composed of Priscilla and Gerry. 'Where's Jimmy? I hope you two didn't frighten him off.'

'*Au contraire . . .*' Priscilla replied. 'He's ensconced

in deep conversation with some frightfully dreary cousin of yours – a cat-sitter, would you believe? Much as I love my own dear pets, it's hard to imagine a more tedious job. Cynthia or Clarissa or . . .'

'Celia.'

'Right, yes, Celia. Well, you couldn't prise them apart with a can-opener right now. Look.'

Hat followed the direction of Priscilla's gaze and saw Jimmy sitting at one of the tables next to a dark-haired, chunky-looking woman. They were in the middle of what looked like an animated conversation. Hat was delighted that the unlikely pair had met and, by the looks of it, found some fascinating subject of huge interest to them both. Although she didn't feel guilty about Jimmy – there was no reason to, she hadn't broken his heart – she cared for him. She didn't want him to feel like a spare part at their defunct wedding reception.

'Never mind about those two, match made in heaven, if you ask me. Have a look over there – they're in the middle of a right old barney!'

Hat did as Priscilla instructed. The sight that greeted them was of Sam and Gloria sitting at a table on their own having a row. Hat couldn't help wondering if it had something to do with her. Perhaps Gloria had had enough of Sam's role in Hat's games and hadn't wanted to come.

'Let's go over and interrupt. I mean, this is hardly the place for a marital dispute, is it?' Priscilla said. But Hat had misgivings about muscling in. She was considering hanging back when, out of the corner of her eye, she caught sight of her mother marching towards her. She didn't feel quite ready for that one-sided battle yet and decided that Gloria and Sam's company, albeit stormy, was the lesser of two evils. As the trio walked towards their table the disco started up. The insistent, irresistible beat of 'Groovejet' filled the room as the three friends reached the couple's table.

'Hi!' Sam barked. 'Sit down, join us, please.'

'*Quiero bailar. Quieres bailar conmigo?*' Gloria leapt up at Gerry's approach.

'*Sí, claro!*' he replied, as he took her hand and led her on to the dance floor.

Hat looked at Sam and wondered what he was thinking. She couldn't tell from his expression.

'Oh, good. Thank God, you've got a full one,' Priscilla said, sitting down on a chair opposite him and leaning forward to replenish her glass from the bottle of champagne sitting in the middle of the table. She was impervious to the almost palpable tension between the pair at the table.

'Oh, no.' Hat sighed, as she saw her mother stalking towards her.

'What?' Priscilla said, peering over her shoulder. 'Oh, it's Maggie. My giddy aunt, she's absolutely chomping at the bit to get her teeth into you. You should have heard her sounding off in the car on the way here. Dear God, anyone would have thought you'd beheaded the vicar and drunk blood out of her gaping neck. Don't worry I'll head her off at the pass.' She stood up and hurled herself at her strident friend.

Hat was deeply grateful for this, but she felt awkward left alone with Sam. Evidently he felt the same: he didn't speak for what felt like an eternity. Eventually she decided she had to know. 'Sam, were you and Gloria rowing about me?'

'Yes, as it happens, we were,' he replied matter-of-factly.

Hat's hopes soared then crashed back down. She was racked with guilt and shame at having come between them. 'I'm really sorry I got you involved. It was stupid and selfish of me. And now I needn't have bothered. I've put you to so much trouble over being my beard. If only I'd –'

'Oh, we weren't rowing about that,' Sam interrupted.

Hat didn't know what to say. She couldn't think how else she might feature in a row between them, if not as his pretend fiancee.

'She wants me to tell you something. I *don't* want to tell you because it might put her at risk, but she thinks I'm being over-cautious. Anyway, you may not be interested,' Sam said, straining for a casual tone. After a pause he continued: 'Although, she insists you would be.'

Hat had no idea how to respond. Her heart was beating wildly. She was filled with dread and anticipation.

'Right, you two. I want some explanations,' Margaret said, planting herself in a chair next to them. Hat hadn't seen her coming, so engrossed was she in what Sam had been saying. Her mother's bosom was in shuddering overdrive. Priscilla threw Hat an apologetic smile and went off in search of more booze.

'Were you deliberately trying to make a fool of me? Is that what this whole thing has been about?'

'Of course not, Mum! Why would I want to make a fool of you?'

'Well, whether or not that was your intention that is what has happened. I'm not going to be able to hold up my head in front of half of the family for the rest of my life. And let's not begin to talk about the money! To think of how I put myself out for you! Can you imagine what this has been like for me?'

'Mum, it hasn't been a bowl of cherries for me either,' Hat replied sulkily. She was determined to square up to her mother but not now: now she wanted to hear what Sam was going to say.

'And as for you,' Margaret said fiercely, turning towards him, 'I assume you had your own personal motives for leading me a merry dance.'

Hat felt dreadful. Not only had she caused Sam to row with his wife but now he was getting grief from her formidable mother into the bargain.

'Actually, Mrs Grant, none of this has anything to do with you – specifically.'

Hat's eyes nearly popped out of her head as she listened to Sam give her mother what-for.

'Of course, I'm sorry, as I'm sure Hat is too, that you've been misled but it was no one's intention to hurt you. You, I'm afraid, don't figure in the whys and wherefores of this situation. Now, if you don't mind, I'd like to dance with your daughter. So, if you'd excuse us . . .' Sam stood up and stretched out his hand to Hat. She took it, avoiding her mother's astonished gaze. Margaret's ample bosom was shuddering so hard that Hat was worried she might start an earthquake.

'I thought you couldn't dance.'

'I can't, really, but I didn't know how else to get away from your mother.'

'I don't think anyone's ever talked to her so . . . erm . . . directly before.'

'You don't mind, do you?'

'No, not really, although I do feel a bit sorry for her. It's not her fault she's like that. I'll have to give her an explanation at some point, she deserves one, but I don't feel up to it right now.'

Sam smiled.

'And when I do it might be quite a long talk because I guess I'll have to tell her that the whole thing started with her making me feel like a loaf of uncooked bread next to my sister's exquisitely handcrafted after-dinner biscuits.'

The pair shuffled around each other, secretly longing for a song with a less energetic beat. Trying to dance and have a conversation at the same time isn't the easiest thing to do at the best of times and Hat was desperate to hear the rest of what Sam had to say. And then an awful thought occurred to her. What if that was it? Maybe he's already told me that he didn't want to tell me whatever it was that Gloria wanted him to tell me! So maybe he's not going to say anything else! Now I'll never know what it was. Fuck, I've got to know. Hat was so preoccupied that she didn't hear the music change to a slower number.

A look of relief came over Sam's face as Aretha's 'I Say A Little Prayer' began to play. The reluctant jiggers fell, without awkwardness, into an infinitely easier sway. Still, though, Sam didn't speak. Hat was crushed: he wasn't going to pick up where he'd left off. She couldn't think of how to start up the conversation again. And there was only one thing she wanted to hear.

After a few agonizingly uncomfortable moments when neither of them could speak or even look at each other, Sam took a deep breath and burst forth as if he'd been holding the words in his mouth like a bunch of sharpened nails. 'All right, OK, look, seeing as you didn't go through with your wedding to that guy you apparently wanted to marry *so* much I may as well say my piece. But you have to swear not to tell a single soul.'

Hat nodded. She didn't dare to speak, fearing that any utterance might break the thread.

'What I told you about Gloria being a political journalist in Colombia and in danger is true, but there's something else that I didn't tell you. And I'm sure it's the reason the authorities here are so interested in our marriage. I think they know.'

'Know what?' Hat asked anxiously. She thought she was going to burst with apprehension.

'Gloria's gay. She's a well-known gay-rights activist

in Colombia among other things, none of which makes her very popular over there,' Sam explained.

Hat tried to take it all in. 'Why . . . why . . . would she want me to know that?' she asked.

Sam looked away in exasperation before he spoke again. 'Because despite my protests – which she insists are silly, she reckons we can easily work something out – she thinks it's important that you are made aware that our marriage . . . ah . . . *isn't* a real one.'

For a moment Hat couldn't make sense of it at all. And then a deep blush covered her face. Her head was swimming. She was having the weirdest, most eventful day of her life. She was aware of utter delight surging through her but she didn't know how to express it. Adding to her inability to speak was the nagging fact that she still wasn't clear what Sam was saying. Had Gerry and Mish been right? Had they seen something she'd missed? She suspected she knew the answer but she didn't dare take it for granted. She decided that she had to keep pressing, just to be sure.

'Why . . . erm . . . why would I need to know that?'

'Oh, Hat, why do you think? I'm in love with you. I fell for you the day we met, when I watched you try to drown yourself in your soup when Priscilla forced you to tell us about your botched wedding plans.'

Hat was dumbstruck, but an enormous smile broke out on her lips.

'And, you see, Gloria reckons you're in love with me,' Sam continued.

At last, Hat found her voice. 'She might be right.'

Sam coiled his arm around her waist, pulled her towards him and squeezed her tight, laughing. 'You know your trouble?' he said. 'You can't see the wood for the trees.'